NOT SO ALONE

"Amadou."

"What?"

She holds up her wrist.

"I want you to know I'm not going to try to run today."

"What?"

"I heard what Moussa said to you this morning." Her face is serious. "I want you to know that, even though I don't want to be here, I'm not going to do something that would put Seydou in more danger."

I feel a tightness inside that, for once, isn't due to feelings of guilt or fear or anger. The wildcat is looking out for Seydou too again, like she did when he was sick and she stayed with him.

I'm startled to realize that that's how I'm thinking of her now: as someone who takes care of Seydou, not someone who betrayed him. As one more set of hands to keep my cricket safe. I wonder whether we could ever be a team. A little family, just us three, sharing things and looking after one another. I want to tell her how much it means to me to have someone to trust so that I'm not all alone, but the words won't come.

Instead, I nod.

She nods back, picks up her machete in her blistered hand, grabs the other end of the sack, and follows me into the trees to find another section to work in until dusk

OTHER BOOKS YOU MAY ENJOY

THE BITTER SIDE OF SWEET

TARA SULLIVAN

speak

SPEAK
An imprint of Penguin Random House LLC
375 Hudson Street
New York, New York 10014

First published in the United States of America by G. P. Putnam's Sons,
an imprint of Penguin Random House LLC, 2016
Published by Speak, an imprint of Penguin Random House LLC, 2017

THE LIBRARY OF CONGRESS HAS CATALOGED THE G. P. PUTNAM'S SONS EDITION AS FOLLOWS:
Names: Sullivan, Tara.   Title: The bitter side of sweet / Tara Sullivan.
Description: New York, NY : G. P. Putnam's Sons Books for Young Readers,
an imprint of Penguin Group (USA), [2016]
Summary: "Kept as forced labor on a chocolate plantation in the Ivory Coast, Amadou and
his younger brother Seydou had given up hope, until a young girl arrives at the camp who
rekindles the urge to escape"— Provided by publisher. | Includes bibliographical references.
Identifiers: LCCN 2015038251 | ISBN 9780399173073 (hardback)
Subjects: | CYAC: Slavery—Fiction. | Child labor—Fiction. | Chocolate—Fiction.
| Blacks—Cãote d'Ivoire—Fiction. | Cãote d'Ivoire—Fiction. | BISAC: JUVENILE
FICTION / People & Places / Africa. | JUVENILE FICTION / Social Issues / Violence.
| JUVENILE FICTION / General.
Classification: LCC PZ7.S95373 Bi 2016 | DDC [Fic]—dc23
LC record available at http://lccn.loc.gov/2015038251

Speak ISBN 9780147515094

Printed in the United States of America

Edited by Stacey Barney
Design by Annie Ericsson

9 10

For Aidan, Evan, and Anna.

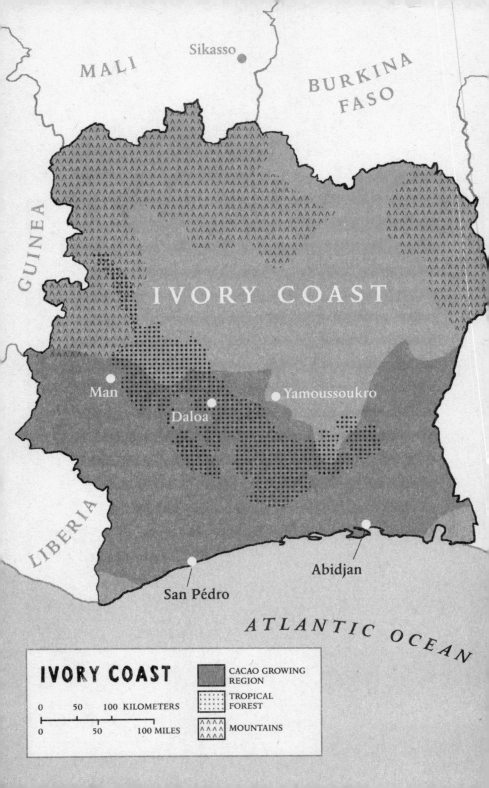

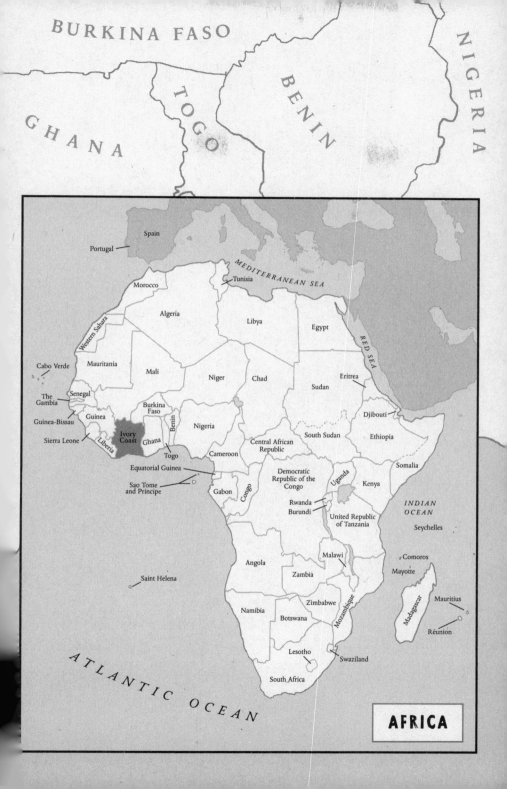

I count the things that matter.

Chop, twist, toss, check. Chop, twist, toss, check. Two more pods make twenty-five total.

Neither Seydou nor I have eaten anything since breakfast, but Moussa is working too close for us to be able to sneak one of the *cacao* pods out of the sack. I take a moment to wipe the sweat off my forehead. You'd think it would be cooler up here, but some days there isn't a breeze even halfway up a tree.

I scrub at my face with my wrist and look out over our work area. Moussa is collecting pods off to our right, though he'll leave in a second to make another sweep to be sure everyone's still here. The other boys on crew with us today are just smudges of noise through the green. Directly below me, Seydou scrambles around as quickly as he can, picking up the pods I've cut and putting them in our sacks. They're lying worryingly flat right now.

Only twenty-five pods. Our sacks need to be full, at least forty or forty-five each, so I can get Seydou out of a beating. *Really* full if I want to get out of one too. The bosses usually look the other way when I give Seydou lighter work since he's

slaves on a cacao farm

only eight, but that kindness only goes so far. We still need to bring in about the same as the other boys.

I slide to the ground and push the sack onto my shoulder. The bunched bag digs in, pressing through the bruises there, but I don't let Seydou carry things that are too heavy if I can avoid it. Instead, he carries the machetes.

"Moussa! We're finding new trees!" I call out.

"*Awó!*" he shouts, looking to see which direction we're going. In a few minutes he'll wander over to check on us. I try not to let it bother me.

Seydou and I walk past tree after tree. They taunt us with their clustered pods, all the wrong size, none of them ripe enough to cut. I don't count how many trees we pass because I don't count the things that don't matter.

I don't count unripe pods. I don't count how many times I've been hit for being under quota. I don't count how many days it's been since I've given up hope of going home.

In the next grove I heave the sack onto the ground and shake out my arms. Seydou stumbles a little as he shuffles up behind me. His thin shoulders slump. I can see how tired he is and it makes me mad, because I can't do anything about it. More than seventy pods to go and it's already late morning.

"Give me my machete."

He scowls at my tone, his thin eyebrows scrunching down in his round face, making him look like a cranky old man, but he hands it to me even so. Then he heads straight to the nearest

2

tree with low pods and gets to work, a frown line still between his eyes.

I clench my machete between my teeth and pull myself up a smooth trunk with my bare feet and hands, counting the shiny pods that are the right size for cutting. When I get high enough to reach some purple-red ones, I knot my legs around the trunk, grab one in my left hand, and hack at the tough stem that holds it to the tree.

One strong chop and with a twist it comes off, surprisingly light in my hand for its size. *Twenty-six.*

I turn to toss it to the ground and check on Seydou. I notice that he's still trying to saw through the stem of his first pod. His skinny little body is sagging from exhaustion and his blade keeps slipping. I want to scream at him to be more careful. Instead, I slip down the tree and don't add the pod to my sack.

"Come on," I say, walking to him. "Let's take a quick break before Moussa gets too close again. Then we'll get to work. How does that sound?"

"I can keep working." He straightens and glares at me as if I've just called him a baby in front of the whole camp.

I grind my teeth in frustration but keep my face smooth. Tremors of exhaustion are making his blade wave slightly in the air as he argues with me.

"I need a break," I lie, and sit deliberately in front of him. Balancing the pod I just cut in one hand, I aim the machete and swing. One, two hits, and it cracks. I wedge the pod open with the blade until the whole thing splits in two. Inside the thick rind, the seeds are packed together in a tube, each in a squishy skin. I drop my machete, scoop the seed-mess out with my fingers, and shove some of it in my mouth. Then I hold out the other half to Seydou.

"Eat."

"Okay," he says, and slides down beside me, resting against the tree.

While I chew on the slimy, crunchy *cacao* seeds, I look for a place where the leaf litter is deep, to hide the empty husk. There's no way I want Moussa catching us eating the crop, but all of us boys do it when we can. We don't get fed much and chewing the seeds makes you feel better and gives you enough energy to keep working.

Seydou chews his handful, a little at a time. I'll let him finish it before I make him get to work again, but I get up. I need a new twenty-sixth pod and the day is only getting shorter.

I'm halfway up the next tree, my hand already wrapped around it, when the unusual sound of a motor surprises me. Giving in to curiosity, I climb higher until I can see out over the treetops. The growing groves and the wild bush beyond them stretch like a green sea in every direction. There are little pockmarks of brown in it—the clearing where the bosses have their house, the clearing where we husk the pods, ferment and dry the seeds, eat and sleep—and a long tan-colored scar pulling across it: the track that the *pisteurs* use to come here and collect the seeds we've harvested.

4

And along that track, a plume of dust announces that a car is coming to the camp.

I slide down the tree as quickly as I can. Seydou looks up in alarm, his hand halfway to his mouth with the last few seeds.

"What is it?"

"A car. There's someone coming."

Seydou finishes and wipes his hands on his pants. He wrinkles his nose, thinking. "It's too early for the *pisteurs* yet," he says. "I thought Moussa said they're not coming until next week."

That's what I had been thinking too.

"More boys?"

I shrug.

Not many people come all the way out here to the middle of nowhere, Ivory Coast. There are the *pisteurs*, and every now and again someone else, someone delivering fertilizer or insecticide or food for the bosses. But usually, when a car comes by in the middle of the day, it's because they're delivering more boys to work.

Over two years ago it was Seydou and I who were part of that batch, leaving Moke and Auntie, thinking we'd be home after a season of work; Seydou and I who were about to get dumped at the *cacao* camp and learn that we now had to work all day, week after week, season after season, never getting paid. I rub my bruises and wonder what poor boys are currently peering out the bug-spattered windshield for their first glimpse of their new work site.

"We'll find out soon enough," I say. But Seydou darts past me and shimmies up the tree I was just in to see for himself. I wait for him at the bottom, considering.

"I wish we could see them." His whine filters through the leaves to me.

"Wishing doesn't make it so," I remind him, moving to the next tree. Moke used to say that to us all the time when we complained at home. And he's right. I've wished for a lot of things: first, to make my family proud by earning a lot of money; then, that my family would come find us; finally, simply that my family would know what had happened to us before we died here. "Wishing doesn't make it so," I mumble to myself again, and start up the tree.

I'm cutting through the next stem when the shrill double blast of a whistle makes me jump. Moussa wants us. For a moment I sit there, straddling the branch, cradling my new twenty-sixth pod against my chest. A distraction is the last thing I need.

No, I correct myself. *The last thing you need is to get Moussa angry.*

I drop the pod to the ground and slither down the trunk until I'm standing at the base. I shove the pod into my sack. When I hear the *swish* of Seydou's bare feet on the tree, I grab the sacks, and we trot to where Moussa is waiting for us.

We're the first ones there. Curious, I walk to where Moussa is standing. Tall and broad, Moussa is the oldest of the three brothers who run the farm. His face is handsome, though he has deep lines on his forehead from worrying. At fifteen, I'm

6

one of the oldest boys in the camp. Even so, I have to tilt my head to look him in the eye.

Seydou tucks himself behind me a bit as we stand there waiting for the other boys to join us. He won't talk to the bosses if he can avoid it. Seydou is the youngest at the camp by far. I grimace as the old guilt twists in my stomach. It's a number that matters, but in all the wrong ways.

I turn my attention back to Moussa. I look at his face carefully, gauging whether he might be angry. His stance is relaxed; there are no muscles bunched at the corners of his jaw; his hands hang loosely by his sides. I take a chance. "I didn't know we were expecting new boys," I say.

Moussa's eyes cut to me. I try not to flinch. Then he looks away and shrugs.

"Neither did I." He pulls a whistle from inside his shirt and blows it again. "Help me get my things."

Seydou scrambles to get Moussa's tools and I put the rest of his pods in his sack. Yussuf, Abdraman, and Konaté arrive just as we hear a blaring sound from the direction of the clearing, like someone is leaning on a horn, then two quick honks.

Moussa grabs his sack from me and leads the way.

I fall into line with Seydou and the other boys and follow Moussa. It's not like he would trust us to work in the field alone while he took care of business. I grind my teeth in frustration at the thought of daylight slipping away.

"*Aw ka kene?*" says a voice beside us.

"Oh, we're fine," Seydou answers. "But, Yussuf! We think

there might be some new boys from Mali coming to the camp! What do you think?" My crazy cricket of a brother is bouncing on the balls of his feet as he walks, excited to be able to share a secret.

Yussuf smiles indulgently at Seydou, his thick eyebrows almost comical on his thin face. I've never been too friendly with the other boys. It just hurts too much to care, and all of my caring is used up with Seydou. If I had to, though, I would trust Yussuf above the others. He smiles a lot like he means it. In a place like this, that's rare.

"*Awó,*" Yussuf whispers. "You're probably right. More mouths at the stew pot, hmm?"

We all go back to walking in silence. How little food we get is never something to laugh about.

When we get to the edge of the clearing where we live, Moussa walks straight to the Jeep to talk to the driver, a bulky man in khaki pants and a sweat-stained shirt. The five of us don't really know what to do with ourselves, so we stop a little ways away. Always glad for a break, we sink to the ground and wait to be told what to do. Seydou stands on his tiptoes trying to see in the windshield, but there's a glare. With a huff of frustration, he settles beside me.

Only a few moments behind us, the other two bosses and their crews trickle in, one after another from the areas they were harvesting, until pretty much everyone is here. The three bosses, Moussa, Ismail, and Salif, stand in a loose ring, talking with the man from the Jeep. The boys float over to join our crew.

I'm contemplating whether or not this would be a good chance to sneak in a nap, when the driver pulls a struggling kid out of the Jeep. Instantly, the thought of napping, along with all others, is jolted out of my head. I hear a low whistle of astonishment from Yussuf.

"Is that a *girl*?" whispers Seydou.

I nod, still trying to wrap my head around this. First of all, girls never come to the farm. Second, I've never seen or heard of one kid being brought alone, ever. Seydou and I had to wait a while in the halfway house in Mali before we crossed the border because it was just too expensive to move us until the drivers had enough kids to make the trip worth it for them. What on earth are they doing, bringing only one kid, and a girl at that? None of the girls at the Sikasso halfway house came with us to the farms. They were all driven somewhere else.

I watch, fascinated. You can tell the kid is a girl because of the plain blue cotton dress she wears, but the thing that the big man pulls out of the Jeep is more like a wild animal than any girl I've ever met. She whips around in his hands, thrashing her head from side to side. Her arms are tied behind her, so when he drags her out, she hits the hard-packed ground with a *thud*. In a heartbeat, she's on her feet and running for the trees.

Biting off a curse, the big man in khakis is after her. He catches her by her wrist and yanks her sideways. She loses her balance and falls, crying out. The big man sinks a knee into her spine. She lets loose a stream of curses that would curl a man's hair and doesn't even stop when he slaps the side of her head. He hauls her to her feet and pushes her before the bosses.

Moussa looks wary. I agree. This girl's crazy.

I notice I'm standing and that I've taken a few steps toward them without realizing it. Moussa crosses his wiry arms, and the four of them begin a heated conversation.

I try to think like the bosses: Would I take her on? Given her height, she's probably a little younger than me, maybe thirteen or fourteen, but she's not as skinny as most of the girls I knew at home. Maybe the drought is over if people have food to spare on girls.

I pull my thoughts away from home and pretend I'm helping them decide to take her on or not. *She looks healthy and strong enough to work, but I wouldn't trust that wildcat.*

Yussuf and Seydou and the others are whispering among themselves, wondering where she came from, why the middlemen in Sikasso would be willing to transport only one kid, and what it might mean to have a girl in the camp. I'm just about to sit, joining the other boys, when the girl's eyes snap off the ground and lock into mine. I take a step away. Wide and dark in her oval face, her eyes are asking for help. But I have enough to worry about with Seydou and myself. I have no more help left to give. And so I look away. When I glance at her again, her eyes have turned hard.

There's nothing I could do anyway, I remind myself.

As I sink into the rough circle we've formed, I'm distracted by the pity in Yussuf's eyes. *I wonder whether he has sisters at home.*

The thought takes me by surprise. After two years working with Yussuf, I have no idea who he left behind. I don't usually wonder about people's pasts. Thinking about someone else's past only makes me remember mine, and that's too much to bear.

"I wish we could get back to work," I hear myself say.

"Wishing doesn't make it so," Seydou parrots.

I'm annoyed to have him sass me like that in front of the other boys, but Yussuf laughs, so I let it drop.

Until the bosses give the word, we can't do anything, so even though we're all losing time on making quota, we sit together and wait.

Wait while the men finish their deal.

Wait while the big man in khakis drives his Jeep away.

Wait while the girl screams curses after it.

Wait while Moussa and the other bosses beat her for the first time.

Finally, Moussa comes over to where we're sitting, dragging the girl with him.

"Okay, enough lazing around," he says, waving us all onto our feet. The other bosses round up their teams too, and we all head back to where we were working earlier this morning.

I trudge with my crew into the underbrush, sneaking glances sideways at the girl. Up close, she doesn't look like a wildcat. Her cheekbones are high and fine in her oval face, and the lashes ringing her eyes are spiky from crying. Her hair is braided in slightly uneven lines and knotted at the base of her head. She looks pretty, and kind of soft around the edges. She's clearly not a village kid like us. Her cheeks are round and her skin is dark and shiny. You can tell that she's been eating well for years. Her family must have landed on hard times for a girl who could eat that well to be looking for work in a place like this.

I tell myself that it doesn't matter where she came from; she's here now. Her full lips are split open and her blue dress has blood on the front of it. Fresh bruises are swelling her almond eyes shut and her hands are tied in front of her. I shake my head to get rid of all this useless thinking and set myself to the task of counting things that matter. She's not my problem. Quota is.

When we reach the area we were working before, I'm the first one up a tree.

Grab a hard red-orange pod, smooth and ribbed and as long as my forearm.

Chop with the machete raised, careful not to miss the stem, thin as my fingers.

Pull the pod off the tree and toss it at the bag.

Twenty-seven.

Check on Seydou, make sure he's all right. Begin again on the next pod.

Chop, twist, toss, check.

Twenty-eight.

the 1st girl is brought to the farm

12

2

When I've taken all the ripe pods off that tree, I drop to the ground, expecting Seydou to have collected them. Instead, I find him harvesting his own pods in a way I told him never to do.

I stalk up behind him, watching him swing his machete in wide arcs. He knows better. Seydou is young and clumsy. When we're harvesting, I make him hold the blunt side of the blade with two hands and saw it across the stem. I don't let him use the machete any other way, and he's not allowed to climb trees with it.

"Seydou!"

He turns and looks at me, his machete freezing in midair.

"What do you think you're doing?"

I see his grip tighten.

"I'm working," he says.

"You know better than to do it that way!" I point at his machete. He lowers it, still glaring at me.

"I'm trying to help us make quota!" he snaps. "Your way takes forever and we already lost an hour."

I glance at the girl, who's sitting in front of a tree, arms crossed, silently glaring at me. She's no longer tied to Moussa's waist. It must have been too difficult for him to move around. Instead, he tied her here. The knots are tight, complex, and out of her reach. Seydou's right, of course. We did just lose valuable work time, and because they're machetes, not saws, it does take him a while. But, even if it slows us down, I won't see him get hurt.

"This isn't a discussion," I say. "Do it properly."

Seydou's face gets hard and flat. He's furious.

"I'm *helping*," he insists.

I roll my eyes. "I don't care. Pay attention, and do it right." I turn away to collect the nine pods I got off the last tree and shove them in my sack.

"You never let me help!" Seydou yells at my back. I can hear the tears clogging his voice. I'm sick of arguing with him, sick of telling him he's too young, too small. Sick of it always having to be my job to keep him from getting hurt. I grab my sack and look sideways at him.

"If I see you being reckless with your machete again just to impress a stupid girl, I'll beat you myself."

Then, to make sure that Seydou doesn't follow me while I'm still mad, I carry my sack to where Moussa is working, and climb the tree next to his. I know Seydou won't get closer to the bosses even to have the satisfaction of yelling at me.

As I hack at the next pod, I hear a low laugh from the greenery off to my right.

"Always on the lookout, aren't you?"

Hidden by the leaves, Moussa's voice sounds oddly friendly. For a moment I think about how nice it would be if he actually were. But without being able to see what the rest of him is doing, I don't feel entirely safe.

"*Awó,*" I mumble.

Moussa's low laugh rolls over me again and, with a pang, I wish for Moke. My grandfather didn't laugh very often, but when he did, his laugh was like warm honey.

In the early days here I used to think all the time: *How can I run away? What is my family doing right now? Is Moke worried about us? Are they searching? How much longer will we have to work before we pay off our debt and the bosses let us go home?* The questions would seethe through me, twisting on themselves in new shapes again and again like an injured snake. I soon learned the price of thinking. It slowed me down, and I didn't make quota. Now I count instead of thinking and I'm able to get through most of my waking hours in a daze. It's better this way.

Chop, twist, toss, check.

Thirty-seven.

I don't say anything else to Moussa and I refuse to think of anything other than the rise and fall of my machete. After a while, I manage to enter my empty place: that strange state of mind I get to when I'm working, where the burn in my muscles is the only way to track the passing of time. It's like being half-asleep or feverish. I move without having to think about it. Without having to think about anything.

The sun has sunk about a hand lower in the sky when I'm finally not angry with Seydou anymore and I decide to go back and try to talk to him again. Numbly, I've followed Moussa for the past few hours and we've wandered well away from where I last saw Seydou. I heft my comfortably full sack (*sixty*) high on my shoulder to avoid the old bruises as I walk. It hurts to carry, but its weight feels good. Between what I've got and whatever Seydou managed on his own, we might actually have a chance of making quota today, even with the delay the girl caused by her arrival.

I'm still a little ways off when I hear a soft sobbing filtering through the trees. My heart pounds as I break into a run. It was stupid to leave Seydou working alone just because I was mad. If he's gotten hurt when I wasn't there to help him, I'm never going to forgive myself.

I break through the last bit of underbrush and rush to Seydou. At first I can't tell what's wrong. A quick glance around the nearby trees shows me a chest-high ring of sloppily cut stems. In the near-flat sack at his feet there are maybe a dozen pods. I can't see his machete, or any obvious injuries. I drop my sack and grab his arms, turning him this way and that.

"What's wrong?" I shout. His eyes are terrified. Set in his round face, they make him look very young and breakable.

Sobbing, snot and tears running down his face, Seydou points behind me. I turn, and for a brief second I don't really know what I'm looking for. Then I see the rope dangling from the tree, empty. It feels like the world stops. I face Seydou again, my eyes as wide as his.

"What did you do?" I manage, my voice barely a whisper.

"I—I—" Seydou gasps.

I'm shaking my head because, no, *no*, this day did not just get worse. We had the chance to make quota. Everything was going to be all right. Now there's no way we're going to be okay. If we helped a kid escape, Moussa's going to destroy us.

"She . . . asked me to cut her free . . . as soon as you . . . and Moussa . . . were out of sight. I said . . . I said no . . . but she . . . she tricked me." Seydou is beyond panic. "She asked me to come over when we were talking . . . and then . . . she knocked me to the ground and took my machete . . . and she . . . and she . . ." He trails off, pointing at a spot in the bush to his right where the branches are bent at odd angles, then starts sobbing again. "A-A-Amadou, I'm sorry! I'm so, so sorry!"

I wave my hand at him to shut him up so I can think. Of course he's sorry. I'm always the one bailing him out when he makes mistakes. I bet he knew, the minute this happened, that I'd figure out a way to take care of this. I try to think over the panic churning in my belly.

I can't believe that she would put Seydou in this situation. Already I'm right: the girl's not worth the trouble she's causing. That little snake. I'm so angry at her I feel I'd like to kill her myself. But my terror quickly overrides my anger. Any minute now, Moussa is going to come here to check on all of us. I look

17

at Seydou, curled on his nearly empty sack, his breath wheezing in and out of his skinny little ribs as he sobs. I imagine Moussa's rage at losing the girl. The kind of beating that's likely to follow this disaster could kill Seydou.

Not every boy survives here. Some have fallen sick and died of their diarrhea; some have been bitten by poisonous snakes or spiders while they worked in the bush. And one, a stringy boy named Yacouba, got beaten and went unconscious and never came out of it.

I think of the scars that already crisscross Seydou's back and I make up my mind. I reach over and smack him hard across the face.

He reels, surprise cutting off his crying. I never hit Seydou.

"You were an idiot to trust her," I snarl, low and fierce. "Now pull yourself together and *shut up.*"

Then I throw my machete at him, whirl on my heel, and race back the way I've just come. "Moussa!" I yell at the top of my lungs. "Moussa!"

I nearly ram into him. I was right; he was on his way to check on us.

"What?" he says, "What is it?"

I try to catch the breath my fear has knocked out of me.

"The wildcat escaped," I manage.

"*What?*" he roars. "How?"

My mind races.

"When I went to check on Seydou, she tricked me into

coming over to her. She knocked me off my feet and stole my machete. She cut herself loose."

"She knocked you over? A *girl*, a girl who was *tied up*, knocked *you* over and stole your machete?"

Maybe that wasn't the best way to put it.

Moussa's meaty hand slams into the side of my head.

"You make me sick." He grabs me by the ear and drags me to Seydou. Since I'm almost as tall as him, his grip on my ear makes me bend nearly double. Head still spinning from being hit, I have a hard time keeping my footing. But I'm still here, still standing, and even if he believes an embarrassing story, at least he doesn't know the truth.

When we burst through the bushes, Seydou jumps, holding my machete out in front of him. Tears are streaming down his face and his lower lip is trembling, but he's stopped sobbing and I hope that Moussa will assume his distress is from being generally afraid and not from being responsible.

Moussa lets go of my ear and examines the tree with its dangling rope. Reaching up, he slices through it near the knot and winds it into loops. My ear throbs but I know that I have to keep up my side of the story.

"She ran that way." I point.

Moussa scowls, looks at the afternoon sun, and lets loose a tight curse. He takes a moment, fingers fisted in his hair, and then seems to come to a decision.

"You." He points at Seydou. "Keep working. Harvest as

much as you can. We're going to lose a lot of time chasing her and it will be your fault if we don't bring in enough. Do you understand?"

Seydou darts a glance to me, frightened, and I take a step forward, my mouth open to argue for him even though I don't know what I'm going to say, but Moussa shoves an open hand in my direction, stopping me in my tracks.

"I said, *do you understand?*" he repeats, softly.

"*Awó,*" says Seydou, hearing that softness for the danger it is.

Moussa looks at me and holds out the rope. "You, you're coming with me."

My heart drops into my stomach. We'll never make quota now. With one last look at Seydou, I take the rope from Moussa and follow him into the trees.

Moussa wastes only a moment looking at the place where she disappeared and then he's off at a lope, following the direction the girl has gone. I feel vulnerable running through the bush without a blade. Not only is *la brosse* full of pythons, vipers, and poisonous spiders, there are also leopards, panthers, and vicious wild pigs that will rip you to pieces with their tusks as soon as look at you. Even if no animal bothers us, I'm sick of branches slapping me in the face. But the wildcat took Seydou's machete, and the only way to get it is to capture her.

Also, I need to get back to Seydou. A hundred terrible images flash through my mind. *What if he falls? What if he cuts his thigh open and bleeds to death? What if he steps on a snake?* I shake my head and run faster. What's more likely is that he'll sit on the ground crying, too scared to move, until we return. *And then, when neither of us make quota* . . . I run faster still.

Moussa doesn't break his pace, checking her trail as he runs. As I jog after him, jumping over low plants and dodging between trees, I try to figure out what he's tracking in the ground that I'm missing. It's not an easy task and soon I find myself drawn in by the challenge. Even when we were still at home, I never really went hunting; I just set snares around Moke's fields for rabbits. In front of me, Moussa takes a quick left and I slow. What made him turn? At first I see nothing. Then, as I'm passing the bush, I notice where a sandaled foot has pushed the leaves aside.

I follow Moussa, eyes on the ground, scanning for telltale signs. Little by little, it gets easier. The ground tells a story: feet trod here quickly, here slowly. She's getting tired: look, a line from a dragged machete tip. I have entered my empty place and the ground seems to shout its secrets. Pretty much every time Moussa turns I know why: a footprint in the soft loam, a smashed fern. Abruptly, Moussa veers off to the left again, but I see a track to the right. I'm so wrapped up in the task that I don't even consider that he might not want my opinion, that he might not want my noise. I blurt out, "Moussa!"

He turns around and glares, and his hand cuffs me on the ear.

"Shush!" he says in a heavy whisper. "We're getting close to her now, you idiot! Do you want to go shouting where we are, helping her escape?"

"I . . ." I trail off, remembering what we're tracking. I had forgotten, for a few moments there, that it's a person we're after: the difficult girl. That this isn't just one more job, one more thing to count, but another kid. The rest of the words come out shaky, unsure. "I think that's a false trail. Look."

For a moment Moussa is quiet as his eyes follow my pointing finger, taking in the slight scuffing of moss that shows careful steps leading away from the trail of broken branches. A slow smile creeps across his face.

"Good work," he says, and rubs his hand on my head as we turn to follow the real trail. Inside, my heart soars at the praise. It's been so long since someone told me I did a good job at anything. I always have to be the one in charge with Seydou, always the one telling him it's all right, that he did well. I'd almost forgotten how nice it is to be the one to hear those words.

It's not long before my new trail shows its worth. We are turning around a tree when I see a glint in the bushes. I act purely on instinct, calling Moussa's name and pointing, and then the girl is exploding out of the bushes and sprinting away. For a brief moment I think she might make it, but then Moussa is after her and I know that the chase is over.

Very aware of the fact that I am still the only one without a machete, I hang back and let him catch her. She lashes out wildly with the machete. A cold, distant part of my mind criticizes her swing. It wobbles with her exhaustion. It is poorly aimed. *A few months working in the field would cure that,* I think, and a small part of me smirks that that's exactly what she's about to

22

get. Another part of me is ashamed of the thought. A third part of me, one that has slept dormant for months until this crazy girl showed up, wonders quietly how my work-trained swing would do if I were the one trying to escape. I brush the thought away like a bug near my ear, but a tiny echo of its buzz remains.

Moussa leaps sideways, avoiding the blade, and then rushes forward. He uses his machete to beat hers aside and then grabs her other arm with his free hand. He's shouting at her, shaking her, but I don't look, don't listen. Instead, I walk around them to where Seydou's machete has fallen into the undergrowth and pick it up. I'm glad to have it again. But I can't help noticing, as I take the loop of rope off my shoulder and help Moussa bind the struggling girl, that the handle is still warm from her hand.

We arrive at the grove hot, tired, and cranky. I've worked all day and then chased a wildcat on nothing but the thin soup of breakfast and I'm starting to feel weak. I want to lapse into a deep, colorless sleep, but instead Moussa blows a double blast on his whistle and, one by one, Yussuf, Abdraman, and Konaté join us with their bags.

Seydou arrives last, dragging both of our sacks. He runs over and throws his arms around me. He doesn't need to say anything: I know he was scared. Scared to work alone in *la brosse* full of animals, large and small, that could kill him. Scared I wouldn't come back, and he'd have to do this every day. It's a terrible thing to be here. It would be worse to be here alone. I often think of what it would be like if I hadn't taken Seydou's side and convinced Moke to let him come with me into the Ivory Coast. I feel awful about it every day, but if I'm honest with myself, I know that I wouldn't have made it this far if I didn't have him. Without Seydou to protect, and to make me laugh, I'd have given up a long time ago.

I squeeze him gently.

"Let's go!" Moussa's in no mood to be trifled with and sets

a punishing pace, dragging the offending girl behind him. We follow along, the others baffled as to the change in mood, and there is nothing I can do but put one foot in front of the other, and dread what's coming next.

In the two years I've been here, only a handful of boys have tried to run. The punishments have always been terrible. Unbidden, memories flood through me of my one and only attempt at escape. I cringe away from them and try to count the steps it takes us to get back to camp, pretending it's a number that matters.

It doesn't work.

We trundle into the clearing, Moussa and the girl in the lead. Ahead of us is the long, low sleeping hut, with the water pump off to its side. To our right is the large, clear area with the drying platforms for the seeds. To our left are the toolshed and the storage lean-to. Because we're all carrying bags that need to be stacked against it, we turn and walk there. I feel damp and chilled across my neck and on my upper arms. My skin prickles with waiting.

When it's my turn, I hand my sack to Ismail, the youngest of the brothers, who hefts it in his hands for a moment and scrunches up his long, skinny face, considering. Ismail is the one who decides every day whether or not we've made quota. He makes his decision based on how much he thinks the bag weighs and a quick look inside. It really bothers me that he never counts the pods, because even on days I come in high, I'm still never sure if I'll have enough.

"*Ayi*," he tells me, no. Not a surprise since I handed him a near-empty sack. I'm in trouble anyway and making quota wouldn't have helped me out of it, so I poured most of my sack into Seydou's while we waited in line.

I go to stand in the middle of the clearing near the fire pit with the one other boy who didn't reach quota today. Everyone else begins to make dinner. Moussa is talking with his brothers, still holding on to the tied girl. My only comfort is seeing Seydou join the group of boys who made quota. But knowing that I have to take his punishment for him, again, makes it a small victory, laced with resentment.

"How close were you?" asks a voice at my elbow.

I turn in surprise, then shrug. The other boy who didn't make quota is Modibo, a skinny boy with a big head but not nearly enough brains to fill it. He hasn't been here very long, and he's not learning quickly enough what he has to do to survive. He's sloppy with a machete and reckless with pesticides. He gets hit nearly every day, though he's too stupid to do anything big enough to get beaten very badly. He needs to learn fast, though, or the bosses will get frustrated with him. Then, who knows how much he'll be hurt.

"Not close," I say in a tone that I hope ends the conversation.

Waiting for a beating is almost as bad as the beating itself. Having to stand still and see it coming nearly drives me insane every time it happens. I think the bosses do it on purpose. It's twice the punishment and it gives all the other boys time to look at us sideways and decide to work harder tomorrow.

The bosses finally finish talking. Moussa hands the girl to Ismail, and picks up a large stick. He walks toward us, holding it loosely in his hand. Beside me, Modibo has started to whimper. I don't let myself shrink away. For all my bravery around Seydou, though, I hate to get beaten.

Stay strong! I tell myself. But it's no good. Once he lays into me with the stick, and fear turns into pain, I lose my resolve. He's going out of his way to show the girl how bad it will be. By the time he's finished I'm sobbing and begging him to stop, cowering on the ground. I hate that the others can hear me, can see me, but I can't help myself.

Finally, he's done.

"Let that be a lesson to you," says Moussa, and he turns to deal with Modibo, hitting more softly now that most of his frustration is out. He leaves the girl till last. When it's her turn, she shrieks and lurches, but Ismail holds his end of the rope, and she can't get away.

The beating she gets is bad, but not as bad as the one when we tried to escape. I gingerly pull myself into a sitting position. He must be going easy on her because she's a girl. I wonder again how she ended up here. Her family must have sold her against her will for her to be fighting this hard to get away so quickly. But then my curiosity leaks out of me. It hurts to think.

I draw my knees to my chest and tuck my head, moving slowly, trying not to pull at the long, open welts across my back and shoulders. I let myself cry because I can't help it. Besides, tears are like pus in a wound: either you get them out quickly or they fester and make you sick and weak. My tears dribble across my bare knees, leaving tracks in the dirt that has caked on me from scrabbling on the ground.

Let it out. Tomorrow you'll need to be strong again. I tell this to myself over and over, like a lullaby. I give myself until Moussa's finished with the others to be weak, then I make myself stop. I lift my face and rub the wet off, then I gingerly brush the dirt off my clothes and hair. Then, even though it hurts like dying, I straighten and look up.

I'm surprised to see that my team from today is coming over. I wonder why. Yussuf leads the way. Abdraman and Konaté look frightened, but they come anyway, and that's worth something. Seydou is pale and shaking.

"Amadou, I'm sorry! So, so sorry!"

Annoyance seeps into me through the pain. I'm sick of taking his beatings for him. Tired of taking care of him all the time. It hurts so much, and once, just once, I'd like for someone to take care of me. But that's never going to happen here. I try to pretend that wish doesn't exist.

Usually I tell him it's okay. But right now I'm in too much real pain to care if Seydou's feelings get hurt or not.

"Next time, don't be so stupid," I manage.

Seydou snivels, but Yussuf barks a laugh.

"Well, I see that another beating didn't improve your personality," he jokes. "Come on." He slides his arm under mine and across my chest, where he grabs hands with Abdraman, who has come around on my other side. Bracing off each other, careful not to touch my cuts, they help lift me to my feet and bring me to the circle of boys sitting around the fire.

I'm shocked by the help. Usually no one helps, for fear of making the bosses angry. My beating today really must have been worse than usual. Then again, today I'm being punished for two things, not only for coming in under quota.

I guess I got my wish. For once, others are looking out for me.

"*I ni cé,*" I murmur. The thanks feel strange in my mouth.

Out of the corner of my eye I see Modibo's team help him to the fire too. The girl is still tied to Ismail, so no one goes near her. When Ismail comes to sit at the fire, he drags her along with him. She curls into a ball, her back to us. Moussa drops his heavy stick by the water pump to wash off.

"Are you going to be okay?" Seydou asks. "That was bad."

I nod. It was. And I will be. There is no other choice.

"That stupid Khadija!" Seydou mutters. "I can't believe I let her trick me!"

Khadija? I'm doubly surprised. First that this wild thing has a name and second that Seydou knows what it is. How long had they been talking this morning before she betrayed him?

I start to shrug, then think better of it when my back screams from the tiny movement. Moussa, finished washing up, joins the far edge of the circle. The reflection of the flames dances in his cold stare. I shudder and look away.

When the soup is ready and the bosses have eaten, the boys surge in to grab bowls.

"No food for the three who got beaten tonight," Moussa says, as Seydou is about to hand me one.

I try to hide my disappointment. Eating always helps me forget, just for a moment, about everything else. Plus, after a long day I'm always really, really hungry.

"Water?" I ask.

Moussa shakes his head.

Seydou sits beside me, putting his soup to one side.

I slant a glare at him. I want him to suffer like I'm having to suffer for his stupid mistake. I want him to learn, want him to stop doing things that get me in trouble. From beside me I hear his stomach whine.

"Eat," I order.

He looks at me. He shakes his head.

"No." He sniffs. "I'm not going to eat when you can't."

"Eat."

Finally, used to being the younger brother, he does as I tell him.

I lean forward, trying to find an angle where everything doesn't hurt. I don't find one. I look at the ground between my feet and try to pretend I can't hear Seydou slurping guiltily beside me.

When they're finished, the bosses sit by the fire, talking and laughing together in low tones, and the boys clean up and prepare everything for the morning. I try to stand but, again, my work crew covers for me. Sometimes the bosses let us help each other out, sometimes they don't. Tonight no one tells them not to, so when Abdraman says, "We've got it," I sit.

It's worse to sit than to work, really, because then I have nothing to take my mind off the things I don't want to think about. How badly everything hurts. The bosses relaxed and content across the fire. The blue-dressed back curled beside them. The yawning black shadow of tomorrow and all the days after it stretching over me.

Finally, it's time to go to bed. I let Seydou pull me to my feet, sucking in a breath when the movement causes a fresh wave of agony to wash through me. I sway a little, and Seydou keeps me upright while I wait for it to pass. I have no idea how I'm going to work tomorrow. Just the thought of climbing a tree makes me wince.

"Okay, let's go," I say to Seydou. I hate that he has to help me instead of the other way around, but even leaning most of my weight on him I can barely walk, so I don't tell him to go away.

"*Ayi.*"

Seydou freezes. Slowly I shuffle my feet around and face Moussa.

"You sleep in there tonight." He points at the toolshed.

I shake my head wearily, not wanting to go. It's common for them to put kids in there overnight for punishment: it's small and cramped, full of bad-smelling chemicals, and there are ants that nest between the cracks of the wooden beams.

Moussa walks over and takes my upper arm in his hand and pulls me away from Seydou. My back screams at the jolt, but I don't pull away from him either.

"But . . ." manages Seydou, before he's silenced by a glare from Moussa.

"Get in the sleeping hut," Moussa says to Seydou, then he half drags me into the toolshed and lets go of my arm. Without his support, I crumple to the ground with a groan, still not able to fully support my own weight. I land next to something soft that yanks away from me with a hiss and I realize that they've put the girl and Modibo in here too.

Moussa stands there for a moment, framed in the doorway by the purpling light of evening, his face in shadow.

"You allowed her to escape today," he says, "so you're being punished. Since I don't think you'll be able to keep harvesting tomorrow, I'm putting you on shelling duty until you're better."

My brain struggles to process why this is a punishment. I know the reason is there somewhere, but I can't quite find it.

"Also," Moussa goes on, "you won't be allowed in the sleeping hut with the other boys until you're on your work crew again. Until then, you sleep here."

Moussa waits. He wants to make sure I really understand. I force my sluggish brain to work. Why is this all so bad? Then it hits me. If I'm locked in here, I won't be able to look after—

"Seydou . . ." I manage, trying desperately to force my brain to cobble together a sentence.

"Exactly," says Moussa, and locks the door behind him.

Seydou! In all the time we've been here, I've rarely slept apart from him, never left him for more than an hour or so as we worked. He'll never survive a day without me. I want to get up, want to pace and yell, but even the slightest movement hurts and I feel light-headed from not eating.

Gritting my teeth against the pain, I scoot until I'm able to lean sideways against a wall. A sigh of relief escapes me. *That's better.* At least now I don't have the impossible task of holding up my own head.

Weak threads of moonlight struggle through the tiny cracks around the door. Even so, it's almost completely dark in the toolshed. As my eyes adjust, I become aware again of the other forms hunched against the wall. Modibo and . . . what did Seydou say her name was again?

"Modibo. Khadija?" I try aloud, more to see if I was right in my guess than to really start a conversation.

Modibo is sniffling, clearly not in a mood to talk.

"Go away," comes the retort from the girl. Her voice slurs as she tries to talk through swollen lips.

For a moment I feel a pang—we're all locked in here, all hurt. Then I remember that all of this is her fault and my pity turns to rage.

"Go away? *Go away?*" I snarl. "You've pretty much made that impossible, haven't you? I just got one of the worst beatings of my life and I'm stuck in this stupid, stinking shed instead of being able to sleep comfortably with the other boys, all because

33

of you. *You* were certainly happy enough to *go away* this morning." I choke out a bitter laugh at my joke. "Just trick a little kid and run, huh? Did you even think about the price other people would have to pay for what you did? Well, now you see what that gets you. I hope you're happy."

I want to say more, but even that small rant has exhausted me. I turn my face from both of them, each too stupid to see what they've done wrong, and try to fall asleep.

I jerk awake in the middle of the night, gasping. My quick movement dislodges some of the ants that were crawling on me as I slept. I brush off the rest of them, then swipe the ground in arcs, checking for snakes, spiders, or anything else that might be within reach of biting me, but there's nothing. I settle back and wonder what it was that woke me.

I lie there for what feels like a long time, on high alert without knowing why. My noise and movement caused a sudden silence to fall around the toolshed. Slowly the sounds of the bugs in the trees and the machine-gun roaring of the tree frogs picks up where it left off. I feel another ant crawl across my arm, but I ignore it, straining for the sound that woke me. Then I hear it. A faint scratching sound, too rhythmic to be natural. I strain my ears to hear.

Scritch. Scritch.

Scritch. Scritch.

For a few moments I'm baffled. Then I puzzle it out. It's the girl. I don't know where she's found her hope but there she is, in the dark, rubbing her rope-bound hands against the edge of the concrete foot of the shed's corner post, trying to weaken the thing holding her there. I briefly consider handing her a machete from the far side of the shed. Then I shake my head, brush the bug off my arm, and try to fall back asleep.

4

It hurts too much to sleep more than about an hour at a time, and so I hunch against the wall, dozing between the waves of pain, until daylight seeps through the cracks in the shed door. I know that with the sun my courage will return, and I force myself to straighten so that, when Moussa opens the shed, I'm sitting unsupported.

I see the surprise in his eyes. I take the small victory. I need all the help I can get if I'm going to change his mind.

"Moussa, I want to work on a crew today," I say.

Behind him the boys are craning their necks to see into the shed as they clean up from breakfast. My stomach whines, but I ignore it, not breaking eye contact with Moussa.

For a moment he stares at me with something that looks like admiration, but then he laughs and pulls a machete from the pile. He hands it to me and points to the edge of the grove.

"Go cut me a piece off the top branch of that tree and I'll let you," he says.

Limping, I walk to where he pointed. I can feel the stares of the other boys as they form into their work crews. I rest my fingers for a second against the irregular bark of the tree and take a deep breath. Then I clench the machete in my teeth and reach for the lowest branch.

It's a good thing I've got the blade between my teeth because it keeps me from screaming at the pain that rips through me when I try to pull my body weight up using my arms. I scramble with my feet to get a hold on the trunk, but only about a meter off the ground the muscles in my back give out and I can't go any higher. Arms trembling, drenched in sweat even from that little bit of a climb, I rest my forehead against the tree, trying to swallow my frustration before turning around. Then I drop to the ground and limp to Moussa.

"Thought so," he says. "Let me show you what you'll be doing instead." He waves me in the direction of the storage lean-to.

"Seydou!" I call around him. Seydou looks up from where he's getting ready across the clearing with Yussuf, Abdraman, and Konaté. At least they let him work with the same team as yesterday. I see Modibo shuffling out of the clearing with his work crew too. He must have managed to prove to the bosses that he's ready to go back to the fields. I scowl. More proof that I got the brunt of Moussa's anger yesterday. "Be careful today," I say. "Promise me."

He nods. "Get better, Amadou."

I turn back to Moussa. He points again and I walk to the storage area. On the far side of the lean-to a metal ring is sunk in concrete in the ground. Moussa heads into the shed and comes out a moment later, bringing a long chain with the girl attached to one end of it. Just my luck. Modibo is in the fields and I'm left working with *that* one.

She stumbles along beside him and he lets her fall next to the ring. Next to me. Then he threads the other end of the chain through and reattaches it to her.

I glance at the girl I helped recapture. She's glaring daggers at me. I look at Moussa. He arches an eyebrow. I realize he has to manage the farm and he can't have feuds between kids, so he's going to leave us here, armed, for a day to work it out. If we fight, if we argue, if we do nothing, we will have found a way to be together by the time he gets back. He doesn't have to be involved, and his problem gets solved.

A distant part of my mind acknowledges the genius behind this plan, even as I now doubly dread my day.

I rub a hand over my face. "So what are we doing?" I ask.

"Good choice, Amadou," Moussa says. He rolls an empty plastic rain barrel to us, then points to the sacks stacked to the roof of the lean-to. "We're behind on shelling pods. You and the girl here will work on that. One of the *pisteurs* should be by any day now, and we need to have the seeds fermented and at least four days dry for him to be willing to take them. Get started."

With that, he tosses two machetes at us and then turns on his heel and walks away. I scramble forward, expecting to race the girl for the weapons, but she doesn't move and I get there first. Now I'm left with bad options. I can keep both machetes and have her tell Moussa that I didn't let her work, or I can give her one and have to watch myself all day so that I don't stumble close enough for her to stab me. I've already hesitated too long for it to be friendly when I hand one to her. I chew my lip, then consider the two blades. I pick the better one and toss the other so that it lands with a *smack* in the dust beside her.

"That one's for you," I say, and turn away. Moussa disappears across the clearing into the trees, following Seydou and our crew from yesterday.

When I hear the soft *shush* of the blade leaving the ground, I turn to face her. She's standing, holding the machete tightly in her left hand. I balance forward, ready to fight if it comes to that. The moment lengthens. The only sound filling the silence of the empty camp as we stare at each other is the whirring of the bugs.

"Well?" I finally ask, breaking the silence. "Are you going to stand there all day like a wildcat waiting to pounce?"

"You're the one pointing a machete at me." Her face is swollen from the beating yesterday, one eye nearly shut, and her words come out thick and garbled through her puffy lips.

"I'm not going to attack you. I want to get going on these pods."

"Oh, right, because you're such a *good* boy," she sneers. I want to punch that tone out of her voice, but don't. There's not much space to fight, and we're both armed.

"And why are you so bad?" I ask. "Do you really think this is the right way to start off here? They're just going to beat you until you work. Why did you even agree to come across the border if you're going to be so awful about it?"

She looks at me stonily.

"I'm going to escape," she finally says, not answering my question. "I suggest you keep out of my way. I'll do what I have to."

I scowl at her again.

"Well, *I* have to fill that bucket," I say, making up a quota to keep myself on track, pointing with my machete to the impossibly large plastic barrel, "by the time Moussa gets here. I don't care about you. I don't even really care about myself. But the sooner I do what he wants me to, the sooner I can get back to taking care of Seydou, that little boy you tricked and hurt and abandoned yesterday. And I need to know whether you're going to try and stop me because if I'm always looking over my shoulder at you, it's going to slow me down and I can't afford that."

At the mention of Seydou, her eyes flick from me to the edge of the clearing, where the path twists into the trees. Then they flick to me again, hard and flat as roof metal.

"If you really wanted to do what's best for him, you'd get him out of here."

My anger flares.

"You think it's so easy? To get away from here?"

"At least I tried!"

"I've tried too! But all you have to do is think about yourself. I have to find a way that's safe for two." I count off reasons on my fingers. "Seydou can't run very fast. Seydou can't climb very high. Seydou isn't good at keeping secrets. Seydou is afraid of the dark, afraid of snakes, afraid of the bosses . . ." I throw up my hands. "We didn't make it ten meters before they caught us."

She stares at me, unreadable.

"Besides," I continue, "as soon as we earn out the money the bosses have spent on us, we can leave."

"Says who?" asks Khadija.

"Say the bosses. All I have to do is work hard and make sure Seydou doesn't get hurt and then we can walk out of here, free."

I think I've hidden the quaver of uncertainty in my voice, but I'm not sure. It's true, that's what the bosses *said*, but in the two years I've been here I've never seen a boy earn out the money that the bosses paid the middlemen from Sikasso. Plus, I don't even know what they paid for us, how much I earn a day, or how much I'm being charged for food and shelter. All of these numbers matter and I don't know any of them, which means I have to trust that Moussa is keeping track of all of them. I don't like trusting.

"Believe what you want, just stay away from me," says Khadija. "I'm going to take care of myself."

With that, she turns. A moment later I hear the high *screech-screech* of her working at the chain links with the blade. I roll my eyes. Good luck to her. She can get beaten and starved until she learns her lesson. I've already learned mine and I need to not waste any more time.

I drag the chest-high barrel closer, then grab the first bag out of the towering pile beside me and settle into the pattern of the day, working as quickly as I can.

The sun climbs the sky and sweat is running down my face and back but I keep working. The pod is shiny purple-red in my hand. *Thwack-thwack-crack*, I split it open. I tuck my machete under my arm and scoop the *cacao* seeds out with my fingers, throwing them into the big blue barrel. I have no idea why we grow these seeds, no idea who wants them. Why have so many trees growing the same thing? The bosses never talk about it; they only say that the seeds leave our farm and go to the coast, where someone else buys them. *For what?* I asked once, but they all shrugged. No one here knows. All we know is that people in the city want these seeds, so we grow them.

The seeds make a depressingly hollow *splat* as they hit the bottom, but I try not to notice. Once they're in the barrel, I throw the empty half husks into the bush as hard as I can. By the time they clatter to the ground in the distance, I've reached into the sack beside me and taken out another pod. I do all this in silence. Except for the sound of my machete against the pods and the sound of her machete against the chains, we make no noise.

Over an hour later, I finally get to the bottom of the first sack. The storage area is too full for me to take advantage of its roof's shade. I shake the sack inside out to clear the twigs and bits of leaves and dust, and then I drape the burlap over the top of my head and shoulders, like a giant floppy hat. The smell of dirt and pods sifts onto me, but the shade is so welcome I don't care. I put my machete point into the ground in front of me and close my eyes for a moment. Black spots dance behind my eyelids.

The *scritch-scritch* in the background never wavers.

"*Hakéto,*" I call to her.

"What?" She doesn't pause.

"Are you going to be gone by the time they come back?"

"What do you care?" she mutters. "Are you going to come catch me? Again?"

"If you're not going to be gone by the time they get here," I say, "you should start working. You can explain away some of the lack of work based on how new you are, but if they check tonight and you haven't done anything, then you're going to be beaten again. And they'll probably figure out what you were doing instead and make it impossible for you to keep doing it."

I don't mention that if she's done nothing other than try to escape again all day, it will probably somehow turn out to be my fault and I can't afford many more nights on Moussa's bad side.

The girl stares at the chain link she's been working on and the machete in her hand. I see her squint at the sky, judging the passing of time, estimating how long it will take her to finish.

"Do they always stop at dusk?" she asks.

"*Awó.*"

She sighs, then digs a little hole in the ground and buries the few metal shavings she managed to work off the chain and turns to me. She looks at me silently, her head cocked. She reminds me of a bird, considering whether the object in the grass in front of it is a worm or a snake. "Show me what to do."

I look at her like she's no smarter than Modibo. It's pretty clear what we have to do. I wave vaguely at the sacks.

"You shell them." It really doesn't get any more basic than that. Plus, I've been doing it all morning. It's not like it's a secret.

She scowls.

"And just *how* am I supposed to do that? I'm not an expert on all this like you are."

Somehow she makes that sound like the worst of insults.

I grind my teeth and remind myself that we need to work together at this if we're to have a good showing by the end of the day.

"Take a pod in the hand you don't hold your machete in and hit it hard, like this." I demonstrate, thwacking the blade into the thick rind and pausing to show how I'm holding it.

She picks up a pod in her right hand and swings the machete at it. I don't know whether her blade wasn't entirely straight or if she simply didn't put enough force behind the swing to cut it, but the blade skims off the curved ridges of the pod and bites into her hand.

"Dammit!" With a curse, she drops both the pod and the knife and scowls as she sucks on the fat part under her thumb where the knife cut her.

"You have to hit it harder," I say.

"And have it cut off my whole hand when I miss? No thank you!"

"All right, all right! Try doing it this way." I hold the pod by the stem stump, bracing it on the ground. I swing the machete over my head and land it, *thwack*, in the middle of the pod. I pause again, letting her get a good look at how I've done it, before I lean away and signal with the tip of my machete that she give it a try.

Awkwardly, Khadija copies me. But again, her swing is off and her blade angles sharply to the left. Luckily, this is away from the hand that was holding the pod, so she doesn't get cut again, but her machete clangs into the dirt and the scratched pod goes flying, hitting off a sack and then rolling around a little before coming to rest near me.

"Any other great ideas?" she snaps.

"It's not my fault you're a weakling and can't do it!"

"I am not a weakling!" She throws the machete down. "I just don't know how to do it right and you're not helping!"

"Well, I can hardly tell you how to do it right when you don't have enough muscles to even use a machete! Useless girl; didn't you do any work at home?"

"No! Of course not! I went to school! How nice for you that *you're* so good at this! I'm sure it comes from *years* of staying here, letting them tell you what to do." She gets to her feet and takes a step toward me.

"What's that supposed to mean, rich girl?" I'm on my feet too, shouting in her face. I don't know where she's from or how on earth a creature like her ended up here, but she's clearly rich if her parents were throwing money away sending a girl to school. I still have my machete in my right hand and my knuckles are aching from how tightly I'm gripping it.

"It means that I'm not the weak one here! I may not know how to cut pods like you do, but I don't plan to learn! I'll be out of here so soon that I'll never have to learn, and you know what? I'm okay with that. I'm okay with not being an *expert* on cracking some horrible fruit open!"

I tighten and loosen my grip on the machete in my hand. This girl, this *stupid* girl, is making me so mad. I want to lash out, shut her up forever. I wonder briefly what it would feel like to cut another person, then I turn away, sick with my own thoughts.

I stand with my back to her and look across the clearing, up, over the tops of the trees and into the sky. I pretend that I am pouring my anger into the sky and, slowly, it drains out of me. This is a trick I learned when I was little, from my grandfather.

Oh, Amadou, he had said, *you get angry so easily. Just like I did at your age.*

Really, Moke?

Awó. *But you must learn to let it go.*

What do you mean? I had asked him, and that's when he told me the secret of pouring my troubles into the sky.

There is no problem so big, no anger so great that it can fill the sky.

I try to remember Moke's words when I feel like my anger is about to make me do something dumb.

"We're wasting time," I say, and sit.

"What?"

It's funny how confused and frustrated she sounds, ready for a fight and not getting one. But I have left myself floating in the clouds, and I can turn to her with nothing but air in my eyes.

"Fighting won't help us get this done." Then, as usually happens when I let go of my feelings, I find an answer. "You're not going to be able to learn to go fast enough today without hurting yourself." She takes a breath in, ready to shout again, but I just keep talking. "So I'll crack the pods and give them to you, and you'll open them and take out the seeds and put the seeds in the barrel and throw away the husks. This way we'll work as fast as possible."

For a moment she stands there, then she sighs and sits next to me.

"Fine," she says.

"Also, if you chew the seeds you can get some energy, and the pulp around them has some water in it. Moussa didn't leave us any food. I can bring us water from the pump, but we'll have to eat some of these to be able to work all day. As long as we don't eat too many, Moussa won't notice they're missing." I see her eyes sparkle a little with interest when I tell her this, and she looks at the sacks of pods in a new way.

"Not too many," I repeat. I reach over, pick up the pod she had been butchering, and split it in one clean swing. I toss it to her.

"You are a strange boy, Amadou," she says. She pulls the two halves apart and scoops out the seeds.

I shrug.

"Eat the first handful, then put the rest in the barrel," I say. Then I find my empty place and get to work.

We go on like that for hours, both sunk in a silent routine. It's easier to work with her than with Seydou, and this surprises me. I find that I don't have to heckle the girl to stay on track. Nor do I have to keep a close eye on her so that she won't eat too much. Instead, she seems to be taking her cues from me, eating when I do, stretching when I do. This keeps us in almost perfect time. She even put a bag over her head like I did to get some shade.

I dart a look at our garbage area. The pile of husks is growing steadily into a small mountain. The smell of them is strong in the sun, and the sap has attracted all kinds of bugs. The flies and mosquitoes buzz around my sticky hands but I try to ignore them. Swatting them all away would be a full-time job, and we don't have time for that. When I look, Khadija is doing the same. She's letting flies crawl on her arms and face and she only flicks her head to the side to dislodge them when they get near her eyes. My right arm burns with fatigue from the non-stop cutting, but there are seven folded sacks at our feet and I have to admit I'm pleased by our progress. I squint at the sun, just a little past straight overhead.

"It's midday," I say. "Do you want to take a break?"

"Do you usually take a break?"

"Only if I'm sure the bosses won't catch me at it but, yeah, usually Seydou needs a rest in the middle of the day and we take a break."

"I'm not some little ten-year-old."

"Eight," I correct her without thinking, then kick myself.

"What?" She pounces on the error.

"Eight," I mumble, picking slivers of pod off my wrists and flicking them away. "Seydou is only eight."

"He told me he was ten."

"I told him to tell everyone that. He's tall for his age, so he can get away with it. Some of the other boys can be rough. I don't want people taking advantage of him because he's so young."

"That makes sense, I suppose," she muses. "He doesn't really act ten, does he?"

I'm thrown off balance by this.

"No, he acts very young. He *is* very young. He was only six when we first got here. That's why I have to take care of him. He's far too young to be doing this kind of work. And he's sloppy."

I scowl off at the tree line. I should be out there with Seydou. Instead, I'm stuck here, wishing away the hours until I can see him return to camp all in one piece to set my mind to rest.

"I don't need a break."

I turn around, surprised to hear Khadija speak, I was so

49

deep in my wishing. Her eyes jump from my face when I turn and she too stares out at the tree line. She stretches her wrists and cracks her knuckles.

"I'm thirteen, not eight. Let's keep working."

I can see the tremor in her hands from the unfamiliar work. But she's managed to keep up so far and, even though I don't say it out loud, I'm grateful to this strange girl for helping me meet an invisible quota for Seydou's sake. I reach for my machete.

"Okay," I say. "Let's get back to work."

5

The hours pass. The shadows of the trees lengthen and reach for the fire pit on the far side of the clearing. Slowly, oh, so slowly, the blue plastic rain barrel fills with harvested seeds.

By dusk, the fingers on my left hand are cramped so completely from clutching the pods that I can no longer straighten them fully. My right arm has gone beyond burning, beyond pain, and is now just weak. My swings are wobbling like Khadija's did in the morning, but I don't know how much I need to do to get Moussa to allow me on crew again, so I force myself to keep going. Any minute now the bosses will be here and will judge the worthiness of our entire day's work. I raise my arm to take one more swing and then, as though my thoughts have called them, they are here.

The boys dribble into camp in twos and fives, carrying sacks heavy with pods on their heads and backs. I scan the incoming teams anxiously for Seydou, but I don't see him yet.

"There he is," comes a soft voice from beside me, and I follow Khadija's pointing finger. Sure enough, I see the tall form of Moussa and a familiar little shadow, bent double under the weight of the sack he's carrying. My heart soars: he's all right! I try to see whether he has any injuries but, from here, the dusky light hides his features. I let the machete slip out of my hands and I stand up.

"Seydou! Seydou!" I wave. It's unnecessary, really, since he has to bring his sack to the lean-to, but I do it anyway.

Beside me, Khadija stands too, but she is only a vague shape that I ignore. My eyes are completely fixed on Seydou, who has turned at my call. I shuffle toward him, stiff from a day of sitting, drinking in the sight of him. His little legs are trembling, whether from the weight or exhaustion, I can't tell, but he's *walking*. Before I'm able to offer to help him, Seydou drops his sack with a *thump* beside the others hemming us in. The rest of the boys line up behind him, each beside his own sack, waiting for Ismail.

"Hello, Amadou," he says. The weariness in his voice makes my heart tighten, but I don't let him see this. "How are you doing?"

I think about the swollen muscles and broken skin of my back, how the cuts split open again and again because I wouldn't stop working. How I had to cover up with sackcloth at midday and how it rubbed me raw. I think about how hungry I am and how tired. I look at Seydou.

"I'm okay," I say. "How was your day?"

"I kept up, Amadou," he says with a weak smile. "I told you I could keep up."

"That's great," I say. "And you were super careful? You only cut pods the way I taught you?"

He looks away.

"I'm fine," he says, and I know he wasn't doing it the way I told him to. Although, really, the fact that he kept up with the rest of the team should have told me that already.

I'm furious with him.

"No, it's not fine! You got lucky today, but that's no reason for you to think you'll be so lucky again. If I'm not put on crew with you, you *do it right* tomorrow, do you hear me?"

The other boys have stopped chatting with each other and have turned to watch us fight.

Seydou is furious now too.

"You're always telling me what to do! Well, today you weren't there and I was just fine! I kept up, so I don't want to hear you telling me what I can and can't do anymore! You treat me like a little kid!"

"You *are* a little kid!" I roar.

Ismail arrives. Seydou grabs his sack and stomps away from me, to where Ismail is hefting the boys' sacks to check quota. When Ismail tells him he's made quota, Seydou pointedly turns his back on me and goes to the far side of the fire, plopping on the ground between Yussuf and Modibo. He wraps his arms around his knees and scowls into the flames.

I haven't had my work checked yet by the bosses, so I don't chance following him.

I stalk to the blue barrel and grip the edge roughly.

"That went well," Khadija murmurs dryly.

"*I ka da tugu,*" I mumble, rubbing my hand over my face in frustration. But she doesn't shut up.

53

"Do you think they're going to feed us tonight?" she asks, changing tack.

My stomach rumbles loudly and I grimace. A few handfuls of *cacao* seeds aren't enough for a whole day.

"I hope so," I say, and leave it at that.

Ismail must be in a good mood. Today, everyone makes quota.

When he's done hand-weighing the sacks, he and Moussa come lean over my barrel. Our barrel. I know, from having watched our progress creep up the sides hour after hour all day, that it's slightly more than halfway full.

"Hmm," says Moussa.

I hold my breath. Finally, he turns and looks at me.

"This is what the two of you have done today?"

"*Awó,*" I say.

"And how many did you eat?" Ismail asks, narrowing his eyes.

I freeze. How many does he think we've been eating? Will he believe me if I say none? I decide to be honest and hope that it won't earn us both another beating.

"A couple handfuls each, no more."

Moussa and Ismail stare at me for a long time. I don't blink or glance away. That's what a boy would do if he were lying or ashamed. I want to show the bosses that I'm neither. Finally, Moussa says, "I believe you. Very well, stay here. I'll have someone bring you some dinner." I sag with relief. Moussa turns to

Khadija. "And you, wildcat? Have you learned to work calmly instead of acting like a crazy girl?"

Khadija stares at him, her eyes like river stones. But then she looks down.

"I did the work," she answers.

If Moussa notices that she didn't actually answer his question, he doesn't point it out.

Moussa and Ismail join Salif and the boys by the fire. We stay put. I can hear Khadija's stomach whining to my right, and my own stomach feels like it has fallen in on itself like the thatch roof of an old house. It's the hope that has made me hungry, I realize. Without the promise of food, I would have ignored the feeling and gone to sleep. But Moussa's promise of a hot dinner keeps me awake, leaning forward.

Finally, after most everyone is done eating, I see Moussa walk to Seydou, a bowl in each hand. For a moment Seydou hesitates, then he takes the bowls from Moussa and brings them to us. With the fire behind him, Seydou's shadow stretches all the way across the clearing. If I could eat shadows, I would already be full.

"Here." Seydou puts a bowl in my hands, then shoves the other at Khadija. I want to say something to get him to do things my way tomorrow, but as soon as the bowls leave his hands, he turns on his heel and stomps back to the fire.

I sigh. I guess we're not patching up yet. I promise myself I'll talk to him if I get the chance tonight.

"Eat slowly," I think to tell Khadija before I dig into my dish. "If you eat as quickly as you want to, your stomach won't know what to do with it and you'll vomit." I shouldn't really have to tell her this. In my village, girls always ate last and were used to not getting enough food. But Khadija is a rich girl who went to school. I would hate to see a bowl of stew go to waste in the dirt just because she's soft. She doesn't make eye contact with me, but she pauses between sips, so I know she heard me.

The first bite of banana I pull out of the stew is hot and slick with oil. It burns my tongue but tastes so, so good. I chew it slowly, not only to show Khadija how to be smart when you're hungry, but also to make it feel like I've eaten more. There are chunks of white meat in the stew tonight. One of the boys must have managed to kill a lizard or a snake. The meat is rubbery but it's a rare treat to get such a filling meal, so I savor every bite. Too soon, I'm done. I run my tongue around the inside of the bowl, pulling in the last bits of moisture, and then wipe my face with my arm. Beside me I hear the soft clatter as Khadija puts down her empty bowl. She has timed her eating to end exactly with mine. I don't know why this annoys me, but it does.

With dinner finished, I look across the clearing to where the other boys and the bosses are. They're talking in small groups, half of them in shadow and half of them in the light of the fire. Those assigned cleanup are scraping the bowls and the pot with old ashes and placing them to one side. There is a relaxed air to the camp. Soon everyone will be sleeping. No one ever has much energy left after a day in the fields during harvest season.

I see Khadija rub a finger around inside of the shackle on her ankle. After a day of sweating into it and having the metal rub dirt against her skin, the whole area is swollen and must be sore.

Moussa comes over to us, jingling the key to the manacles in his hand.

"Moussa, can I sleep in the hut tonight?" I ask respectfully when he's close enough that I don't have to shout. I don't want to push too hard. I can put up with a second night in the tool-shed if I have to and I'm still hoping that, if I'm good, Moussa will let me go with Seydou in the morning. What's most important is that I'm there for Seydou tomorrow.

Moussa looks at me for a second, calculating how comfortable I have earned to be.

"I suppose."

"*I ni cé,*" I say sincerely, heaving myself to my feet.

"Hmm," says Moussa.

"What about me?" It's Khadija.

"What about you?" asks Moussa.

"You're not going to leave me out here, are you?"

I'm surprised at her question. It shows, again, just how little she knows about life here. Of course Moussa will let her sleep inside. It's far too dangerous to sleep outside this close to *la brosse.* Anyway, why else would Moussa have brought the keys? I sigh and shake my head. This girl has a lot to learn.

"You're going to let me sleep inside the shed again, right?" she presses. Though she's trying to hide it, she sounds frightened. I see Moussa's face soften slightly.

"*Awó*," he says. "Sit."

Khadija collapses on the new stack of bags from today's harvest and Moussa bends down to release the chain on her leg.

The thought of not having to sleep away from Seydou in the toolshed again soothes my spirit. I'm so happy that I almost don't catch the quick gleam of excitement in her eye. In a split second my feeling of peace is gone. My head whips around to look at them just as Moussa turns the key in the lock and the catch springs free. I open my mouth to say something, even though I don't know what it will be, but no sound makes it out of my mouth before it happens.

The moment she hears the *snick* of the lock opening, Khadija rams her knee into Moussa's face. Moussa, still bent over the lock, takes the impact in his nose. He reels, cursing, and I see blood dripping darkly through his fingers. I take a step forward, my hands outstretched, not sure what to do. But there's nothing I can do. Quick as a fish, Khadija has kicked free of the open manacle, grabbed one of the machetes we used for shelling, and sprinted away from camp, into the darkness of the trees.

I'm so stunned by what happened that for a moment I don't do or say anything. The sight of Moussa struggling to his feet snaps me out of it.

"I—she—" I stammer.

Moussa slaps me across the face so hard I fall to the ground. My lip splits open and when I touch my face, my fingers come away wet with a mixture of Moussa's blood and my own. I scramble to my feet and try to move out of his way, but he grabs me by the arm.

"Oh no, you don't!" he growls. Then he bellows for the other bosses as loudly as he can while pinching his nose shut to stem the bleeding. "She's escaped again! Come help me!"

The camp explodes into activity. One boss herds Seydou and the rest of the boys into the sleeping hut, which is hastily padlocked, while the other grabs torches, machetes, and ropes. Moussa hits me with his free hand. He has to let go of his nose to do this and blood soaks the front of his shirt. *How is this my fault?* I think, covering my head.

Luckily, Moussa doesn't have much time for me right now: he has a girl to catch. After one last ringing smack, I'm shoved, hard, into the toolshed. Losing my balance, I just have a chance to see Ismail and Salif set off into *la brosse*, whacking at the bushes and shouting to each other, before Moussa slams the door in my face and locks it.

After the three bosses' shouts fade into the distance, a tense silence descends. Well, maybe the silence isn't all that tense. But I am. My face is still throbbing from where Moussa hit me, the blood from my lip is dripping off my chin into a small puddle between my legs, and I am winched tight inside, like a metal spring, twisted around myself to the point where it is almost impossible to stay still. And yet I am still. Other than the *drip, drip* of my bleeding, I make no sound. Even my breath is a small, tight thing.

What will happen when the men get back? Does Moussa really think I helped the girl escape? What will they do to me? I flop, groaning, against the rough wooden wall of the toolshed.

Somehow, in Moussa's mind, this is going to be my fault again. I contemplate what it will feel like to get a second beating like the one I got last night. A wave of fury engulfs me. *How could she?* She must have known that I would be blamed. She must have been thinking about escape for hours, not telling me about it, plotting away as she scooped seeds. Why on earth did I ever trust her? I sit up, clenching my fists, wishing I had someone that *I* could beat. Wishing that someone was her. *Oh, just let me get a chance, Moussa, and you won't even have to worry about punishing her. I'll be happy to do it for you.* After all the trouble she's caused me, she deserves it.

I bang my fist against the ground again and again and the anger flashes out of me through the pain in my knuckles. But when I'm done, I'm sorry I did it. Not only are my knuckles now cracked and bleeding too, but when the anger leaves me, there's nothing left inside but the smoldering embers of my fear.

What can I do?

It is a question without an answer. Or at least, it's a question without an answer that I like because, I discovered long ago, the answer to that question is *nothing*. Nothing to help myself, very little to help Seydou. I can't get us out of here. I can't do anything that will make this better. The only thing I can do is count, and wait.

Khadija's earlier words echo in my head: *If you really wanted to do what's best for him, you'd get him out of here.* This girl has no idea what she's talking about. I remember my first week here in the camp: new, frightened, Seydou crying against me all night long, asking for home, for Moke, asking when we would leave. Me telling him all sorts of pretty lies: *At the end of the work season, when we don't come home, they'll come looking for us. We'll be fine. I'll get you out of here soon.* But none of the lies came true. No one looked for us, or at least, no one found us. We are not fine, and I did not get us out of here soon. Now, two years later, it looks like I won't get us out of here ever.

I move to the far back of the toolshed and slide along the wall until I'm sitting in the corner. I don't want to lie all the way down in case that makes me so stiff I can't get up quickly if I need to. And I don't really want to be waiting by the door when they get back.

Because I know they will be back. No one has ever escaped this farm since I've been here, and I'm sure that a well-fed girl isn't going to be the first.

I think over her attempted escapes so far. If I didn't have to take care of Seydou, I could take advantage of situations like she does, I know I could. I'd do a better job of slinking through the forest too. And cutting through the chain? If she had strong arm muscles like me, she would have been through before dusk and there would have been no need for the trick that left Moussa with a bloody face.

But just the thought of leaving Seydou behind makes my

stomach clench. I got him into this mess, and I can barely live with myself for that. I'd rather die than also be responsible for leaving him here while I sprint to freedom.

I sigh and rub my face against my knees.

How far will she get tonight? Will she make it away entirely? I can't decide whether I'll be angrier with her if she escapes successfully or if she's caught and brought back here. *I hope they catch her,* I decide. *That way they may be too busy beating her to have much energy left to come after me.* Although, given how angry Moussa was, the beating she'll probably get may kill her.

I'm surprised by the twinge of sadness I feel when I consider her possible death. Of course it's a shame when someone dies, but she is nothing to me and I am nothing to her, so the feeling of loss comes as a shock. I realize that, although it would be worse for me, a part of me hopes she has gotten away. For whatever reason, for all the trouble she's caused me, I would rather think that the wildcat was out there somewhere in the world, even if she is mocking me for staying behind with every breath, than to think that she has left it.

I sit with that strange thought until, against all odds, I drift off to sleep.

6

I'm woken later in the night, though I'm not sure how much later, by the men returning to camp. Their rough shouts and the sound of blows are punctuated by the girl's crying. I lean forward, trying to see with my ears. I hear the scuffle of feet and the lock clicking free on the toolshed, the creak as the door swings open. The first shaft of light from the torches they took with them darts in through the cracked door and, without even thinking about how pointless it is, I scurry behind the big drums of pesticide in the corner, hiding from them like a child.

The sudden light when they enter makes the shadows of the barrels behind me leap against the wall. They're shouting at her, hitting her, furious and frustrated. I can't see them, and I realize they can't see me.

They've forgotten about you, whispers a small hopeful voice inside me. *They're so mad at her that they don't even remember you're in here. Stay quiet and maybe they won't find you.*

Their shadows dance above me.

I hunker down, trying to squash the uncomfortable feeling I get whenever someone else is being beaten. Then I realize that they're not stopping at beating her.

I scrabble desperately to find my empty place and sink into it so that I can be somewhere, anywhere but here. I curl into a ball, hiding my face in my knees, and cover my ears with my hands. I can't see even their shadows now, but try as I might, I can't block out the sounds. Her cries get more frantic as she fights them, and then, terrifyingly, stop altogether when she gives up. I try not to hear any of it, but my empty place stays just out of reach.

The sounds of angry men fill the space around us until they know they've won and finally go away, locking the door behind them, leaving us in the dark together.

For a while I sit there, shaking, even though I haven't been touched.

She's no one to you, why do you care? I try to tell myself, but the words are a lie. I try to remember that she betrayed Seydou, that she got me beaten, that I'm in trouble again because all she does is think of herself. Then I hear a rustling as she pulls herself back together and a soft, broken sobbing, and all I can think about is how terrible it is to be alone when you're hurting. Without actually deciding to do it, I find myself crawling out of my hiding place and through the dark toward her.

My knees shush against the dirt floor and her crying cuts off. Her breathing is jagged.

"Shh," I say. "It's okay. It's just me, Amadou. I'm not going to hurt you."

"I . . . A . . ." She can't get any farther.

I scoot over and put my hand on her back. She stiffens instantly when I touch her, and I take my hand away, not wanting to make her feel worse. Instead, I pull my knees to my chest again and stay beside her.

We're like that for a long time, two people wrapped up like coils of rope sitting next to each other. Then, after nearly an hour of me not moving, she leans into me. I wrap my right arm around her and let her cry into my shoulder.

"I'm sorry," I say, rubbing her back in small circles like you would a crying baby or a frightened child. "I'm sorry." I don't say anything else because there's nothing else I can think of to say.

We sit like that until the sun bleeds into the night sky and the cracks in the wooden shed door glow pink. When this happens I know we've made it through the worst of it. Pain is like sadness; both are easier to bear in daylight.

"Look," I whisper to her, "it's morning."

When the shed grows bright enough that I can easily see the jumble of objects around us, I stand up, breaking the contact we've had all night, to do some gentle stretches. I have no idea what the morning is going to bring: whether I'm about to get another beating or another test to be put on a crew. I decide to try to be as ready as possible. Khadija doesn't move.

The silence is starting to feel uncomfortable, but we haven't said anything to each other for hours, so I let it stand.

Finally, I hear the rattle of the bosses' old pickup coming over the hill from their house. I bounce a little on the balls of my feet, trying to loosen up, trying to ignore the worry building inside of me.

I hear the *snick* of the padlock on the sleeping hut, the normal tired grumble of thirteen boys asked to get up, the clatter and splash of morning chores. I hear Ismail calling my name. Finally, the toolshed door opens.

"He's in here." Ismail's tone is surprised, his eyebrows high on his forehead.

"Oh, that's right." Behind Ismail I hear Moussa's low rumble. "That's where I put him last night."

I look at Ismail, wondering whether it makes a difference to him that I was here last night. Whether, in some way, this will make things worse for me, or for her. But I don't see any shame in his face. Instead, he turns and gapes at Moussa.

"You didn't count last night?"

Moussa barks a laugh.

"*Ayi,*" he admits. "With all the excitement I forgot to count."

I can see Ismail puff up, ready to shout, but Moussa goes on.

"I was tired. I went to bed. He's here and nothing happened. Let's get on with it. Oumar is going to be here any day now."

Ismail grumbles.

"Seydou was in the hut," Moussa says soothingly, putting a hand on Ismail and steering him out of the doorway. "Even if Amadou had been outside and holding the keys to my truck, he wouldn't have gone anywhere." The way he says it makes it sound like a weakness. I scowl since they're not facing me.

Ismail grunts in response and closes the door behind him, leaving Khadija and me inside. That throws me a little off balance. I turn around to see what Khadija thinks of all this, but she's curled with her head on her knees again and doesn't look up. I shuffle from foot to foot, not sure what to do with my body and unable to settle my mind. The sounds of breakfast swell and fade and then the door is opened again. This time Moussa fills the doorway.

"Come on," he says.

Grateful to have a reason to move, I walk out of the toolshed and stand off to the side, waiting to be told what to do. Moussa follows me out, dragging Khadija with him. I pull in a breath. Though I just spent a night next to her, I haven't really looked at her since yesterday. The change is brutal. Her dress is filthy and bloodstained; her face is swollen from blows. But the most terrifying change is the deadness in her eyes. Moussa shoves the two of us at the lean-to where we were shelling yesterday and chains her to the ring again. As soon as he lets go of her arm, she collapses.

I feel a stab of loss. I helped Moussa catch her the day she had her best chance of getting away. Then last night I hid in a corner and didn't even try to stop what they did to her.

I fiddle with the machete in my hands and try not to look at the hunched form of the thirteen-year-old girl at my feet.

Khadija is still here.

The wildcat is gone.

Both of those things are my fault.

The rest of the boys are split into crews as always and head off into the groves. Like yesterday, the girl and I are left with two machetes and a wall of sacks full of pods. Today she's supposed to shell and I'm supposed to pile the shelled seeds in shallow pits to ferment them.

For a while after the camp empties out, I just sit there, not sure if I have the strength to make quota today. Not that I even know what quota is. I pick at the crusted blood and dirt on my arms, glancing from time to time at Khadija. Other than the slight rise and fall of her rib cage, there's no indication she's even alive.

Working alone, I'll never get as much done today as we did yesterday. But even that realization isn't enough to make me ask her to come back to this world. I sigh and flex my aching muscles. Maybe if I work as hard as I can, I'll get enough done to cover for her.

I pull the nearest sack forward and spill the pods on the ground before me, ready to do my best to cut and scoop them myself. And that's when I find the present. As soon as the top layer of pods rolls out of the sack, underneath I find four wild mangoes. I touch the gifts with my finger, not really ready to believe they're real. They are. I marvel at them. There's only one way these items found their way into this sack. It means that yesterday, not only did Seydou keep up with the bigger boys on a regular crew, but he took time from meeting quota to cut me some mangoes. Small, tired, and scared, even on his first day out alone, my little brother was taking care of me too.

I get myself a big drink of water from the pump and eat two of the mangoes, saving the rest to give to Khadija when she feels up to it. Then I get to work.

Today I am going to make quota.

I will do it for Seydou.

I will do it for Khadija.

I slip into my empty place and start to cut pods.

The day stretches on and the heat builds. I'm working as fast as I can, though the pain from my two-day-old beating still makes it hard to move smoothly. Sweat is running down the sides of my face and neck, making the welts on my back sting, but I don't stop. After the first few hours of not moving, Khadija has slowly relaxed, but she still won't make eye contact with me and we still haven't said anything to each other.

Finally, I've gone through all the sacks I can easily reach. All the rest are behind her and I'm not sure how she'll react to me getting that close.

"Khadija?"

After half a day of not talking, my voice sounds loud and grating even to my own ears. Khadija stiffens immediately. Then, after a moment, when I don't say anything more, she slowly lifts her head.

I wince. Her face is filthy, her lips are split, and her right eye is swollen shut, disfiguring her prettiness. Without her expression declaring war on the world, she looks younger, more fragile. When she turns, she moves stiffly, like the rest of her is hurting too.

"Here," I say, and I hold out a bowl of water. My voice is soft, like you use to approach an animal that might bolt at any second. "Have some water."

She looks at me blankly. I'm reminded again that this beaten thing is not the same girl I worked with yesterday. I'm surprised to find that I want her back.

I put down the bowl and pull my shirt off. I turn it inside out so there's not so much dirt showing and pour a little bit of the water onto the sleeve. I squat in front of her and reach for her face. She flinches when the wet cloth touches her, but she doesn't move away. Slowly, I wipe the dirt from her cuts and eyes and mouth. I pour a little more water on my shirt and wipe at the dried snot and tears and blood until her face is clean. While I do this, I hold her hand and talk to her softly, like I used to do for Seydou when we first got here and he was hurt and afraid. Stupid things, just to fill the silence and keep her from moving.

"You're going to be all right," I murmur. "Look, here you go, you're nearly clean now. No more dirt. Doesn't that feel better?"

When I've finished with her face, I wipe off her hands and arms, then I trace under the chafed ring of the manacle on her ankle. I squeeze her hands and look into her one unswollen eye, but she still isn't there. I'm starting to get worried: I know the place she's wandering. The dry, gray place inside where your spirit goes when you decide you'd rather die than continue to face the world. I've sunk there many times. But I always crawled my way back out, because I knew Seydou needed me.

"I need your help," I say softly. "Can you pass me the bags behind you? I can't reach them."

Still nothing.

I lift the bowl of water to her mouth and tip a little in. She swallows automatically and I tip it a little more. After a few swallows, her eyes clear a bit and she looks at me, really seeing me for the first time all morning. I slip my damp, dirt-streaked shirt over my head, pick up a mango, and slice it for her with my machete.

"Eat," I say, holding it out.

After a few seconds, she takes it from me. I could sing. Her spirit might not yet want to be with the living, but if she'll eat, at least her body doesn't want to die.

When I take her hand again, I can feel the grip of her fingers and I smile.

"Hello, wildcat," I say.

She eats the mango all the way to the peel and I slice the rest of the fruit for her, then hand her the pit to suck the juice from. Wordlessly, she pulls a sack around for me.

"*I ni cé,*" I say, and I get back to work.

⸺

For the rest of the day, I become a machine for shelling. When my muscles cramp, I get up and pile the seeds for fermenting, covering them with banana leaves and stirring the piles that have already sat in the sun for a few days. The stench is powerful, but we don't dry them on the racks until they're well and truly soured.

Though she still won't talk, Khadija watches me work, and whenever I get to the bottom of the sack I'm working on, she pushes another one to me. By the time Moussa walks into the clearing and comes to check on us that evening, everything is done.

"You've finished?" Moussa looks over my work, sounding faintly surprised.

"*Awó,*" I say. "I'm ready to go on a work team now." Moussa looks at me sharply, but I've been practicing what to say in my head for the last hour and I race on. "We're caught up. It would be a waste for you to keep me here when I could get so much more done on a harvest crew."

All day my worry has bounced between the girl beside me and my invisible brother, working far away without any help. The mangoes kept me going, but every time I tasted their lingering sweetness in my mouth, I wondered about Seydou. Even if he can keep up now, I don't want him going any more days alone. I need Moussa to not keep me here for a third day. There's a pause where Moussa looks at me, his face as hard as a tree trunk. I play my last card.

"When we get enough for you to need me to do this again, you can put me back here. But for now, you should put me on a crew."

"Now, you listen carefully, Amadou," Moussa says, leaning his face close to mine. His usually flat eyes are glittering and the muscles of his jaw are bunched into visible knots. I feel my hope trickle out of me. Moussa is still furious. "You helped that girl escape. Twice. I don't want to let you off so easily. But I have no choice but to put you on crew because we only have a few days left to meet quota and we lost a boy today." *Lost,* I think. That one word could mean so many things. *Lost* could mean the boy ran away, or died, or got injured so severely that the bosses don't think he can work anymore. I look at Moussa unflinchingly. He goes on. "So I'm letting you go. But I'm going to be keeping an extra-special eye on you, so don't try anything funny."

"*Awó.*" I gasp with relief. "You'll see, I'll work hard and you won't have to worry about a thing!"

The first of the teams are appearing on the edges of the forest. Moussa goes to the center of the camp to light the fire. I stay sitting beside Khadija because, as evening has fallen and

73

the sky has gotten darker, she has pulled back into her little ball and I feel bad leaving her alone like that.

"Moussa?" I call over to him, my curiosity getting the better of me.

"Hmm?"

"The boy you lost today. Who was he?"

Moussa turns. The firelight behind him makes his face a mask.

"It was your brother," he says.

7

Y_our brother._

The words echo hollowly in my head and, for a moment,
I don't process them. They are nothing but sounds, without any
meaning. Then it hits me. _Seydou._ He's talking about Seydou.

Beside me, Khadija's head snaps up and she makes a small
noise.

At any other time today, this would have made me happy,
but my problems have suddenly gotten so much bigger that I
don't even look at her. I jump to my feet and scan the faces of
the boys who have already arrived. He's nowhere to be seen.
Moussa is still looking at me. I take a step closer to him, not sure
my voice will carry.

"Seydou?" I choke out.

"_Awó,_" says Moussa flatly. "He got hurt today and isn't going
to be able to work until he gets better."

Hurt! My heart starts beating again when he says that word
and it's only then that I can admit to myself that I thought Seydou might be dead. My stomach twists painfully and I want to
throw up, but don't. Moussa gives me a thin-lipped smile.

"I guess he just wasn't able to manage without the help of his big brother. Shame you weren't there to protect him."

"Where is he?" I ask. My voice is tight and shaky.

Moussa waves toward the edge of the clearing.

"His team should be back soon. They're moving slowly since they have to carry him." And with that, he turns away from me and busies himself feeding the fire.

I run to the other boys.

"Did you see Seydou today?" I ask them, but the ones who answer say no.

I pace the clearing by the fire in tight circles, shaking out my hands in nervousness, waiting for Seydou's crew. Every time I look, I see Moussa staring at me. His eyes are mirrors; I can't see anything behind them. Unsure what he's thinking, I don't take a chance on any more questions. I turn away from him and continue pacing.

How much longer will they be? Where are they?

And then suddenly, there they are. The shadowy greenery off to one side of the camp shivers and then Salif and the other five boys who went with him that morning pop into the clearing. Except one of them isn't walking. For a moment I stand there, then I'm sprinting across the clearing to see the limp body that is stretched on a pod sack being carried by a boy at each corner. They leave a dark trail behind them. The cloth is dripping blood.

I run so hard I have trouble stopping and I nearly smash into

Modibo. I grab his arm to steady myself and look into the hammock he's straining to carry. But then I'm frozen again, hand still on his arm, because I don't know what to do next.

Seydou is sprawled in the dip of the sack, his long skinny legs hanging off, his heels covered in dust from where they've been dragging. His head lolls to the side and I can tell he's not really conscious right now, but that's probably a good thing because there's blood everywhere. *So much blood!* It's very wet and very red, so he must have been injured not long ago.

"Get off!" Modibo pulls away from me. "You can look when we get to the fire. He's heavy."

I trail along after them, watching miserably as Seydou's heels bump across the ground.

When they get to the edge of the fire, the boys set down the sack and leave, stretching their arms and cracking their necks, as if they'd carried a large sack of *cacao*, not my brother.

The sack with Seydou on it is now spread in front of the fire. The firelight plays across his face, highlighting his slightly sunken temples and eyes. I try not to think about how skinny he is most of the time, but right now, I can't avoid how little of him there is in this world.

I sink beside him on my knees and rest my hand softly on his forehead. His face looks peaceful, smoothed out in the light like he's asleep. I know it's only because he's unconscious that he looks like that, but it makes my heart twist anyway.

"Oh, Seydou," I manage. Tears are choking my voice, but I

don't even care. Seydou's not awake to hear me, and the rest of them can all go to hell as far as I'm concerned. They didn't keep him safe.

No, you *didn't keep him safe.*

I shudder and force myself to look at my brother more carefully. There. That's why he won't be able to work anymore. I see a dirty rag wrapped tightly around Seydou's arm, soaked in blood. His chest is bare and I realize that the rag must be his shirt. I look over the rest of him, all blessedly in once piece. But there's so much blood I wonder how bad the cut is. A heavy hand on my shoulder makes me jump. I whirl around. Moussa is standing behind me, a small bag in his hand.

"Let's have a look," he says.

I scoot over and Moussa kneels beside me to unwrap the shirt tied around Seydou's arm. I don't know what to do, so I just stay put. The bandage is dripping, soaked through, so it comes off Seydou's arm easily. The wet shirt hits the ground with a soft *slap* and Moussa looks at me sharply. It's the only way I know that I've made a noise.

It's a disaster. A deep, jagged-edged gash slices down Seydou's forearm, biting through the base of his hand. I see the pulp and meat of his arm and a white thing lurking in the red of his wrist that might be bone. When Moussa pinches the two edges of skin together, blood pours out of the sides. Seydou doesn't move. I start to get really worried.

"Hold this here," Moussa says to me, gesturing with his chin to where he's holding Seydou's arm in place. I reach forward tentatively and cup my brother's wrist between my hands. I put my two thumbs around it and replace Moussa's fingers holding the mangled forearm together. I have trouble looking at the wound but I don't want to look away, so instead I stare at my thumbs, examining the dirt under my fingernails. Moussa digs around in the bag beside him. A minute later he leans forward with a spool of black thread and a needle.

"What are you going to do?" I ask, my voice husky.

"I have to sew it shut. Hopefully that will stop the bleeding enough for him to get better." Moussa shrugs. "One way or the other, we'll do this quickly."

Part of me hates Moussa right now, but the rest of me is so grateful to him for showing up and knowing what to do that I don't say anything as he bends over Seydou and binds the edges with large, irregular stitches. It takes a lot of stitches.

"How did this happen?" I ask as he rethreads the needle.

Moussa looks at me before bending over the work in front of him again, pulling the thread slowly through the muscle and skin of Seydou's arm, tying him back together.

"From what I hear, he was reaching around the trunk of a tree to pull at a pod just as another boy was swinging to cut it. The boy cut him instead."

I want to ask who the boy was. A rage so pure and white burns inside of me that I think I'll find the boy and kill him with my bare hands. But I don't let myself ask the question, even though Moussa has one eyebrow raised, waiting for it. I can't trust myself with what I'd do with the information once

I had it. Because really, it's not that boy's fault. Seydou should have known better. But he didn't. I would never have cut a pod when his hand was there, because I'm always looking to see where his hands are, what he's doing, whether he's safe. He's so used to being with me that he's never learned the common sense of a crew: don't put your hand around a tree when other people are cutting in the area. So really, it's my fault the other boy cut him. I look away from Moussa and keep my mouth shut.

Moussa shrugs, then goes back to his stitching. His stitches pull at Seydou's swelling skin and the little black knots look like rows of ugly birds, flying down his arm and onto his hand.

"Find something to wrap it with," says Moussa, "and tie it tight." He wipes the needle off on his pants, puts it and the thread into the little sack, and walks away from us, to where the other crews have prepared dinner.

I cradle Seydou's head in my lap. I'm not sure if I should use his shirt from before or not. On the one hand, it's covered in blood and dirt and it's wet. I'm not sure if you're supposed to wrap stitches in wet cloth or not. On the other hand, the shirt is ruined for wearing, and I don't really have many other options, unless I use my shirt. I sit there for a minute, undecided, and then I take Seydou's shirt to the water pump.

The metal handle flakes rust into my palm as I crank it, but after a few full-arm pushes, I'm rewarded with a gush of water from the spout. I hold Seydou's shirt under the spout with one hand and pump with the other, squeezing the cloth in my hands as I go. The air in the shirt bubbles out through the fabric when I squeeze it and the whole thing froths red over my hands. I try not to let the mingled smell of my brother's blood and my own fear turn my stomach. Instead, I pump harder and scrub the shirt between my fists, imagining it's the face of the boy who cut him.

By the time the water runs clear through the shirt, I'm standing in a red mud puddle that fills the wrinkles on the tops of my toes. I wring the shirt out and head to where Seydou is lying. I want to rip the shirt into strips: one to bandage him, one to wash him off, one to leave, cool, on his face, but we don't have the luxury of destroying a shirt for comfort, so instead I fold it in three and then wrap it tightly around his arm, tying the sleeves in a knot to hold it together.

As I pull the ends of the knot, Seydou cries out.

"Seydou?"

He starts keening in response, a high, awful sound. I look wildly around the camp, but no one tells me what to do. I notice that Khadija has stood up and has come as close to us as her chain will allow, but she's still far away and no one else is coming any closer.

"Hey there," I say, low and soft, pulling him against me. "I've got you now. It's me, Amadou. It's your brother. I've got you now and you're safe. I know your arm hurts, but Moussa stitched it up and soon you'll be all better, I just know it. Shh."

I mumble on with whatever ridiculous things I can think of to calm him, but he continues to sob and tears roll down his face. When he thrashes, he tries to make a fist with his hurt hand, but only three fingers bend. I taste bile in my mouth and force myself to swallow.

It'll get better. It'll get better, I say to myself.

Clumsily, I lift Seydou into my arms, trying not to pinch his injured arm between our bodies. The ridges of the scars on his back rub against my fingers. I carry him to the pump and set him down a little bit away from the puddle I made before. Then I peel off my own shirt and wet it like I did for Khadija. I do the best I can to scrub the rest of Seydou's body. When I'm done he looks cleaner but, without the layer of dirt and blood, he looks almost gray. I don't think I've ever seen anybody look as pale as my little brother in that moment and I'm afraid.

Now thoroughly wet, Seydou is shivering, so I pull on my soaked shirt, pick him up again, and go sit close to the fire. I pull his head onto my lap and stretch his legs toward the warmth. One of the other boys offers me a bowl of stew but Seydou won't eat it and I can't. I shake my head and eventually the boy leaves. I sit and rock Seydou until the bosses come and make us go into the sleeping hut.

Yussuf comes over and helps lift Seydou into my arms. I pull away from him. *You were there today,* my eyes say. *I don't know if I can trust you.*

"I'm sorry," he whispers, and then he walks away before I can let myself think about what Yussuf might be sorry for.

I stagger under Seydou's weight into the sleeping hut. There is a general quiet rustling and murmuring as the rest of the boys settle for the night. I head to our usual corner and lay Seydou gently on the dirty straw. Then I hear the *clink* of a chain.

I look up in time to see Khadija being shoved into the sleeping hut with the rest of us just before the big door swings shut, blocking out the last traces of light from the fire. I feel a small pang. In all my worry about Seydou I had forgotten about her.

"Good luck," says a faceless dry chuckle from the other side of the door, and I hear the bolt being thrown and the padlock click closed.

For a heartbeat the entire hut is silent. Then I hear a whistle from the corner near the door where the oldest boys sleep.

"Hey, pretty girl," says a voice in the darkness, "come sleep over here."

There is a wave of soft laughter among the rest of the boys. I can tell it's a joke, said to break the awkward silence, but Khadija doesn't know it.

She screeches wordlessly. A clatter follows and I realize she must have tripped over someone in her hurry to get away from the whistler. You get pretty good at seeing with your ears after two years in the dark.

"Ow!" Another voice, this time from the person she must have fallen on.

The laughter gets louder.

Khadija sobs.

In an instant I'm standing, following the sound, sliding my feet along the ground so I know when to step over a boy instead of bumping into him. Part of me can't believe that I've left my hurt brother to help a girl I didn't even know existed four days ago. But I have to. The other boys may not know what she went through last night, but I do. And while I couldn't do anything to change what happened then, I can do something about this.

I get to the front of the hut.

"Stop it," I say, loudly, to the sleeping hut at large.

There's a startled break in the laughter.

"Come on, Khadija," I say, and reach my hand through the darkness toward her. I touch her and for a second she recoils.

". . . Amadou?" Her voice is shaky.

"*Awó*, it's me."

A soft hand grabs mine and I pull her forward.

"Try not to step on anyone. Seydou's in the corner."

The older boys recover the quickest, and as we shuffle to the back of the sleeping hut, I get some colorful suggestions about what I can do with my new girlfriend and a few fuzzy threats about what they'll do to me if I ever give orders again. I ignore them. I'm one of the biggest boys here and pretty much every-one knows better than to mess with me.

My foot bumps gently into a leg. It pulls out of my way.

"You're just about there," says Yussuf, helping me orient myself.

I turn slightly and creep forward until I hear Seydou's jag-ged breathing, then I sit. Khadija settles beside me with a jingle. She's close enough that I can feel the heat radiating off her body as well as Seydou's. There's a slim sound from her chains that makes me think she's shaking.

"It's all right," I say softly, hoping none of the others can hear me. "It was only a joke."

She doesn't answer and since the joke isn't really worth defending, I leave it at that.

"We're in the corner now," I tell her. "If you're careful, you can step over Seydou and sleep between him and the wall. I'll be out here." After a long moment of silence I hear her rustle and clank her way to follow my suggestion.

Now that the area around me is clear again, I stretch out beside Seydou.

The whistles and jokes continue for a while, but I don't say anything and, one by one, the voices drop away as the boys in the hut fall asleep. Everyone had a long day of work today and is facing another one tomorrow. No joke is better than sleep.

I only wish I could join them.

Instead, as quiet settles into the hut and the noises of the night bush take over, I stare at the ceiling and wonder what on earth I'm going to do now that I have two hurt people to look out for instead of one.

I don't sleep well that night, waking whenever Seydou moves or cries out. I touch his face in the dark and my hand comes away feeling warm. I touch his arm in the dark and my hand comes away feeling wet. Neither of these comfort me, and when I do sleep, I dream I'm walking across ankle-deep fields of blood while lines of black birds pull together wounds in the sky, only to finally find myself standing by a yawning grave.

I wake up shaking, my heart thudding in my chest and my breathing rapid. I clutch Seydou to me.

When the bosses open the doors the next morning, I feel like I live in another world. I don't see right, don't hear right. It takes Moussa slapping me on the head to get me to move out of the sleeping hut to the fire with the other boys, Seydou still clutched in my arms, Khadija a clanking shadow behind me.

Now that my initial terror is gone, I realize how heavy Seydou is. I walk stooped like an old man, shuffling one foot in front of the other, to the pump, where I peel the bandage off Seydou's arm, wash it out, and put it on again, since I don't know what else to do. He yells and thrashes around when I touch him, but he's so weak it doesn't take much to hold him still. I splash water onto his hot face and try to direct some into his mouth. Most of it dribbles down his chin, but I'm rewarded when I see the bump in his throat move, showing that he's drinking at least something.

I look up when Moussa stands in front of me.

"Eat." He hands me a bowl.

I want to scream at him to take it away. Want to tell him I'm not hungry. Want to beg him to save my brother. But when I open my mouth no words come out. Moussa puts the bowl in my hands and takes Seydou from me.

"Eat," he says again.

I do.

Moussa turns around and walks back into the sleeping hut, carrying Seydou. I get to my feet and follow along behind them, Khadija still by my side.

"Wait," I say, "wait." But Moussa ignores me and I'm not sure what I want him to wait for anyway, so I make myself finish the bowl of whatever it is as I follow them into the semidarkness.

The inside of the sleeping hut is dim, with speckles of bright morning sun slicing through the tiny cracks in the siding and along the ground where the walls disappear into the floor. Because the door is open behind me I can see more than I usually can: the piles of dried grass and cloth scraps that the boys have moved around to make sleeping areas for themselves, the shadow-lined dents in the dirt floor that show where someone has slept for many months. I walk to our sleeping area, where Moussa is laying Seydou, pulling grass from nearby piles for under his head. His movements are gentle, and I'm grateful to him for that. I hover in the doorway and watch. Moussa looks at me.

"Go fill a bucket with water and bring whatever's left of that soup. You," he continues to Khadija, "help me with his head."

To my surprise, she obeys and goes to Seydou.

When I get back to the sleeping hut with the bucket of water and the half bowl of soup I was able to take from the other boys, Khadija is sitting on the ground beside my brother and

Moussa is standing off to one side, looking at both of them in disgust.

"Listen closely, Amadou," Moussa says when I get to them. "In five minutes, we are going to leave for a day of work. You will be coming with us. I am going to leave this girl in here with your brother." He looks at the watch he is so proud of on his wrist. "You have . . . four and a half minutes to persuade her to take good care of him."

With that, Moussa strides out of the sleeping hut and into the morning sunshine. Out of sight, I hear him shouting at the boys to get their tools and form work crews. A distant part of my brain notes that, being the last one in line, I won't get a good blade, but the thought is such a small problem that I actually laugh.

Khadija looks up.

I put the bucket of water beside her and hand her the extra bowl of soup.

"Do your best," I say. "I'll be back as soon as I can."

She doesn't say anything to me, but takes the bowl. I brush my hand softly over Seydou's face. He whimpers. I rearrange the pile of grass under his head, trying to make him more comfortable. Then I lean over and rest my forehead against his burning one.

"You stay alive," I whisper to him fiercely. "You stay alive until tonight. You hear me?"

But Seydou's eyes are wild and feverish, staring past me, and I don't know if he's heard me or not.

"Amadou!" Moussa barks from outside. "Now!"

I turn at the sound of Moussa's irritation and get up to leave. A hand darts out of the shadows and grabs my ankle. I look at Khadija in surprise. She's looking at Seydou, lying there making mewling noises of pain. Her fingers squeeze my ankle tightly. Then she looks up.

"Hurry," she says. "I'll do the best I can."

It's the first thing she's said, other than my name, since it happened.

"*I ni cé*," I whisper, and walk out. Moussa closes the door behind me, padlocking it shut.

"Get a machete," he says, and heads into the trees, where the last group is disappearing into the green.

I walk to the toolshed and pick up the last machete. I was right: it's the worst one. But as I swing the cracked, warped handle in my hand and grab a sack, I feel lighter. Because the wildcat agreed to take care of my brother. And a bad machete is a very, very small problem.

8

The day is a humid ache of work accompanied by the drone of mosquitoes. I smack at the insects when I can't stand it anymore, but others are always there to take their place. Mosquitoes are like bad thoughts that way. All day I swat away thoughts of Seydou and Khadija, but I can't ever make them stop.

Today more than most, I note the slow creep of the sun across the sky and I race to fill the bags, hoping to leave early. It still hurts to work, each swing of my machete pulling on the half-healed welts crisscrossing my back. But I won't let myself slow. I'm on my second sack when someone joins me.

"I'm sorry about your brother," says a quiet voice at my elbow.

I rub my forehead against my upper arm, not wanting to put down my machete to wipe the sweat out of my eyes properly. It's Yussuf.

I don't feel like talking. I keep cutting the ripe pods off their stems and for a minute we work side by side. An uncomfortable silence stretches, with only the *chop* of machetes to fill it. With Yussuf so close, it's hard not to imagine what happened to

Seydou. Why was he even working near someone? Why didn't he get his own tree?

I know that Yussuf is giving me the chance to say something, giving me the chance to talk. I want to think that Yussuf is being nice. But somewhere else in my head, a dark, poisonous voice whispers that maybe Yussuf's conversation isn't based on feelings of kindness. Maybe it comes from feelings of guilt.

Could Yussuf be the one who cut my brother? I won't let myself ask. But I also don't make eye contact and I don't talk to him. I focus on the movements of my hands and resolve not to talk to anyone for the rest of the day. After a while, Yussuf lets his work take him away from me. I don't invite him to stay.

The afternoon passes in a haze of sweat as I worry about Seydou. How is he doing? How is he feeling? Is Khadija alert enough to help him? Visions of the two of them sprawled on the floor, too weak to reach for the water, assault me, making me work faster, sloppier. But I don't care. All that matters is seeing them again and knowing they're all right.

When Moussa finally looks at the orange-striped clouds and says it's time to go, I shove my machete into a loop of rope around my waist, heft a sack, and break into a jog. Moussa lets me run. I guess he knows I'm running back, not away.

I skid into the clearing and dump my sack of pods by the lean-to. I toss my terrible machete into the toolshed and race to the sleeping hut.

"Seydou, Khadija, I'm here!" I call through the door.

When Moussa catches up to me and unlocks the padlock,

I charge across the dusty floor and drop to my knees beside Seydou. He's lying very still, but I can see the soft rise and fall of his chest and I slow my breathing to match it. When I reach out, he gasps as if it hurts for me to touch him. He's burning with fever. The makeshift bandage I put on him this morning is crusted solid. When I left, it was loose, but now it's so tight his fingers bulge out of the top like cassava tubers. I turn and look at Khadija, not knowing what to say. She leans forward and puts her free hand on Seydou's face. He whimpers again at being touched.

"He's been like this for a while," she says.

"Was he awake at all?" I ask.

"A few times. But he was raving, so I think it was just the fever talking."

"Did you give him more water?"

"How was I supposed to do that?"

I remember, too late, that they were locked in.

"I'll go get some now." I reach for the empty bucket and the bowl.

"Bring me some too?" I can hear how hard it is for her to ask.

"Of course," I say.

As I jog to the pump, I see the rest of my group file into the clearing. I fill the bucket with water and head back into the hut. Though it kills me to do it, I hand it to Khadija first, since she's awake. Her eyebrows go up in surprise but she doesn't say anything. She takes a few long, slow swallows and then tips the rest of the bucket over her head and hands. She gives it to me empty and I retrace my steps. This time, as I head into the sleeping hut, a few of the other boys follow me. I ignore them and kneel by Seydou. I hold his head in one hand and try to pour the water into his mouth with the other. He moans and turns away. The water dribbles down his neck. Frustrated, I consider my options. Unless he's awake, I can't make him drink. As long as his fever is this high, he won't be awake. The thin remains of daylight coming through the open door glint off the water I failed to pour into his mouth. That's all the thought I give it before I pour the entire bucket of water over his face.

All I was trying to do was bring down his fever but when the cold water hits his skin, Seydou jerks awake, screaming.

He lurches into a sitting position, then, gripping his arm, falls back again. He's awake now and I try to reach for him, but he hasn't stopped screaming and his writhing is turning the water puddle under his head into a thick mud that coats his face and shoulders. I hear the other boys murmur behind me and shuffle away.

"Seydou!" I say, leaning over him. "Seydou!"

His shouts are formless. I don't even know if he knows I'm here. I want to follow the others out of the hut, but this impulse shames me deeply and I stay put. I look at Khadija.

"He was like this?" I ask.

She nods.

I don't know how she stood it. I crouch there, frozen by my own powerlessness until I hear a grunt of distaste. I turn and see Moussa silhouetted behind me. I hate how small and miserable

I must look, but there's no way I can think to move that would be helpful.

Moussa takes one look at Seydou and hoists him into a semi-standing position, braced against his body. I stare dumbly as Moussa wrestles Seydou out of the sleeping hut.

"Wait!" I say, scrambling to my feet and running after them. "You're hurting him!"

Moussa throws me an annoyed glance over Seydou's head.

"With a fever this high, everything will hurt."

"But . . ." I stumble along beside them, waving my hands uselessly. "But this is hurting him more than leaving him where he was. Stop!"

Moussa ignores me and drags Seydou to the water pump, laying him in the mud. Seydou struggles to get away.

"Get his head up," Moussa says to me. I scramble behind Seydou and hold him against me. He thrashes weakly from side to side. "Hold him still," says Moussa, and then he stands behind the pump and works the handle with powerful thrusts of his arm. Water gushes out. I'm about to tell Moussa that getting Seydou wet was what made him start screaming in the first place, when Moussa reaches around and cups the spout, redirecting the water so that it drenches us both. Seydou lurches in my arms as the water hits his fevered skin.

"Stop it!" I shout.

Moussa stops, but his scowl could rip the sky.

"The water's hurting him," I mumble miserably.

"Would you rather hurt him now, or have him die?" Moussa's quiet question stabs me like a machete. Neither! I don't want him hurt, now or ever, and of course I don't want him to die.

"What?"

"We have to bring his fever down. If we don't, he may die. I would prefer to hurt him now and have him live, than let him be comfortable now and have him die. Which would you prefer?"

I stare dumbly, unable to answer. After a moment of silence, Moussa starts pumping the water again. This time when Seydou bucks and shrieks, I hold him still. After a while, he goes limp in my arms, resigning himself to the pain, crying. I let the hard, cold water hit my face and take my tears away with Seydou's fever.

When Moussa stops, both Seydou and I are soaked and shivering in the early-evening breeze.

"Let's get you by the fire," says Moussa, and he hauls us both up by the arms. He slings Seydou's dead weight between us and we shuffle to the fire, where Moussa lets go of his side. Seydou and I crumple in a heap inside the orange circle of light. I pull Seydou's head into my lap and carefully place his hurt arm on top before I look around the fire. It's oddly quiet as the boys consider us. A soft clanking of chains draws my eyes to where Khadija settles.

I'm still shivering and wet, but Seydou's fever has already dried the water off his skin. I tell myself that the swelling will go down along with his fever, but when I look into Seydou's eyes, he doesn't look out at me. He's awake, but has gone somewhere far, far away inside where I can't reach him. I stroke his forehead, willing him to get better.

Yussuf offers me a bowl of stew. When I take it, he leaves without another word. I try to think of a way to get some food into Seydou, but I'm afraid that if I force the chunky soup into his mouth I'll end up choking him, so I just eat my portion and spend the rest of the quiet evening wetting Seydou's head and trying to sneak little dribbles of water into his mouth.

When they call us for bed I'm not sure how much I've succeeded, but I go and refill the bucket with water for the night and carry it into the sleeping hut. Then I half carry, half drag Seydou in after me.

I don't know how much later it is when I hear the whisper.

"Amadou? Are you awake?"

I sigh and answer quietly.

"*Awó*. What is it?"

"How's he doing?"

Khadija must not have been able to sleep either, though whether this is because of the discomfort of the chains or the discomfort of sleeping in a house surrounded by fourteen boys, I'm not sure. I flush a little in the darkness, wondering if she's been listening to the stupid nonsense I've been whispering to

Seydou for the past hour or so. I guess she has. I push the thought away.

"Still hot." There's not much more to say than that.

"Have you gotten him to drink anything?"

"*Ayi.*" The frustration of it roughens my voice. "It just dribbles off his face."

A pause.

"I can take over swabbing him with water if you want to sleep."

"No. We're fine."

Another pause.

"You should try to sleep."

"What does it matter to you?" I ask dismissively. She doesn't answer my question, but goes on as if I hadn't spoken.

"I was able to rest yesterday, and they'll probably keep me here tomorrow too, so I can sleep during the day. You were in the fields all day and they'll probably make you go out again tomorrow. You should sleep if you can."

"I can take care of my own brother," I bite out, but the words are sour in my mouth and I can taste the lie in them.

"You'll be no good to him if you get hurt because you're overtired," she says.

"Why do you care?" I ask again, this time truly curious.

At first she doesn't answer. But then she mumbles, "You can't help me either if you're hurt."

"What?"

"The boys leave you alone. Right now they're leaving me alone too. If you and Seydou were both hurt . . ."

For a few minutes there's only the irregular sloshing sound of me dipping my hand into the bucket. I've done it for so long that my fingers have puckered and my ridged fingertips drag across Seydou's eyebrows when I rub the water on his forehead.

"Maybe Moussa will let me stay with him tomorrow." I don't even realize I've said it out loud until I hear a snort from over by the wall.

"You trust him too much." There is a hard flatness to her voice when she says it. I remember how, that first day, she criticized me for not getting Seydou away from here. I feel a deep need to prove her wrong.

"He cares about Seydou," I say, scrambling to find facts to make what I said true. "He had him carried to camp, stitched him up, tried to bring his fever down this evening with the water. He left you here with him all day today instead of leaving him alone."

She snorts again. "You can't really believe that."

I stay quiet, angry now. The wildcat goes on in the silence.

"He doesn't care about Seydou, or any of you!" I want her to shut up, but she keeps talking. "He doesn't want Seydou to die because he's still hoping to get more work out of him. But you can do the work of a man in a day. There's no way he's going to lose that by letting you stay here."

I'm so angry now that I'm clenching my fists. I won't listen to what she's saying. I won't. It's not true.

98

"He'll take care of Seydou all right, but only if it doesn't cause him too much trouble and only because he cares about the money." There's a pause. Then, "Amadou?"

But I refuse to answer and although she calls my name a few more times, I don't talk to her again for the rest of the night.

And I don't let her help Seydou.

And I don't sleep.

By the next morning, I've passed beyond tiredness to a place where it takes me a few seconds to process sound into words and grainy colors into shapes. I move to the water pump to refill the bucket, which I've emptied overnight. But I haven't made it there when Moussa appears behind me, carrying Seydou, who is hanging limply in his arms, still hiding in that place where I can't find him.

Moussa sets him by the pump. I splash a little water onto Seydou's face. The water spatters over his eyes and dribbles off the curve of his cheeks onto the ground beside him. He doesn't even flinch. Moussa frowns. He lifts Seydou's shirt-bandaged arm under the pump and runs water on it until it soaks through. Then he unties the knot and unwraps it.

The stench is overpowering. Blood, sickness, and rot merge with the smells of sweat and dirt as Moussa peels the shirt off Seydou's arm. The last part sticks, pulling an infected crust off the wound, causing it to seep freely into the dust. I have to force myself to look at it. Swollen, oozing pus and blood, with angry streaks stretching from the tight stitches toward his elbow, Seydou's arm is so horrific I turn away and vomit.

He's not getting better. It's worse, so much worse than I could ever have imagined. I turn to Moussa, ashamed of myself. He's still frowning at the arm, pushing at the edge of the swollen stitches with one finger. I don't know how he can stand to do that. The smell of my vomit mixing with the smell of the infection makes me wish I was anywhere but here.

Moussa looks at me then and his face seems to soften.

"Your brother's arm is very bad," he says. "Go to your crew. I'll stay and take care of him today."

My body sags with relief. A part of me is ashamed at how glad I am to leave my brother, but I can't fight my feelings of helplessness when I look at that awful wound. Moussa knew how to stitch Seydou up. He'll know how to make his arm better today. I look at the corner of the sleeping hut where Khadija is leaning in the shadows and send a glare her way. *Moussa will take care of everything,* I think. She turns and hobbles to the breakfast fire. Perhaps she heard me.

I walk to the other side of the fire, away from Khadija, and bolt my breakfast of cooked green bananas. No stew this morning; Moussa was too busy with Seydou and me to organize it. As I pull off the hot, starchy peel and eat the insides, I see Moussa talking to the other bosses. A few minutes later when the call goes up to form crews, Ismail and Salif divide Moussa's usual crew between them.

I'm assigned to Ismail's team and I grab a machete from the shed and run to get in line. Ismail is not known for his patience. Even so, I don't end up with the worst machete. I almost smile. Tired as I am, today is looking up.

My mood is ruined when I see Moussa walking toward me, dragging a chained Khadija with him. I look behind me, sure they must be heading somewhere else, because, really, why on earth would he be putting us together when she's escaped twice when I've been around?

Moussa stops in front of me. He changed Khadija's chain. It's now almost a meter long, connecting two cuffs. One of them is around her wrist. Moussa holds the other out to me.

"Put this on," he says.

"W—what?" I stammer. "Why?"

Moussa gives me a look that says he has all the patience in the world and I am slowly using it up, one drop at a time.

"The *pisteurs* will be here soon. I have to have all the hands working in the field that I can. If I'm staying here to take care of your brother, she has to go and work."

I stare at him blankly. How does he expect me to be able to make her work? It's not like *I'm* a boss, or her brother, or anything.

"How . . ."

Moussa reaches out, grabs my left wrist, and slaps the heavy metal cuff onto it.

"Figure it out," he says to me softly. I gaze blankly from his receding back to the shackle on my hand and the girl at the end of the chain. A few steps away Moussa pauses as if he's just thought of something. "Oh, and Amadou?" He half turns.

"*Awó?*"

"If you let her escape today, I'll kill him."

With that, he walks away.

9

I stand there for a moment, frozen by Moussa's words.

They're not sinking in. I can't process them.

At the far end of the chain, Khadija moves. Reflexively, I grab the chain, causing her to take a stumbling step forward.

Scowling, she takes a second, very deliberate step toward me. She leans in until her thunder and lightning eyes are all I can see.

"You trust him too much." She says it quietly, fiercely, her eyes slicing into my carefully crafted shell. She holds my gaze for a moment, and no words, no thoughts spring to my defense, only a terrible dread.

I close my mouth and break away from her stare. I yank at the chain to make sure it will hold, bile churning in my stomach at the feel of metal against my skin. When I'm sure it's locked and won't come off, I let the length of chain slip through my fingers like water.

Neither of us says anything.

Why would we? There is nothing to say.

I walk to where Ismail's team has vanished into the bush and follow their trail. As I jog to catch up with the crew, I try to ignore the irregular tug that pulls my left arm behind me every time I take a step.

We still haven't spoken a word when I reach the last boy in line. He turns his head when he hears our jangling approach and I see his eyebrows shoot up as he takes us in. I want to say something to show that this is not what I wanted. I want him to say something that shows that he understands how unfair this whole thing is. If he had done that, I would have told him what Moussa said about Seydou. That awful thing he said that is still lying like a venomous snake at the bottom of my memory. I want someone to tell me that I couldn't possibly have heard right, or that Moussa didn't mean it. The wildcat heard it too, but I know she thinks Moussa would happily kill Seydou in a heartbeat. I look at the boy and try to remember how to smile.

Instead of smiling, he gives a low whistle.

"Well, I knew you two were close, but I didn't realize you wouldn't let yourself be separated more than a meter." He waggles his eyebrows when he says it, and laughs. Ahead of him, I see another boy repeat the joke. Anger hardens into a tight knot in my chest and I scowl at the row of boys. Why did I believe even for a second that any of them would be any help at all?

"*I ka da tugu,*" I snap.

The boy laughs again, softly, careful not to let Ismail hear. I'm furious with him, and my uncertainty over Seydou and my lack of sleep make me stupid. I take the flat of my machete and smack it into his chest, pushing him against a tree, pinning his arms flat by his sides. Khadija is pulled after me by my sudden movement, but I push forward anyway.

The boy's eyes dart to my face and his mouth drops open. His machete is on the ground a few arm's lengths away, knocked there when I hit him. I push my body weight against the machete so that the edge presses into him. It's not hurting him yet, but if he moves or struggles he'll be cut badly. I see his pupils expand in fear as he realizes this. I lean forward so that my face is barely centimeters from his.

"You are going to stop making jokes about me," I say quietly. I've learned that quiet words are often more frightening than loud ones. "Today especially, you and your friends are going to leave me alone. Is that clear?"

He nods, trembling slightly.

You're turning into the bosses, whispers a little voice in my head. I shake off the thought. I'm not like the bosses. I only do what I have to do to keep Seydou safe.

Seydou's not in danger here, comments the voice.

I feel my gut twist uncomfortably and I step away, letting the boy go without putting a mark on him. He scrambles to get his machete. His friend loops an arm around his shoulder and they run off into the trees, both of them shooting me ugly looks as they run. From up ahead I hear Ismail's whistle. This is far enough; we're to start here. I turn to find a group of likely trees to work on, furious with myself.

I find the wildcat standing behind me, the machete gripped

in her left hand. In the scuffle, I had forgotten about her for a moment. Forgotten that I'm going to have to spend the day making sure that she doesn't get cut like Seydou, as well as making sure she doesn't run away.

I stare at the ground, chest heaving, finding it hard to breathe. I want to yell. Tell her I have no room in my life to protect her, that I'm too busy trying to protect Seydou and, even with just that, I don't always do the best job.

A pull on my left wrist makes me look up.

"Come on," she says softly. "Let's get to work."

I try to settle into my usual routine of cutting pods, but the mismatched tug on my left wrist every time the girl moves is making it impossible for me to sink into my empty place and lose myself in the work. Since her chain only reaches so far, we have to work on the same tree, one on each side, or on two trees that are really close together. We also need to time our swinging, even though she's using her left hand and I'm using my right. Otherwise, we run the risk of cutting each other or twisting our wrists.

She's a sloppy worker. Like when I tried to teach her to shell—only three days ago, though it feels like years—there's no power behind her swing and her blade wobbles from side to side when she chops. When she throws the pods into the bag we're dragging behind us, the stems are mangled and splitting, not cleanly sliced like mine. Even so, we're making good progress. She doesn't get distracted like Seydou would and even though she's slow, the bag is filling much faster than it would if I were working with my brother. It reminds me just how young he really is.

I grind my teeth and keep chopping.

Because of my earlier outburst and because of Ismail's different work style, we're all pretty spread out. Khadija and I could imagine we were alone in the world if we didn't hear the steady chopping of the other boys. After about three hours of working I feel a different movement through the chain. I look over and see Khadija using a fold of her dress to wipe at her palm.

"*Mun kéra?*" I ask.

She looks up.

"Nothing's wrong, I guess. I'm getting blisters." She looks at her hands again.

I grimace in sympathy. I remember my first week of working in the fields. The long days of nothing but the same motion over and over again raised blisters really quickly. I had been surprised because I was used to farmwork, but we never had fields so big, and we grew many different crops to keep us fed. Not trees upon trees of *cacao* pods.

"The harvest months are the worst time for blisters," I tell her. "When they're waiting for the *pisteurs*, the bosses make us work longer than normal. Other times, we still have to cut pods, but we get to do other things too. We spray the trees to keep the bugs off them, chop down dead trees, plant new ones, clear the ground . . . the work is different enough. It's only when they're due for a pickup that we do nothing but chop pods all day long."

"What are *pisteurs*?"

"Not what. Who. The *pisteurs* are the ones who drive their trucks along *les pistes*, the little trails around here, and take the pod seeds we've harvested. They bring money and stuff the bosses need. You can pick *cacao* all year round, but twice a year, a lot of them come ripe at the same time. This is when the *pisteurs* visit and the bosses get really nervous, because they only get paid for what's fermented, dried, and ready to go."

Khadija wipes her hand and the handle of her machete one more time and grips it again.

"Lucky me for my timing," she says dryly.

I surprise both of us by laughing.

"Well," I say, feeling generous, "Moussa said the *pisteur* would be coming by tomorrow or maybe the day after. So, after that, things will get better for a few months, until he's due to come by again . . . Of course," I add with a wry smile, "there are only two months of the year when we pretty much *can't* harvest, so you'll get used to this pretty quickly. For now, wrap your sleeve around your hand. It helps a little." I hold out my hand in front of her, showing her the hard shell of my palm and fingers. "Soon you'll have calluses and won't even feel it anymore."

She looks at me as I settle my machete into my hand. My fingers wrap around the handle and lock into a hold made comfortable from long hours of practice. I swing it around idly a little, then pick up the sack we've been dragging between us. It's time to move on to another section of the grove. The remaining pods here are still thin and stumpy, not nearly the length or roundness that I need. When I straighten again to suggest we walk on for a bit, I'm shocked to see there are tears in her eyes.

"*Mun kéra?*" I ask again.

"It's just . . ." She looks away over the trees and scrubs her wrists into her eyes. Then she drops her hands to her sides. "I don't want to get calluses," she says.

I'm a little thrown off by this, because I hadn't pegged her in my mind as a girl who would cry over losing soft hands, but before I can open my mouth, she corrects herself.

"I mean, I don't want to stay here long enough to get calluses."

I stare at her. The whites of her eyes are red and underneath them is puffy, but the fierceness that's been missing for the last two days is back.

"I hate it here," she says simply. "I don't want to learn how to be better at work I hate doing in a place I hate being. I don't want to think about what it would mean for me to have hands like yours. I can't imagine living here that long."

I consider that for a moment.

"The bus drivers in Sikasso told us it would just be for a season, also," I say, finally. "We didn't come here thinking we'd live here this long either.

109

"I hate it here too," I admit. "But the faster you get used to it, the better off you'll be. You've seen what happens when you try to run away. They catch you and bring you back."

She flinches when I say this. Then, after a moment, she asks, "What happened when you ran?"

The images rush at me from a place in my mind where I've tried to crush them down. Me, grabbing Seydou by the hand and pulling him through the darkness as we ran from the camp, our hands slippery in each other's grip from the fresh blisters we both had. The chest-pounding terror of hearing the whistles behind us, the sign that we'd been missed. Running so hard I thought my lungs would explode from the effort, dragging a gasping Seydou with me as I saw the beams from the men's electric torches bounce off the branches of the trees around us. The heavy hands falling on us as we ran out of air and energy, shoving us to the ground, binding our hands, smacking us around as they dragged us to camp. And then, the worst of it. Moussa and the other bosses tying me up, off to the side, and making me watch as they whipped Seydou senseless with a bike chain. They forced him to say, after every lash, *This is Amadou's fault. This is Amadou's fault.* I knew he was being forced to say it, but that didn't make any difference. Every time I see the scars crisscrossing his back, I hear the echo of those words in my head.

"What happened?" she asks again, jerking me out of my memory.

"They caught us." My voice is rough as I say it. "I didn't run again."

"What did they do to you when they caught you?" Her arms are wrapped protectively around herself and her eyes are far away, probably remembering what they did to her.

I don't want to talk about it. It makes me sick to my stomach to even remember that night.

"Nothing." I surprise myself, hearing my own voice. I give a hollow laugh. "They never touched me." I know my smile has turned ugly.

She looks at me for a long time. I don't know what it is she sees but finally she says, "They knew what to do to break you."

It's a harsh statement, but probably true.

"It's okay," she whispers, and I'm startled to feel the warmth of her hand on my arm. "I think they know what to do to break everyone."

"Did they break you?" I ask.

She looks away, but doesn't take her hand from my arm.

"I don't know," she says finally.

I'm not sure how to tell her a part of me cries inside to think that they may have broken her. I'm not sure how to tell her, again, how sorry I am that I didn't do anything to stop it, even though I know it wouldn't have made a difference. I shift my arm to hoist the corner of the bag onto my shoulder. Her hand falls away.

"We should move on and try to get this bag filled before we stop for a midday rest." I start to walk, but I only make it a step or two before I have to turn around. She hasn't moved.

"Amadou."

"What?"

She holds up her wrist.

"I want you to know I'm not going to try to run today."

"What?"

"I heard what Moussa said to you this morning." Her face is serious. "I want you to know that, even though I don't want to be here, I'm not going to do something that would put Seydou in more danger."

I feel a tightness inside that, for once, isn't due to feelings of guilt or fear or anger. The wildcat is looking out for Seydou too again, like she did when he was sick and she stayed with him.

I'm startled to realize that that's how I'm thinking of her now: as someone who takes care of Seydou, not someone who betrayed him. As one more set of hands to keep my cricket safe. I wonder whether we could ever be a team. A little family, just us three, sharing things and looking after one another. I want to tell her how much it means to me to have someone to trust so that I'm not all alone, but the words won't come.

Instead, I nod.

She nods back, picks up her machete in her blistered hand, grabs the other end of the sack, and follows me into the trees to find another section to work in until dusk.

When the day finally winds to a close, I find that, though she hasn't been able to keep up with my pace, Khadija has worked hard without stopping, and as we walk in the direction of camp, each balancing a large sack filled with pods on our head, I'm confident that, as a team, we'll come in above quota.

On the main path we merge into the middle of the line of boys, each staggering under the weight of their day's work. The boy I pushed against a tree this morning stays well clear of us but the rest act normally, talking and joking. Khadija and I don't say anything to each other or the rest of the boys, but as we walk I notice that I no longer feel the irregular pull of metal on my wrist. Over the course of the day we've learned to walk perfectly in step with each other. For some reason, this makes me smile.

We're still a little ways off from camp when I first hear the crying. I wrinkle my forehead, trying to place the sound—a monkey? A bird? Beside me, I feel Khadija stiffen. It's definitely coming from the camp. My heart plunges into my stomach as I wonder if it's Seydou. I walk faster. Khadija matches my pace, not complaining.

The closer we get to camp the more sure I am that the sound is human. However, the cries aren't the fevered shrieks that Seydou was letting out yesterday when Moussa splashed him with water and I start to hope, quietly, deep inside, that Moussa kept his promise and was able to do something.

We break from the trees into the clearing and at first I think I'm right. Moussa has made a fire and is standing in front of it, arms crossed, staring into the flames. Beside him is a small, hunched figure that must be Seydou. The fire blocks my view of them, but the fact that he's sitting unsupported is such an improvement that I turn to Khadija with a smile.

"Look! He's sitting up!"

She doesn't say anything, just keeps staring at the pair by the fire, her forehead wrinkled in concern.

"Amadou—" she starts, but I don't want to hear it. I veer off, dragging her with me to the storage lean-to, where I drop our sacks, then spin around and trot to the fire, not even waiting for Ismail to come and tell us whether or not we've made quota.

"Seydou!" I call, but he doesn't answer me.

It's only as I get closer that I can see something is wrong. Though he's sitting up, Seydou isn't acting normally. He's twisted himself into a tight knot, and he's rocking back and forth, seemingly unaware of what's going on around him. I run over to him, Khadija only a half step behind me, and I pull him into my arms. Seydou falls against me, keening. I use the fact that I'm bigger to force him to uncurl his body, trying to get a look at the wound and see if it's doing better.

And that's when I see that his arm is gone.

10

For a moment I can't process what I see, can't understand what's happened. I hear a gasp and feel the weight of the air shift beside me as Khadija falls to her knees next to Seydou. She reaches out and touches his face lightly.

"Oh, Seydou," I hear her whisper, "what did they do to you?"

I want to scream at her. *What do you think they did to him? Don't you have eyes? There's only a rag-wrapped stump of his arm left past his elbow. You can see what they did to him!* But I don't because some part of me realizes that screaming would be ridiculous. She wasn't here with him all day; she was with me.

Seydou pulls out of my arms and crumples to the ground. I let him go, spinning to face Moussa, who hasn't moved. My wrist jerks when I do, and I hear Khadija's hiss of breath when my action pulls her onto her feet behind me, but I don't even care.

"What did you do to him?" I shout. A small part of my brain registers that the only words that make it out of my mouth are almost the exact ones that Khadija used just moments before, but I can't seem to come up with any others, so I use hers and let my volume speak my anger.

Moussa glares at me.

"What needed to be done," he says. His voice is tired and annoyed.

"You . . . you . . ." *You took his arm,* I want to say, but the words catch somewhere in my chest and won't come out.

"It had to be done, Amadou." Moussa is still talking in that quiet, I'm-the-elder-here voice, and hatred for him washes all over my skin, burning like spilled pesticide. "His wound was festering. He didn't have another day in him. If I had left his arm on, you would be coming home to a corpse."

An acid feeling twists inside me. The gratitude he's trying to make me feel mixes with my rage, creating poison in my belly.

"You cut off his arm!" I finally scream, the words breaking out of me, tearing big holes in my soul as they do. Moussa stares at me as if I've lost my wits.

"Of course I did. What did you think I was going to do when I told you this morning I would take care of it?"

And then I can't help myself. I curl my hand into a fist and punch Moussa in the face with all the strength I have.

Of course, after a stunned moment of cursing and grabbing his bleeding nose, Moussa does the same to me, repeatedly, and then tosses me again into the toolshed, the evening resting place for all problem children, locking it behind me.

I lean over in the corner, with my head tipped forward so I'm not choking on the blood from my nose, and spit until it clots. I lift my hands to my face to wipe off the mess and it's only when my left wrist jingles as I do so that I realize Khadija is still chained to me.

"Why are *you* here?" I manage, my words muddy because of my plugged nose.

"Because I'm still attached to you, silly," she says.

I look at her sideways.

"Apparently this time it's *my* fault for not stopping *you*." She gives a half smile.

And I don't know why, but for some reason this strikes me as the funniest thing I've heard in weeks and I start laughing, deep belly-clenching laughs that make me bend double and force tears out of my eyes. Khadija seems surprised at first, but then she laughs softly along with me.

"It's really not that funny, you know," she says after a while.

I huff some air through my nose to clear it.

"Yeah, I know."

For a while the two of us just sit there, our backs along the wall of the shed, our chained hands resting on the floor between us, listening to the sounds of dinner and cleanup happening outside. No one opens the door to give us any food but I wasn't really expecting them to. As the shadows deepen, Khadija's eyes begin to dart around the shed and she picks at a tear in her skirt, making it worse.

"They sound extra busy tonight," I say, to get her mind off the things she's thinking about. Her hands still. I tip my head to the side and listen for a moment, trying to identify the chores being done. "Sounds like they're collecting the seeds from the drying racks and filling burlaps. The *pisteur* is due tomorrow."

"You know, I never thought you'd hit him."

For a moment I'm confused because I've never hit a *pisteur*, and I'm pretty sure that this soft little kid has never met one in her life, but then I realize Khadija has changed the subject and is talking about Moussa. I pick at the dried blood on my face until it flakes off under my fingernails. I don't know what to say. *I* never thought I'd hit Moussa either. Since disrespect is treated harshly, I always figured a physical attack would be the same as committing suicide. I rub my face again. Really, for what I did, Moussa didn't hurt me very much at all. He must be feeling bad.

"He cut off Seydou's arm," I say. The image of the firelight flickering off Seydou's upper left arm and then being swallowed by the bloody bandage below his elbow assaults me as I say it.

That's all we say until after the sounds from outside stop and we hear them lock the sleeping hut door. The rev of the truck engine fading tells me the bosses have gone home for the night too. Beside me the tension goes out of the chain. With the departure of the bosses, Khadija has relaxed again.

But I tense up. Though I wasn't expecting the door to open for food, I was expecting them to put my brother in with us for the night so I could look after him. His absence is like a physical pain, a lack where there should be feeling. Who will hold him if he cries? How will I know if he makes it through the night?

"He'll be fine," says Khadija. I wonder how much of what I was thinking I muttered out loud.

"How do I know if I can't see him?"

"The others seem to like him. He's such a nice little boy."

My cricket.

"But how do I *know*?" I ask again. A pause.

"You don't. For tonight you'll just have to trust that they'll do the right thing, I guess. It's not like you have much of a choice. And if you spend all night worrying you'll drive yourself crazy and you won't get enough sleep to be able to help him tomorrow if he needs you."

It's good advice, but hard to swallow. I'm haunted by images of Seydou the way he was the last two nights, tossing around in pain, but I force myself to remember Yussuf's soft apology and take a deep breath.

"You're right," I say, "he will need me tomorrow."

"Of course he will," she says soothingly. But I shake my head.

"No," I say, my voice hard, "not like that." I've been trying to take care of Seydou in little ways for years, and clearly, today showed that it's not enough. Now it's time to take care of him in a big way. Because when I really think about it, Khadija was right all along. Living here is nothing more than killing Seydou slowly. I turn to her. "He's going to need me tomorrow because I'm going to get him away from here. We're getting off this farm."

There is a brief second of complete silence.

"It's not that easy and you know it," she says bitterly.

"I know," I say.

"So what makes it different this time?"

"A couple of things." I smile into the darkness. "For one, I finally understand that I have nothing to lose by running." My voice falters. "It's hard to work here. I don't think that, even if he gets better, Seydou is going to survive very long with just one arm."

Beside me, I feel Khadija shiver.

"For another thing, I know a lot more about how the farm works than when I was new. Plus, I have you to help me." I say it half as a joke, because, really, what can a weak thirteen-year-old girl do to help me? But Khadija takes me seriously.

"Me? You're crazy. Three are so much easier to catch than one! No, thank you, Amadou. The next time I run I'm going to make it. When I run, I run alone."

"It was a joke," I say coldly, masking my disappointment. "I wouldn't expect help from someone as selfish as you."

I turn away from her and try to think.

Slowly, I feel a giddy excitement building in me, so different from the empty place I've put myself into for the past two years that it feels odd. Like stretching old muscles that haven't done a certain job in a long time and finding out that they still work, still remember what to do.

"One way or another," I say, holding up our chained wrists,

"whether you're coming with us or not, the first thing we need to do is get this off."

"*Awó*," she agrees. Her tone is off, but I don't have time to care.

"Let's see what we can find in this shed to help us."

And so we shuffle around the small space in the dark, on our hands and knees, using our fingers to try to figure out what everything is.

"Machetes," I report.

"Rope," she replies.

"A box."

I'm trying to figure out a way to open the latch when Khadija gives her next update.

"Metal barrel."

"Don't touch that!"

At the end of the chain, I feel her recoil.

"Why?" she asks. "What is it?"

"Poison."

I remember when I was first here. It was one of the two months of the year when we weren't harvesting. Instead, it was cleaning season. The time of year when the main job for the boys is to take pump-cans of pesticide and spray the trunks and branches of all the trees in the grove. Moussa had brought me into the shed and showed me the great one-hundred-and-fifty-liter drums of pesticide. *These,* he had said, *are poison. They are a very special kind of poison, one that kills the insects that would eat my*

trees. But you should never forget for one minute what you're carrying.
Don't drink it. Don't let it get in your food. Don't let it get near fire.
Don't touch it and then rub your eyes. Do you understand? And I had
said, *Yes, I understand,* and as soon as we got out into the grove I
had strapped both canisters on and made Seydou stand far away
from where I was working. And I tried not to show him my fear
as the poison mist settled onto my skin.

"Pesticide," I clarify. "For the trees. It kills the bugs, but it's
bad for you too. Don't touch it." I feel her carefully put distance
between herself and the drums, so I know she's taking me seriously. "Come look in this box."

When we pry the lid open with a machete, what we find
inside makes the whole night of searching worthwhile. Because
inside are tools. Real tools. Strong tools. Screwdrivers and hammers and clippers. I look at the dark form in front of me that
must be Khadija and a smile splits my face.

"We're free," I say.

It's too dark to tell for sure, but I think she smiles back.

It's difficult to do it in the darkness, but I get Khadija to wedge
the tip of the screwdriver into the latch of the manacle on my
left hand.

"Now hold still," I say, hefting the large hammer in my right.

"What if you miss and hit me?" she asks.

"I'll try not to," I say, "but if you let go and that screwdriver
goes sideways, it will go into my wrist and probably kill me."

There is a pause while she processes this information.

"All right," she says finally, "even if you hit me, I won't let go."

"*I ni cé.*"

I take a few practice swings with the hammer, bringing it slowly over my head and tapping it onto the top of the screwdriver. I miss a few times but I keep doing it until I'm consistently hitting the handle. I'm going to need to use a lot of force and what I said to Khadija is the truth: if I miss, it's likely one of us will get seriously hurt. After a few minutes, I feel my muscles relax into the new pattern. Hammering a point in the dark is not so different from splitting pods with a machete. I turn to Khadija.

"Okay, this time for real."

I feel her grip tighten on the screwdriver and I try not to change the angle of my body as I lift the heavy hammer.

The blow sends my wrist shooting sideways. The screwdriver is wrenched out of Khadija's hands and scrapes against my leg, and the hammer hits her knuckles. I hear her gasp in pain. But mingled in with all those sounds is the sound of a snapping clasp, and when I feel the manacle, it now has a large gap in it.

"Are you okay?" I ask the darkness.

"*Awó.*" Her voice is muffled because she's sucking on her knuckles.

"Did I break any bones in your hand?"

A pause.

"No. I can move all my fingers. It just hurts."

I let a breath out, relieved. Pain is something we can handle.

"Are you out?" she asks.

I shove my hand against the gap in the metal, twisting my wrist painfully and scraping the skin.

"*Awó!*"

"Good," says Khadija, handing me the screwdriver. "Now me."

I pick up the hammer again.

"Use your other hand to hold it steady," I say.

This time, since I can grip the handle of the screwdriver in my left hand, it's much easier. After only two swings, the lock gives and we're both free.

"Now what?" A twinge of breathless excitement has crept into her voice.

I still don't know whether she'll stick around or run on her own once we're free, but I know she'll help me until we're out of this shed.

I walk to the rear of the shed, toolbox still in my hands, and put it by the wall closest to the forest and farthest from the fire. The one that, hopefully, no one will notice has been tampered with until it's too late. I hand her the screwdriver.

"Help me loosen these boards," I say, and we set to work. Though our movements are slow and clumsy with exhaustion, neither of us talks of sleeping.

It takes much longer than I think it will to loosen the boards to the point where the hole is big enough for us. By the time we've crawled out, the crescent moon is past the midpoint of the sky.

It's eerie to stand at the edge of the camp in the half-light and see places that are usually filled with people. The fire pit is a darker gray hole in the middle of the light gray clearing, like a cigarette burn in a piece of cloth. The fermenting *cacao* seed piles are ghostly lumps in the landscape. The drying racks, shadowy skeletons. In front of us, the sleeping hut looms, quiet and still; you'd never guess there were more than a dozen boys inside. And over everything, a hush, filled only by the haunting night sounds of *la brosse*.

I clutch the toolbox to my chest and we creep across the packed earth of the empty yard to the sleeping hut. I shuffle around until I find a splintered piece of board. I press my lips to the crack and whisper-shout, "Seydou!" Then, realizing that Seydou is probably in no condition to answer me, I switch to, "Yussuf!"

After what seems like forever, but is probably only a minute or so, I hear a tired scuffle on the other side of the planks.

"Amadou?" My name is half a yawn.

"Yes! Who's this?" I ask, splaying my fingers on the wooden boards as if it will get me closer to my brother.

"It's Yussuf."

"Yussuf! How's Seydou? Is he all right?"

There's a brief pause.

"What do you mean?" asks Yussuf. "He's not with you?"

"What? No!"

Another pause, then Yussuf's voice again, this time very much awake.

"Amadou, I don't know what to tell you. He's not in here with us either. There are only twelve of us in here tonight. I counted."

For a brief moment I feel an odd kinship with Yussuf. I never knew anyone else was counting the things that mattered. But then I remember my real kinship—Seydou—and the fact that he's in neither of the places he should be. I shake off my daze and realize that Yussuf is still talking.

". . . at their house, but really, Amadou, you should get back into that shed. I don't even know how you got out, but you should go back. It won't do you or Seydou any good in the morning if the bosses don't find you in there. I'll figure out where he is tomorrow, okay?"

"*I ni cé*, Yussuf," I say, and ease away from the sleeping hut. I'm thanking him for offering to help, not saying I plan to accept it, but Yussuf doesn't know that and I hear him shuffle to his sleeping spot and lie down. I feel like I'll never be able to sleep again. I have to find Seydou. Why did the bosses not put him with the other boys or in the toolshed with me? Where is he? I feel as if my soul has been hacked to pieces with a machete. *What if he's dead?* What if the reason he's not in the sleeping hut is because he's in a new grave somewhere, dug by the bosses while Khadija and I played around at escaping?

A hand on my elbow makes me jump.

"*Mun kéra?*" Khadija asks.

My mouth moves, but no sound comes out. I clear my throat and try again.

"Seydou's not there," I manage.

Khadija looks as stunned by the news as I am.

"Where is he, then?" she asks. She whips her head from side to side, her oval face creased with concern, scanning the camp as if Seydou might be somewhere there, sleeping out in the open.

I shake my head.

"I don't know, but I have to go look for him." Aside from the storage lean-to, there's only one other building that has a roof: the bosses' house. I've gone ten paces down the beaten-earth track that leads over the hill to their house before I realize that Khadija isn't beside me. I turn and see her standing exactly where I left her, facing into the forest. A cold finger of fear traces my spine as I imagine being entirely alone.

"Khadija?"

She glances in my direction.

"I could go now," she says softly. The finger turns into an icy hand that grips my heart and squeezes.

"You could," I admit.

She looks away over the hills again. Then she turns around. She walks to me as if every step hurts. When she's level with me, she speaks.

"Going to the bosses' house is the stupidest thing I could possibly do if I'm really trying to escape," she says.

I wait.

"But"—she sighs—"the only reason you weren't with Seydou the day he got hurt was because you were tied up. The only reason you were tied up was because I ran." She takes a deep breath. "You called me selfish a while ago. I guess I am. If I had the chance to do that day again, I would probably run again. *But*, I will do this thing now. I owe it to Seydou."

With that, she pushes stiffly past me, spine straight, and leads the way up the moonlit track. Grateful beyond words, I follow her, staying one step behind all the way, just in case she changes her mind.

11

As we walk along the track, the trees around us change. There are some *cacao* trees like the ones we spend all year tending and harvesting, but I see many more green banana trees and even a few fruit trees. I know where the green bananas go since that's sometimes all we get to eat for weeks on end, but we've never been given any papayas, mangoes, or coconuts. I guess the bosses keep those for themselves.

I'm just wondering how much farther we have to go when the track ends and there, sitting in a clearing, is the bosses' house. The thin moonlight shoves the house's blocky form forward and shadows what might be a vegetable garden off to the left. The house has a good tin roof and looks plenty big enough for a family, let alone three men. When I think of how so many of us are crammed into the sleeping hut every night, it makes me want to go over there and tear that nice tin roof off with my bare hands.

I stand for a moment, taking it in and letting the unbroken night noises of the bush soothe my nerves. Khadija is a shadow rooted to the spot beside me. I reach out and take her hand and pull her forward. Once she's moving, I let go again.

We slink to the side of the house and slowly creep around it. I wave my hand in a circle in front of her face, trying to tell her that I want to look around the house before we do anything else. I don't know if she understands, but she nods and we set off.

The short grass and little rocks are prickly under my bare feet. I try to sneak without a sound, but I'm not doing a very good job of it. With every step, I knock loose some pebbles, or scuff my foot on a chunk of masonry hidden in the grass. I cringe, but don't stop. Other than the vegetable garden, a pit latrine, and a small generator, there's nothing on the outside of the house. Definitely no Seydou. I steam quietly to myself in frustration.

"What now?" Khadija's whisper in my ear is so soft even I can barely hear it.

I shrug angrily. Then I lean my face into her ear and whisper, "Only thing for it is to check the windows. Don't get caught."

We circle the house again. I push my face against the bars covering the first window and see a central living area. In one corner there's a propane tank and a little stove. On a crate in the far corner, a television sits next to a car battery. The bulb hanging from the center of the ceiling shows that the bosses could even have light if they wanted to use the generator.

"Wow, what a dump," whispers Khadija beside me.

I turn to her, eyebrows arched in surprise, because I was just thinking that this is one of the best-built houses I've seen. I guess even in the low light, Khadija is able to catch my expression.

"Well," she says defensively, "it is. There's hardly any furniture. They don't have doors to the bedrooms, there's no glass on any of their windows, and they're using a car battery to run their TV. I mean"—she crosses her arms and looks around again—"I kind of thought that, being in charge and all, they'd have a nicer place."

I wonder what on earth she's comparing it to. It's so much better than my family's house in our village. Glass in the windows? Either she's richer than I thought or her mother worked in a rich person's house as a maid. I decide the mystery can wait until we're not in so much danger. She wouldn't tell me her story when I asked her before and even if she would tell me now, this is not the place for storytelling.

"Come on," I say.

The next two windows we look into are bedrooms. They're almost identical: a gray, hollow-looking mattress sits on the floor with a boss sprawled across it, asleep. The walls are bare except for a few pictures ripped from magazines and newspapers. There's only one window left and it must be Moussa's bedroom. I lift my face slowly over the sill, heart hammering, and peek in.

The room is much the same as the other two: gray mattress, torn pictures. But this room has one addition that makes me whole again. Because the person sleeping on the mattress, his left elbow stump wrapped in a bandage and propped on a pile of crumpled newspaper, is my brother. I look around the room again and see Moussa lying across the doorway on a blanket.

It's where I would have slept if I was being careful to keep the other bosses away from Seydou and I feel an odd warmth in my heart for Moussa.

I feel a pull on my arm. When I turn, Khadija points away from the house. Though it feels like going in the wrong direction, I follow her until we're both crouched in the thick shadows where the yard turns wild. I'm breathing hard. Beside me, Khadija is completely calm.

"We have to get him out of there," I say. Even though we're more than five meters from the windows and the night breeze is blowing in our faces, taking the sound away, I keep my voice pitched low.

Khadija chews on her thumbnail, pulling with her other hand at the fraying knot of braids at the top of her neck.

"There are bars on the windows," she points out unnecessarily. I know there are bars.

"What if I went in and carried him out?"

She shoots me an unbelieving look.

"He's in the same room as Moussa! You think Moussa's not going to notice you dancing around him to grab your brother?"

I imagine Moussa waking and catching me with Seydou in my arms. Trapped in that little room, there would be nowhere for me to hide; no way to run. With the added weight and awkward bulk of my brother, there's little hope I could get out of the house without him catching us.

"Maybe he wouldn't wake up," I mumble.

"You're willing to risk all of our lives on a *maybe*?"

I stare at the window. To be so close to Seydou and unable to get to him is so frustrating I want to punch something. Instead, my frustration washes out of me, taking the last of my energy with it and I surprise myself by yawning.

"What else can we do?" I ask around the yawn. How long has it been since I've slept? A day and a night? More? How long since I've slept well? Forever. I yawn again.

"I don't like our options," she finally says, around a yawn of her own. "You can sneak in now and probably get caught, or we can wait until tomorrow and try to get him away from them sometime during the day. Waiting means we get to sleep before we run, which we need, but we can't be sure that we'll have another chance to get him, especially once they see that you're not in the shed where you're supposed to be." She shoots me a fierce look. "And I'm not going into that shed again, no matter what."

I chew on my lower lip while I consider. I imagine all the terrible ways this could go wrong. Then I imagine not ever having this opportunity again.

Khadija sees the look on my face.

"You're going in," she says. It's not a question.

I nod.

She shakes her head slowly. "All right, let's go."

"What do you mean, *let's*?" I ask. It's too dark to see the look she gives me.

"We do this together" is all she says.

I shrug, slap my hands against my cheeks a few times to

clear the sleepiness that is making it hard to make decisions, and creep across the yard to the house, heading for the front. I'm grateful the door has no lock, but remembering the padlock on the boys' sleeping hut makes me angry. I'm grateful for the anger because it burns off the sluggishness.

We step carefully into the main room of the house. Instantly, Khadija heads to the table near the simple stove. When she touches the stuff on it, it rattles softly. I race over and grab her hand.

"*Shh,*" I whisper, shaking her wrist. Does she not have any idea how dangerous this is? She wrenches her hand away from me and points. I look more closely at what's on the table and see a small open box beside a half-sliced papaya. Spilling out of the box are various small canisters and rolls of bandages. Khadija points between the stuff on the table and the room that Seydou's in. I see the need for bandages, so I shrug an apology.

Leaving her to find whatever she's looking for, I tiptoe to Moussa's room. At the darkly shadowed doorway, I freeze. The gray mattress on the floor under the window looms in my sight. Seydou's not moving. *Why is he not moving?* Moussa's back is centimeters from my toes. I find that I'm having trouble breathing normally. All my doubts about this come rushing over me, making me reconsider.

A soft clatter from the front room makes me jump.

What is that idiot girl doing? Sorting through their silverware?

Heart hammering, I turn my attention to the situation in front of me again and note, to my horror, that Moussa's breathing is shallower and more irregular. Khadija's noise is slowly waking him up. I don't have any more time.

Stretching on my toes as high as I can go, I step over Moussa, as far away from his face as I can get. Holding my breath, I walk toward the bed slowly, oh, so slowly. Lifting each foot straight up, and then lowering it, toes first, rolling silently onto my heel. It is the quietest way to walk. All the while, my eyes dart between Moussa's face and Seydou's. I keep dreading seeing Moussa's eyes fly open. I can nearly touch Seydou. I can smell my own terror. Another step. Another jingle from Khadija. *I am going to kill that girl myself if we all get away from here.* And then I'm at the end of the mattress, and Seydou is sprawled below me.

Now is the time to move fast, whispers a voice in my head, but I can't obey it. I touch Seydou's face. I'm terrified that he's going to startle awake screaming like he did in the sleeping hut. Instead, touching him is like pushing on river mud—he doesn't move or give any sign that he's alive. Only the shallow movement of his chest tells me he's not dead. Even though the evening is cool, I'm sweating. Any second now, Moussa or Seydou could wake up and we'd all be done for. I squat beside Seydou and slowly work my arms between his body and the mattress. He's still hotter than he should be, but not as hot as he was before.

After what seems like hours, my hands work free on the far side of my brother. Slowly, even though my back screams in agony at lifting so much weight at such an angle, I roll Seydou against me and lift him off the mattress. His good arm is

135

sandwiched between our bodies and his wrapped elbow hangs free.

Cradling him against me, I turn around and stare at the form blocking the doorway. Behind Moussa, through the door, I can see Khadija, biting her lower lip in terror. I look at Moussa's face. There's a furrow between his eyebrows now and his breathing is light and very irregular. The hairs along my neck rise and prickle, but I'm committed now, and I keep walking. One step. Another. I'm close enough to feel Moussa's body heat. My sweat is making Seydou slippery in my arms.

Taking a deep, silent breath, I clutch Seydou to me as hard as I can, and step over Moussa. As soon as my two feet touch the floor of the main room, I head toward the door. Khadija slips out a second ahead of us. I follow on her heels and find myself outside.

I feel a lightness in my chest, an opening up. The sky is high and clear and covered in the last few stars before dawn. It's what I imagine my soul looks like right now.

Khadija comes up beside me.

"Is he okay?" she asks in a whisper.

"I don't know. Can you help me get him in a better position to carry?"

"*Awó*," she says. "Let me just find somewhere to put all this . . ." I glance at her. I hadn't even noticed until this minute how much she's carrying.

"What's all that?" I ask, bending backward to hold Seydou's weight while she shoves things into my pockets.

"A water bottle, the medicine kit I found, and some money." I feel the irregular bulges press into the sides of my legs. The weight of the water bottle pulls one side of my pants down lower on my hip than the other. "I'll take them in a sec. Here, what do you want me to do?"

"Put his hurt arm up and get his head onto my shoulder . . . yeah . . . and—" But I never get any farther than that because suddenly Khadija's eyes go wide. I whip around to see why, and there, framed in the shadowed doorway to his house, is Moussa.

For a split second, we all stare at each other. Then Moussa lunges after us. Reflexively, I grab Seydou tighter against me and run, but I haven't made it a dozen steps when Moussa grabs me.

Seydou jolts awake and twists in my arms, screaming in fear and pain. I stagger off balance, but don't drop him. Moussa's fingers cut into my biceps, and I struggle against him, but can't get free. He backhands me across the face and I stop struggling as my world spins. It was crazy to run, crazy to hope. Now I've doomed Seydou to a horrible life, and Moussa is probably going to kill me. I waste a moment wishing I could have seen home again, just once more, or at least that the people I love knew what happened to me, but then I sink into my empty place and wait for the worst to happen.

Suddenly, Moussa lurches away, leaving me unbalanced. I see small arms wrapped around his neck, and my empty place explodes into sound—Moussa, yelling his head off, and Khadija, grabbing on to him and kicking at his legs with all her might, screaming at me to run.

Over Moussa's head, my eyes meet Khadija's and hold for a moment. She's frightened, but isn't letting go.

Seydou is warm and heavy against my chest.

I turn on my heel and run as fast as I can.

For a while I run through the bush fueled purely by fear. I absolutely expect to hear the bosses getting closer and closer to me as I pound away, but instead I hear only an ever-increasing hum of bugs and the loud thrashing of my own clumsy feet through the dead leaves on the forest floor. As the terror of the night burns off, exhaustion takes over. Seydou feels heavier than anything I've ever carried, and the damn water bottle Khadija put in my pocket slams against my leg with every step.

When I can't run anymore I collapse on the ground with Seydou. I'm panting from the jarring run and Seydou is clutching his arm to himself and sobbing. As the minutes pass and our breathing slowly returns to normal, I finally feel the truth: they're not coming. We got away.

Sure, they'll probably still come chasing us but this is the best chance to escape that we've ever had. I pick myself off the ground and touch Seydou lightly.

"How are you?" I ask.

Seydou whimpers and shakes his head, but won't talk. That's okay. He should save his strength for later. Right now, we need to use this amazing head start we've been given and run.

I pull out all the things Khadija put into my pockets and rearrange them so that they're easier to carry.

I drink about a third of the water from the bottle, give another third to Seydou, then haul myself to my feet and pick him up again. He cries out in pain, but we have to move, so I try not to listen. I continue away from the camp, carefully now, gently picking my way through the brush so as not to leave an easy trail to follow.

You got Seydou out, I tell myself over and over to keep the pace. *That's all that matters.*

I make it almost half a kilometer repeating that to myself before I stop. Because it's not all that matters, and every step I take makes me wonder what happened to her.

I put Seydou down and rest against a tree while I think. He curls into a ball, making mewling noises. I try to focus. She *could* have gotten away. It's possible. She didn't have anyone to carry, and she's quick on her feet.

Maybe.

"I guess I'll never know."

I can hear the lie in my own voice. I pound my fist into the tree savagely. "There's no way I'm going there again to see what happened to her! It would be suicide!"

The tree doesn't argue, but the voice in my head does. *She tackled a boss for you. She could have run when Moussa had you but instead she gave you the chance to get away. And to think . . .* you *called* her *selfish.*

Beyond the tops of the trees I see the first orange streaks crossing the purple sky. It's dawn. For a few moments I just stand there, letting the exhaustion of too much time awake take over. Then I pull Seydou to me.

"Seydou . . ." I lean my cheek against the top of his head. Hot, too hot. He seems to be getting warmer the farther we get from camp. I want to tell him that we're going to keep running, that he's safe now, and that everything is going to be all right. But what comes out of my mouth is, "Seydou, I'm sorry. We're going back."

12

I wish Seydou could argue, tell me to take him to safety. But his eyes are hollow and glassy again and he's not answering me. I have to make this decision all by myself.

Slowly, over the next few hours, I pick a careful, looping trail through the bush until we're close enough to camp to see what's going on. Far enough uphill to be out of earshot, I lay Seydou against a tree and cover him in leaf litter because he's beginning to shiver. Then I climb the tree so that I can see into the clearing. I've broken into a cold sweat and the morning breeze raises bumps on my arms and legs. We should be far, far away from here by now. We should not be mere meters from returning to that life. We should not be waiting here to be caught, minute after terrifying minute.

The camp is bustling with activity and it's not hard to see why. Parked next to the bosses' pickup truck is another one, even more beat-up looking than theirs. The tailgate is down and the bosses and the boys are working to get everything loaded. The boys carry sacks of the fermented, dried seeds and stack them high in the truck bed, tying them tightly with ropes. They're stacking them so high that the driver's not going to be able to see out his back window at all. I guess it doesn't matter way out here in *la brosse*.

Part of me wishes I was close enough to overhear what the boys are saying, but it isn't worth the risk to get nearer. I don't see Khadija anywhere. I tell myself this means that she must have gotten away, but I stay clinging to my tree, unsure. I think if I even saw Moussa I'd be able to know. After years of watching his face, I know what most of his expressions mean.

Below me, Seydou stirs. I slide to the ground and rest my hand against his face. He's still hot to the touch and he's been slipping in and out of a restless doze.

"Amadou?" he manages.

"Hi, cricket," I say, a big fake smile on my face.

"What . . . Where . . . ?"

"I got you out," I whisper, rubbing my hand on his head like I used to when he was just a baby. "We're running away, Seydou. We're going home."

"Home . . ." he mumbles, but the word sounds hollow when he says it. I wonder whether it's that he's in too much pain to process all this or whether it's been so long that he's forgotten what home is like. There are days when I struggle to remember the texture of the walls of our house or the exact lines of Moke's face. I've never said anything about it because I was ashamed. Now I wonder whether Seydou had those days too.

"Come on," I say, propping him on my arm. "Try to drink some more water." I pull the mostly empty bottle out of my pocket and hold it to his mouth. He sips weakly at it for a few seconds, but then loses interest. The water dribbles over his chin. That frustrates me because he needs to drink. I wedge the plastic rim of the bottle between his teeth and tip his head. Seydou, half-asleep again, chokes on the water and starts coughing. The force of the coughing pushes him into a sitting position and spasms rack his body. He curls forward, spitting the water on the ground.

"Shh! Shh, Seydou," I whisper frantically, rubbing his back. He's howling and rocking. I swing my head around, terrified that somehow they'll hear this in the clearing. I have to make him stop. "Hush!" I shake him gently. "Hush now. I won't make you drink any more."

"It hurts!" he wails, and I see that he's clutching the wrapped stump of his elbow in his other hand. "It hurts! Make it stop, Amadou!"

"I can't," I whisper to him. "Oh, Seydou, I'm sorry." I lower myself behind him so that I'm sitting against the tree and he's sitting between my legs. I pull him gently against my chest and let him sob into my shoulder.

I don't count the minutes we sit there like that, or the hours since I've slept, because in that moment there's only one thing that matters, and it can't be counted.

After what feels like forever, Seydou's sobs calm. He sits up and takes a look at his bandaged elbow. He gently touches the air where the rest of his arm should be.

"I can still feel it," he says.

"What?"

He looks at me, his face a mess of tear streaks and snot.

"It hurts like it's still there," he says. "I can feel it, even though it's gone."

I have no idea how to make that better, so I ramble on about other things instead.

"You were getting really sick from an infection, so Moussa had to cut it off. You'll get better now, you'll see."

Seydou blinks, fading away again. Terrified to lose this slightly-awake-and-talking version of my brother, I rush on.

"I was so mad at Moussa I punched him in the face." I'm rewarded by a glimmer of interest in his eyes at this piece of information. "And then Khadija and I broke out of the toolshed where they put us and came and rescued you."

Seydou looks around.

"Khadija?" he asks.

"Moussa caught her again." I wince. I had meant to say *She ran in a different direction and we're just going to make sure she got away.* "But," I hurry to add, "we came back and I'm going to find her and get her out and then we'll all escape together, okay?"

"Why do we care about *her*?" Seydou asks acidly, stroking the short stump of arm he has left. "*She's* the whole reason all of this happened!" I see the tears well in his eyes and I realize that he may not remember anything that she's done since she knocked him down six days ago.

"Maybe she is," I say slowly, "but she also spent a whole day taking care of you after you got hurt when you were really sick and Moussa wouldn't let me stay with you . . . even though she was hurt too." It doesn't even come close to covering what she must have gone through in that hot, stinking hut with a raving Seydou so soon after what they did to her, but I leave it at that. "And then, instead of running when she had the chance, she came to the bosses' house with me and helped me get you out of there. In fact, the only reason she's caught right now is because she jumped on Moussa to stop him from catching us."

Seydou considers this for a moment. Then he leans against my chest again.

"What about the other boys?" he asks. "Are you going to help them escape too?"

I stare at the round top of his head in silence for a moment. It would never even have occurred to me to try to get the other boys out. How on earth would I get that many people away? Walking through the bush without leaving a trail would be impossible. It would be as good as paving a road for the bosses to come and catch us. I don't even know if we could trust most of them not to turn us in. Plus, if there were no boys here to work at all, then the bosses would have nothing better to do than chase after us, making it all the more likely that we'd be caught. But I don't have time to argue all that out with Seydou, so I just put my mouth near his ear again and say, "No, I'm not. Now stop talking."

Seydou glares at me with a rage I think is ridiculous. We've never been that close to the other boys. I ease away from him and scramble up the tree to look at the camp again. I see Moussa and the *pisteur* come out of the open door of the sleeping hut, shaking hands. The *pisteur*, a big man with a round head and wide shoulders, hands Moussa a thick wad of bills. Moussa is smiling openly. He looks relaxed and content. My eyes flick to the toolshed, locked, even on a loading day. I look more closely. The boards are even again, our hole patched, and I see the edge of the toolbox pushed under a bush nearby. There can be only one reason the tools are not in the shed and the shed is locked.

I slide down the tree, furious at the world, and flop in the uneven leaf litter next to Seydou.

"They got her," I hear myself whisper. Bile rises in my mouth. Yes, the bosses are all smiles now, but I have some idea what they'll do to her once they're finished with more important business.

"What are you going to do?" asks Seydou. He's still angry at me, but he's never been one to hold a grudge or wish a beating on anyone. I look at him for a moment. Even hurt, even annoyed, he expects me to be able to fix things.

"I'm going to set the farm on fire," I say, and push myself slowly to my feet.

I half carry a stumbling Seydou down the hill, until we're out of sight in the forest near the toolshed.

"You have to stay very quiet now," I whisper in his ear. "You can't cry again like you did on the hill or they'll hear you and come get you. Do you understand?"

I hate to see the look of fear darkening his eyes, but at least I know he'll be quiet. I put a hand on his back and give it a little rub.

"Okay, I'm going to set a fire somewhere to distract everyone and then let Khadija out," I say. "You'll be okay here?"

He frowns, but eventually nods.

I slink to the edge of the camp. The bosses seem to be finishing their business with the *pisteur*, and the boys are milling around. Too many eyes. I consider setting the far groves on fire, but the leaves around my feet are heavy and damp. A fire there would be difficult to light and easy to put out.

I drum my fingers against the tree in front of me, considering. Other than for work, I can't think of any time the bosses leave the clearing except to go to their house to sleep . . .

Their house.

And with that thought, I'm off, loping through the bush at the edges of the camp like a soundless shadow, heading for the bosses' house. I make it there in record time. Not able to believe what I'm doing, I light their little propane burner with the matches on the counter. Fingers shaking, I turn the flame up as high as it will go, and then I drag the three mattresses from their bedrooms and lean them so that they're over the flame. The fibers curl away from the heat, blackening, and a horrible smell fills the house. When I see orange flames licking the stuffing, I leave. On my way out the door, I grab a shirt for Seydou, and the rest of the packet of matches. Hands shaking, I tuck the bosses' wadded shirt into my belt and put the book of matches in my pocket. Then, ducking under the billowing black smoke filling the house, I race off again into the bush.

By the time I've made it to where I left Seydou, the pillar of black smoke has caught the attention of the people in the clearing. For a moment I pause to appreciate the sight of the bosses panicking, herding the boys into the sleeping hut and running with the *pisteur* in the direction of the smoke, but then I snap to attention. Time has just gotten more important.

"I'll be back," I tell him again. "Stay quiet and be careful." Then I'm sprinting to the bush where I saw the toolbox.

I pause there, panting, my heart racing as if I have been running for kilometers. Though my gut is screaming at me to *go, go, go!* I slow and take one last look around to make sure no one's sitting at the edges of the camp. I examine every corner and look extra carefully at the *pisteur*'s truck. Everything seems deserted.

I open the toolbox and pull out a hammer. Every nail that I pull out of the boards makes a terrible groaning sound and I grimace at the amount of noise I'm making. But I don't stop until enough of them are loose for me to crawl inside.

I hope I'm right, I think briefly.

"Khadija?" I call softly.

When there's no response, I make my way to the front of the shed. She's lying beyond the light from the hole I've created and she's not answering. I crawl carefully over to her and roll her toward me. New swelling is disfiguring her face. I touch her cheek gently, then remind myself that there will be time to worry about her once we're gone. I turn and root around in the shadows until I find a machete. Then I saw through the ropes binding her legs. The rope frays apart and I untangle the ends. Legs matter more than arms when you're running, so I do them first. But then I get to work on her arms and hands. I tell myself it's because I might need her to do something as we run but really it's because I just can't stand to see anyone tied up anymore. When I'm halfway done, she stiffens under my fingers.

"Khadija," I whisper. "It's okay. It's me, Amadou."

"Amadou? You came back?" Her voice is a cracked whisper, but I smile to hear it anyway.

"*Awó*," I say. "Now keep quiet until I get you out."

She doesn't say anything, but I feel the tension go out of the muscles in her arms. I untie her hands and then, before stepping away, give her fingers a quick squeeze of reassurance. She struggles to her feet.

As we shuffle though the shed, I take one more look at all the things that have made up my life on the farm for the past two years: tools for cutting, tools for pruning; oil for motors, oil for cooking; chains for machines, chains for people. I only realize I've been chewing on my lip when I taste blood. I stop.

Machete. Rope. Poison. Chain.

Anger curls in my stomach. I want to make them all vanish. The faded label on the side of the fertilizer drum with the picture of flames on it flutters. Even though we don't need a second fire, I decide we're going to have one.

"Get into the woods," I whisper to Khadija. "Seydou's there."

I give her a gentle push, and reach through the hole for the toolbox. When I've found a screwdriver I head over to the giant metal drums. I center the screwdriver on the picture of the flames and pound it into the drum with the base of my machete. Then I pull the screwdriver out and do it again. And again. I throw the screwdriver into the spreading puddle that's leaking out of the punctured drum, and uncap the cooking oil and the machine oil and pour them onto the whole mess.

The fumes are overwhelming and I cough and pull the collar of my shirt over my nose. It doesn't really filter out that much, but it makes me feel better about what I'm breathing. I crawl out through the hole, machete clenched in my hand, and, fingers shaking, pull out the matches.

When the first little red head scratches to life, I rip a sleeve off of the shirt I took from the bosses' house and use the match to light it. Then I toss the tiny fireball into the mess of poison and oil I've made and peer in the hole after it as it lands with a splash in the puddle on the floor. For a second, nothing happens and then, with a *whoosh*, the air around the drums catches fire. The flames, unnaturally bright, flare toward me. Plumes of dark smoke billow out the hole in the wall. I scramble away as fast as I can.

The heat at my back pushes me past the edge of the forest, where Khadija is watching, mouth hanging open. I grab her elbow and steer her through the bush to the place I left Seydou. But when we get to the clearing, he's not there.

Panic floods me and I start to hunt furiously through the bushes.

"Seydou!" I whisper-shout. "*Seydou!*" Khadija stands a little way off to the side, rocking slightly on her feet, looking around the area with an unfocused look. Her oval face is lumpy with swelling and her braids are frayed so badly that stray twists of hair surround her like a furry halo. I whip from side to side, looking for tracks, but we've chewed up the area so much with all our moving about that there's no clear trail. My frustration gets the better of me.

"*Why aren't you helping me look?*" I bark at Khadija.

"Because I just found him," she says softly.

Her answer pulls me up short. I wasn't expecting that.

"Where?"

Khadija raises a hand and points through the trees, into the camp. I follow her finger and curse roundly. Because Seydou is not looking for me, not waiting for me. Seydou is not being quiet or careful like I told him to. With only one arm, Seydou is standing in the middle of the clearing, for anyone to see, pounding away at the door of the sleeping hut with a shovel, trying to let the other boys out.

Dammit!" I level one savage kick of frustration at the nearest tree trunk and then I grab Khadija by the hand and we race into the clearing. No point in hiding now. Our only hope is to get Seydou into the bush before anyone catches us. I could strangle myself for giving in to the urge to light that second fire. The smoke will bring the bosses back sooner. The odds of our escaping are getting smaller and smaller by the second. I curse myself, curse my brother, curse this whole misbegotten day, and wish like crazy that I could start again and do things differently.

"Seydou!" I shout. "What the hell do you think you're doing?" With all the racket he's made with the shovel, and the noise from inside the hut, I don't even care that I'm shouting.

Seydou looks at me, his eyes shining with fever and tears, sweat leaving tracks in the dirt on his face.

"You said we wouldn't . . . you wouldn't . . . save them . . ." He's crying now, sobbing the words out between labored breaths. He's barely able to muster the strength to lift the shovel off the ground. He swings it weakly in his one remaining hand. The shovel makes a pitiful *thump* when it slides into the door.

"But I'm not going to leave them here, Amadou. We can't leave them here!"

I want to slap him to his senses. How are we to escape if we waste time like this? But I can see the rebellion in Seydou's face and I realize that there is a quick way and a slow way to get him away from that door. And though it goes against all my better judgment, the quick way is to let him win.

When I grab the shovel from him, Seydou cries out, thinking I'm going to make him leave, but instead I drop my machete, push him to the side, and heft the shovel. I catch Khadija's eyes. She wraps her arms around Seydou, pulling him from me. He struggles weakly against her, but she's bigger than him and she doesn't let go. I glare at the rusted padlock. It whispers to me of all the nights I spent in that hut, heard the *click* of the lock, and despaired. All the anger of the day, all the frustration, all the fear: I put them into my swing, using my whole body to bring the blade of the shovel onto the lock. With a ripping of wood, the screws that hold the latch in place are yanked out. The padlock, still shut tight, falls harmless at my feet and the door swings open. Inside I meet the stunned eyes of twelve boys. They take in the curls of smoke drifting over the hill, Khadija with her arms wrapped around Seydou to my right, and me, with a shovel on my shoulder, standing in the swinging door with its ruined lock, the toolshed a blazing pyre behind me.

Yussuf steps forward, his huge eyebrows raised comically on his skinny face.

"This is the best chance you'll ever get to run," I say, dropping the shovel at his feet and retrieving my machete. "Do whatever you want, but don't follow us."

And with that, I scoop Seydou into my arms, grab Khadija by the hand, and run from the clearing as fast as I can.

We make it past the first line of trees before I look back. The camp is in chaos. A few boys are already disappearing into the bush, each in a different direction. Others seem to have decided not to run and they're sitting in the doorway to the sleeping hut, staring at the burning ruin of the toolshed, looking lost without the lock. Yussuf stands in the middle of the clearing, giving orders to a small band of boys to collect the things they will need. I meet his eyes once more and he nods: *thanks*. I feel a strange stretching in my cheeks and realize that I'm smiling. I nod back, wishing him luck, and then turn into the bush with my little family, and vanish.

Since the bosses are still at their house, I let us walk along the *piste* leading away from the camp for about ten minutes. I'm stumbling from sheer exhaustion, Khadija is injured, and, after his exertions with the shovel, Seydou is barely conscious. Right now none of us have the energy to fight our way through the bush, but when I look over the treetops and see that there is only one plume of smoke, I make us leave the road. The going is terribly difficult, and soon we have to walk with Seydou slung between us. Half an hour later, Khadija stops and rubs her back.

"Amadou? Can we take a break?" she asks. It's the first time she's complained.

"No," I say, sighing. I pull the almost-empty water bottle out of my pocket and hand it to her. "Here, drink this. It might help."

She looks crushed, but she takes the water from me without a word. She drinks and I pull Seydou against me so that she only has to move her own weight. We keep walking.

Seydou is getting heavier and heavier in my arms and I have to keep shifting my grip so that I don't drop him. But as it is, he's barely dragging himself along beside me, clutching his ruined arm in front of him, so I don't ask him to walk by himself. After another hour of this we're tripping and falling every few steps, and even though it still feels far too close to camp to let our guard down, I give in.

"Okay," I say, "let's take a quick rest."

I carefully part the greenery that shoves up against us like living walls and lead us deeper into the bush, smoothing the traces of our passage the best I can. We settle and Seydou slumps onto the damp ground. I groan—it feels so good to let go of him. I'm soaked in sweat from where he's been leaning against me. I didn't realize how hot he was. He must be feverish again. It's too depressing to think about.

I untie the shirt I stole from the bosses' house from around my waist and pull it over Seydou's head. I have no idea what the bosses did with his shirt when they took him to their house.

After it had been used as a bandage for so many days, they probably had to burn it. The bosses' shirt is huge on Seydou and the sleeve I ripped off to start the fire doesn't line up with his injury, so he has a full arm sticking out of a damaged sleeve and a damaged arm sticking out of the full sleeve. I sigh. He looks ridiculous, but at least he's got a shirt on now. If nothing else, it covers the scars on his back so I don't have to look at them anymore.

Then I peel off my own shirt and drape it over a low bush to dry and let the air wash against my skin. Seydou lies where I left him, eyes closed and slightly sunken, chest heaving in and out inside his oversized shirt with the effort of staying alive. Khadija is pressing her palms to her cheeks to cool her face. She pokes the edge of her skirt into the empty water bottle to gather what little moisture is left in it, then uses the corner to wipe away some of the grime on her face.

I look at the trees around us. The bosses' farm stretches in the opposite direction, so we're already past the tended groves, but there are still a few *cacao* trees scattered around. The birds must have carried some seeds out here. I heave myself to my feet and pull myself to the nearest one that has ripe pods on it. I cut one off, split it open, and bring it to Khadija.

Chewing the seeds is gruesomely familiar, but we need the moisture and the energy. Seydou refuses to eat, glaring at Khadija and breathing shallowly. I look up from trying to force him when Khadija sighs.

"We can't keep going like this, you know," she says.

"What?"

"There's no way we can keep running with you half carrying Seydou and me barely able to keep up. We don't have any food or water, and if we don't get far away from camp quickly enough, they'll catch us."

I flop onto my back.

"I know. But I don't know what else to do. We have to keep moving."

The sparkle in her eyes when she looks at me is a surprise.

"I never said we should stop moving." She smiles. "I said we should stop moving *slowly*."

I'm too tired for these games. I want to sleep for a week.

"Well," prompts Khadija, poking me in the side. "Aren't you going to ask how?"

I groan, eyes closed. Life was bad enough when I only had one kid to pester me.

"Fine. How are you going to get us out of here quickly?"
She smiles.

"On the *pisteur*'s truck," she says.

My eyes crack open. She has my attention.

"This has got to be the worst idea ever," I hiss at Khadija from our hiding spot behind a big copse of trees. "Even worse than my ideas."

"Shush," she says. "You're just jealous you didn't come up with it first."

I scowl and hold Seydou tighter against my side. He tries to push away, but I don't let him. I am *not* jealous that I didn't come up with this idea first: it's madness. However, as we crouch here, too near the dusty track for comfort, I have to admit that there is a faint chance I might get jealous—if it works.

There are a lot of ifs. *If* the *pisteur* stayed behind to help the bosses put out the fire for long enough that we're still ahead of him, and *if* he doesn't decide to spend the rest of the day at the farm, and *if* he hasn't joined the search party, and *if* he doesn't take some other trail we don't know about, and *if* we don't get caught or killed before he gets here, *then* maybe Khadija's plan has a chance of working.

When I hear the rumble of an engine in the distance, at first I can't believe my ears. Then all my muscles tense. Seydou stops struggling. Khadija holds her breath.

My eyes dart around the path in front of us. A large branch is blocking the road, as if it had fallen there. All of our footprints are carefully smoothed out. The leaves and bushes to the sides of the road have been carefully rearranged so that it doesn't look like anyone has been through them. The noise gets louder. There's no way he should be able to tell that we set up the roadblock, but even so, my heart hammers in my ears. I duck my head out of sight as the *pisteur*'s pickup truck rounds the bend. When it slows, I have to remind myself that this is what we wanted, this is what we planned.

He's not coming to find you, I repeat in my head, over and over again as I hear the truck slow to a stop a little ways past us. I hear the metallic creaking of the driver's door opening. I hear him curse to himself as he surveys the branch.

A shove on the side of my head makes me focus again. Khadija waves wildly, pointing at the road. Right. This is no time to get lost in daydreaming about what the driver's doing.

I peek around the side of the tree and see the *pisteur* grab one end of the branch to haul it out of his way. His blue shirt pulls across his huge chest as he does so. He's even bigger up close. Focused on the task, he's facing away from the road behind him. I grab Seydou by his good arm and grip my machete in the other, my hands suddenly sweaty. We scramble as quietly as we can through the bush, Khadija behind us.

Carefully, we creep up the red dirt track to the back of the truck. I let go of Seydou long enough to make a platform with my hands for Khadija's foot and boost her into the small space left on the floor of the truck between the tower of burlap sacks and the tailgate.

Moussa won't be pleased we couldn't fill the truck all the way. The thought flits through me like a butterfly through a sunbeam—a flash, then gone.

Khadija safely inside, I hand her my machete and then grab Seydou around the waist. As I do, I peek between the tires, and what I see makes my heart stop. The road ahead is already clear: the *pisteur* managed to move the branch in the few minutes we've already used and now the toes of his boots are walking to his open cab door. I only have a few seconds before he drives off and leaves us. Hurriedly, I boost Seydou as high as I can.

Khadija grabs him under the armpits, looping her arms around his chest. He braces his bad arm away from her, moaning softly. Just as I hear the driver's door close and the engine cough to life, I realize Seydou's not strong enough to hoist himself up and Khadija's not strong enough to pull him inside.

Panic flashes over Khadija's face, mirrored, I'm sure, by mine. I hear the groan of gears and scrabble at the truck, leaving Khadija to hold Seydou's weight alone. The truck lurches forward. Khadija is straining with the effort of holding my brother off the road but I can't help her. I'm gripping the top of the tailgate with only my fingertips, jogging behind the truck, trying to jump up and get a toehold on the bumperless back. I need to get in, but the track is bad, ruined by runoff, and each jostle of the truck over the rough *piste* threatens to knock me loose. The idea of losing my chance for freedom—and my brother—makes me try even harder. I gather every ounce of strength I have left in me and heave myself in. As soon as I land I whirl around to where Seydou is dangling, slapping against the tailgate with every bump. Luckily the *pisteur*'s truck is so old its motor is loud enough to cover his cries. I lean dangerously far out and link my arms under his armpits. Khadija lets go and worms from between us. I brace against the truck and lever Seydou in.

Just then the truck hits a particularly bad pothole and lurches to the side, sending the three of us flying to land in a heap against the wall of burlap sacks protecting us from discovery.

"Amadou?" Seydou gasps, his face pulled tight by the pain. "Ow, Amadou, ow!"

I push myself into a sitting position and lift him off my chest so that he's not lying on his arm anymore. I rub his back with my free hand.

"Shh, Seydou. It's okay." I'm startled to realize that, for the first time in months, I may not actually be lying to him.

"Why does it still hurt?" He sobs. His eyes, glazed with pain and fever, take in the unfamiliar setting. The small clear triangle of corrugated metal we're sitting in. The sacks around him, the sun blazing down.

"I don't know," I say, feeling my panic fade like the nighttime bush noises do at dawn. "But it's going to be okay, Seydou. We're getting out. I'll make it better, I promise."

"Hurry," says Seydou, head resting hot and sticky on my chest, crusty bandaged arm cradled protectively between us.

Looking over his head, I see the rutted trail behind us being slowly swallowed by the bush. I lean against the sacks and feel a smile pulling at the sides of my mouth. I close my eyes and say, "Okay, *now* I'm jealous I didn't come up with this first."

Beside me I hear Khadija laugh. And so we sit, battered and exhausted, propped together in the lurching truck as the *pisteur* unknowingly drives us to freedom.

14

I jolt awake, who knows how long later, when the *pisteur* rattles the truck over a dried riverbed. I can't believe I fell asleep when I should have been measuring our distance from the farm and keeping watch. I shake my head and prop myself up so I can see out. The sun is on the other side of the sky and the shadows' slope tells me it's late afternoon and that we're heading southeast.

I know that we're way past where Moussa or the other bosses would think to look for us. But now I have a new worry: the *pisteur* himself. Soon he's either going to get to his destination or find somewhere to stop. He certainly isn't going to drive forever through the bush after dark: he'll need to eat and rest. I don't know what lies in the Ivory Coast to the south of the farm where we were, but we're moving fast in the wrong direction.

For a moment I hesitate, then I shake Khadija awake.

She bolts upright, slapping my arm away.

"Take it easy," I say. "It's just me."

For a moment her eyes dart around and all her muscles strain against the thin blue fabric of her dress as she gathers herself to run. Then she takes a shaky breath.

"Sorry."

"We need to talk," I say.

"*Mun kéra?*"

"Well, don't get upset, because I think your idea was a great one and this truck has worked really well for us so far, but I think we need to leave."

Khadija considers, staring out.

"Now?"

"Soon, at least. Before he stops and finds us. I mean, it's really good that he's taking us so far from camp, but we're just going to have to retrace our steps to go north. The farther he takes us south, the more we're going to have to walk to get to where we need to be. If the *pisteur* catches us, we're done for. And if he pulls into a town to get something to eat or to spend the night, then we're even more likely to be seen jumping out."

Idly, I rest my hand on Seydou's head. Instantly, I forget about needing to get out of the truck. We have a bigger problem.

"He's burning up," I gasp.

Khadija puts her hand on his face, then leans away.

Under both of our hands, his eyes open sluggishly, but he looks glazed.

"If only we hadn't lost the med kit," Khadija mumbles helplessly. "Do you have any water left?"

"*Ayi.* We drank all the water when we were on the trail." I reach into my pocket and pull out the water bottle. Then, because it felt good to get rid of that, I empty out my other pocket as well.

"Oh!" gasps Khadija. I tense and glance around, trying to find the danger.

"What? Where?" But when I look at Khadija, she's not scouting the woods. She's holding up the two little bottles from the small box that was in my pocket.

"The med kit!" she squeals. "You didn't lose it!"

"Woo hoo," I say acidly. "It's tiny. He's missing *an arm*. I also have half a box of matches and a machete if you're going to get so excited about the stuff I'm carrying."

Khadija makes a face, then shakes a pill from each of the two little orange bottles into her hand. She leans forward.

"Here," she says to Seydou. "Take these."

"What are they?" I ask as he pushes against me, recoiling from her.

"One's an antibiotic. The other one is something that should help with the fever and the pain. I don't know if this is the right dose or even if they're expired, but he can't keep fighting off infection without a little help and it's all we've got." She turns to Seydou. "Come on, Seydou, open your mouth."

"*Ayi!*" His voice is hard to hear because he has buried his face in my shirt. I hold out my hand and Khadija puts the pills into it.

"You're sure this will help?" I ask her, over his head.

She nods.

I look at the little box with a new respect.

"Should we give him more?"

"No. You don't take pills all at once—it could make things worse!"

"Oh," I say, feeling stupid. Then, curious, I ask, "How do you know so much about pills?"

She looks away. "I want to be a doctor when I grow up," she admits.

I stare at her blankly. Big dreams for a girl. Bigger dreams than anyone I've ever known would dare to dream, boy or girl. I wonder again where exactly she came from to have dreams so big. Seydou pushes his head harder into my chest, reminding me why I'm holding pills in the first place.

With my free hand I turn Seydou's head so that he's looking me in the face.

"You need to eat these pills," I tell him.

His jaw sets stubbornly, but this time I'm not going to give in like I did about the sleeping hut door.

"This isn't a choice," I say. "Take them." It's the same tone of voice I used when I would tell him how to cut pods in a way that wouldn't hurt him. The one I used when I would tell him to take pods out of my sack so that I would get punished instead of him. Seydou's eyes darken, but he opens his mouth. Even in the midst of a fever, he knows that tone too.

I pop the two pills in. He gags a little, but swallows, then opens wide to show me they're gone.

"Happy?" he grumbles.

I ignore his tone and look at Khadija.

"Are we happy, doctor?"

"Well, actually . . ." Khadija says, fingering the roll of gauze from the kit. "While we're at it, we should change the bandage, don't you think? That one that's on there now is really dirty."

"*Ayi!*" Seydou pulls away from me, grabbing his elbow stump to his chest. "Leave me alone! This is all your fault anyway! I took your stupid pills, now just leave me alone."

Khadija looks as though he slapped her. Seydou's face is contorted with pain and anger. Khadija leans forward, laying her hand on his knee. He pulls it away.

"I'm sorry," she says.

"Sorry doesn't bring my arm back!"

"I know," she whispers. "But I want you to know that I'm sorry anyway." She takes a deep breath. "I didn't know what it would be like here. I had no idea what they would do to you . . . to Amadou . . . to all of us when I ran. I never wanted anyone to get hurt, I only wanted to get away." She gives him a watery smile. "I'm glad that, when I finally did, you got away too. But I am sorry."

I hold my breath and keep out of this conversation. Seydou stares at her. Then, finally, he mumbles, "I guess, whoever cut me, it's really his fault." He looks at me. "Do you know who did it, Amadou?"

"*Ayi,*" I answer, truthfully, glad beyond measure that I never asked. "You didn't see who it was?"

"I wasn't paying attention," he admits. "I was talking to Yussuf, who was working behind me, and reaching around a tree in front of me at the same time. Then I just remember the pain and waking up back at the camp."

My happiness at finding out that Yussuf wasn't responsible surprises me.

"You're very brave, Seydou," Khadija whispers, "and very fair. *I ni cé.*"

He glowers at her.

"I'm still not happy with you for tricking me that first day and making Amadou get beaten. And I still don't want you messing with my arm."

I'm kind of on his side for that one. Seydou's shoulder and upper arm are thin, but wiry and strong from working in the fields. Then his elbow, scratched and scabby, but still there. And then nothing beyond that but a few centimeters of filthy bandage, peeling at the edges. I don't want to take it off. The last thing I want to do is look at what's left of Seydou's arm.

"Isn't it good enough that it's covered?" I ask, without much hope that she'll agree.

Khadija rolls her eyes. Then she turns to Seydou.

"You probably don't remember, but I was there the day your fever got so high you thought your eyes were being eaten by yellow spiders and you screamed for half an hour straight. The reason you got so sick from that first cut was that no one kept it clean. Do you want that to happen again?"

I feel stupid once more.

Seydou's eyes dart between Khadija and me. His forgiveness of her is still awfully new and raw and he may not remember much about being sick, but he knows he almost died before. He's not letting it out, but I can almost hear the fear screaming inside him as he remembers Moussa cutting off his arm.

"Let's get you better," Khadija says softly, and touches his good side. This time he doesn't pull away from her. Maybe he remembers more of his day with her than we thought.

"Okay." His voice is barely a whisper.

Swallowing hard to fight the feeling of wanting to vomit, I look at Khadija again.

"Let's do it."

Khadija scoots over until she's kneeling facing us.

"Hold him." She sighs. "Just in case."

I lock my arms around Seydou's upper body, caging him against me. Khadija leans forward and picks at the edges of the bandage. Dirt and ash flake off and settle in his lap as she unwinds the gauze. Seydou turns his face into my chest and whimpers. The last layer of gauze lifts off and I'm left staring at the shiny stump where my brother's arm should be.

"Oh," murmurs Khadija, "no stitches."

I look more closely. She's right. The skin below his elbow is a tight, domed mound, smeared with something that looks and smells like papaya, but there are no stitches crossing it.

"How—" I start.

"He must have cauterized it." She's still mumbling, but then she sees the look I'm giving her and catches herself. "Um, Moussa must have used something to burn the wound shut. The flat side of a machete pulled out of the fire, maybe?"

Seydou nods, not meeting our eyes.

The image makes me sick. I can only imagine how much that must have hurt. Khadija is still talking.

". . . a good thing, really, because it's kept the wound so clean under all that gauze. I really think it was the stitches before that caused it to fester."

I have trouble understanding her happiness. The skin is tight and angry and swollen and Seydou is arching against me, trying to be brave through the pain as his burned stump is exposed to the air. I have trouble thinking that anything about this is a good thing.

Khadija lifts the bandage near her face and sniffs.

"What is this?" she asks.

"Papaya," I say, glad to finally have something to say that Khadija doesn't know. She looks quizzical. "Papaya or banana leaves. That's what you use to wrap burns so that they don't get too dry." I point to the gauze she pulled off; dirt crusting the outside, blood and mashed fruit crusting the inside. "That way it doesn't pull the skin off every time you change the dressing. That's what we did at home anyway. Isn't that what you'll learn when you're a doctor?"

Khadija blinks.

"I don't know," she says. She goes and looks into the little kit. "There's nothing else in here," she tells me, sounding disappointed.

I shrug. It was too much to hope that box would solve all our problems. Khadija squints at the bandage we just took off.

"Should we reuse some of the papaya?" she asks.

"I guess. For now."

Gently, Khadija spreads a little of the mashed papaya over Seydou's stump, and then uses some of the fresh gauze to wrap it again. He hisses with the pain, but doesn't pull away.

"Okay, I'm done," she says softly to him once it's wrapped. "That's the best we can do for now." She rubs his back. "You were really brave," she whispers.

Her face is still beaten up but her expression is gentle behind the swelling. I see Seydou grudgingly meet her eyes and his frown softens. Seydou's not used to having a girl look out for him. Our mother died when he was born and Auntie was pretty strict. And, until Khadija, there were never any girls at the farm. He doesn't seem to know what to do with her attention, and hasn't quite let go of being angry at her for betraying him that first day. But I can tell that somewhere deep down inside, he likes her being nice to him.

I clear my throat.

"Well, if that's all we can do for now, we should probably move on. We still need to get off this truck before we're caught and work our way north."

Seydou slumps against me again as if the very thought of moving has exhausted him.

"Amadou, really?" he whines. "Can't we stay here just a little while longer?"

"It's not safe," I say, but even I can hear that my voice lacks its earlier force.

"I don't think it's the best idea for any of us to jump out of a moving truck, do you?" Khadija counters. "Can we at least wait until he slows?"

I roll my shoulders stiffly. Small amounts of sleep in a bouncing truck bed haven't made my injuries feel any better. I'm sure the same goes for her. I look at Seydou again and decide not to put him through anything else if I can.

"Okay," I say. "Let's wait."

⸻

Not long later the *pisteur* finally slows down. I shake both Khadija and Seydou awake. The falling dusk will help cover our exit. It's perfect.

"This is it," I say. "Let's go."

Khadija grabs the med kit and the empty water bottle and I reach for Seydou, who's lying against one of the sacks.

"Come on, Seydou." I pull on his good arm, trying to get him up.

"No," he says, pulling away from me, still half-asleep. "No, I don't want to go."

We don't have time for this. I shuffle closer to him and try to lock my arms around his chest so I can drag him with us.

"Seydou! Wake up! We have to go now, stop it!"

But Seydou thrashes around in my arms.

"No! I don't want to!" His voice is rising in pitch, whining loudly. I'm glad the noise of the clunky old engine covers us, but even so, he's endangering us with his shouting. Even with Khadija's pills in him, he's still hot to the touch, though not as hot as he was earlier.

"Shh!" I whisper desperately, but it's no good. Seydou is screaming now.

"I want my arm back! It's not fair! It hurts!"

Behind me I hear a quiet whisper from Khadija.

"Too late."

I look out and see that the narrow path we were on that ran past rambling farms and thickets of untamed bush has turned into a real road and opened into the square of a town. I duck reflexively. Seydou struggles out of my grip and snuggles against the sacks. I glare at him, angry that he made us lose our opportunity to get out unnoticed.

Khadija crouches beside me. I risk peeking over the top of the tailgate. Across a dusty stretch I see a few houses. There's a baby and a dog lying on the ground together and people are moving around the village now that the heat of the day is past. I hide again, flattening myself on the floor of the truck, hoping none of them saw me.

The truck shudders to a stop beneath us. I put my face close to Khadija's ear and whisper. "We'll have to wait until it gets dark, and then we'll make a break for the bush when we see the street clear."

Khadija makes a face.

"I don't want to go into the bush in the dark."

I stare at her, not believing what I'm hearing.

"I mean," she goes on, "why not sleep here and wait until early morning? Why take the chance of getting eaten by something in the dark when we could stay here, safe in the truck, and then head out when it's light?"

I don't say anything. In principle, of course I agree with her: it's not a great idea to head into *la brosse* in the dark and of course I'd rather not do it. But it doesn't even seem like she's processing that it's much more dangerous to stay here. And it's not like we could make it home to Mali in a day anyway. If she was so upset about sleeping in the bush, she should have let us jump out earlier so that we didn't have as far to travel.

I'm just opening my mouth to say something to her, when a new voice chimes in.

"Hello, children."

Khadija and I whip our heads toward the voice and there, leaning his crossed arms on the tailgate of the truck, is the *pisteur*.

15

I leap to my feet and grab my machete, hauling Seydou into my arms and bracing against the wall of sacks behind us. He flails around, which makes him hard to hold, and I realize that I don't have very good odds of making it past the big man, especially carrying a fighting eight-year-old. I stutter to a stop. Khadija is on her feet too, clutching the med kit and our empty water bottle to her chest, her whole body pressed into the sacks of *cacao*, as if she's trying to vanish into them. I see a small crowd forming behind the *pisteur* and my hope of getting away trickles out of me. It's like losing blood: it makes me feel weak and shaky. I sink to the bed of the truck with Seydou in my lap and hang my head. Khadija moves to stand behind me.

"What are your names?" asks the *pisteur*.

He's speaking Bambara and his accent makes me think he might be from Mali originally, like us, but I'm not about to tell him anything. *Tie us up and take us back, I don't even care anymore,* I think. Now that I know we're caught, I just want it to be over already. Hoping hurts too much.

"Do you not speak Bambara?" he asks, confused by our silence. Of course we do, but still none of us answers him.

The *pisteur* doesn't move, but leans against the tailgate, looking at us. I glance warily at the muscles cording his thick arms and the stretch of his shirt across his wide chest. He's every bit as big a brute as I thought he was when I first saw him in the clearing at the farm. But when I lift my head and look at his face, I'm surprised to see that it's broad and open and that his eyes are gentle. He looks like he could have come from my village. Those eyes take me in at a glance and then spend a long moment on Khadija's bruised face and Seydou's missing arm. His smile, when it comes, is forced.

"Well, I'm Oumar," he says, "and it looks to me like maybe you three could use some food. Come on."

He unhooks the tailgate with one strong tug of his burly arms and it flaps down with a *clunk*. None of us move. I sit numbly clutching Seydou and my machete. Khadija makes a small noise behind me. I wish I could do something to comfort her, but I don't see any way to get out of this.

The man's big hand closes on my elbow and, as my options narrow to *move* or *be dragged*, I scoot forward and climb carefully out of the truck, holding Seydou tight against me. He's gone still in my arms and his eyes are round as coins. The *pisteur* puts his other big hand on Seydou's shoulder and steers us away from the truck. Oddly, he doesn't try to take my machete. I shrug off his touch and turn back.

I tuck the blade into my belt and hold out my hand to Khadija.

"Come on," I say softly. "Let's stay together."

Shaky with fear, Khadija slides to the end of the tailgate and grabs my hand in a death grip. Then she jumps out and, with Seydou in one hand and her in the other, I follow the *pisteur*, walking stiffly to one of the little houses that line the road. The villagers move out of our way, whispering to each other.

Feeling like each arm and leg weighs a hundred kilograms, I head into the small, dark front room. The shadow of the big man cuts off any hope of escape. Entering the little house after us, the *pisteur* is so tall he has to duck to avoid hitting his head on the rotting crossbeam. The floor is bare and there is one table in the center of the room with mismatched chairs and stools around it. Khadija, Seydou, and I turn and look at the *pisteur*.

"Sit, sit," he says, waving at the table.

Khadija sits on a low stool and pulls Seydou against her. It's a testament to how scared he is that he lets her. I refuse to sit. Instead, I stand behind them and cross my arms over my chest, staring at the *pisteur*.

The big man sighs as he sits across from us. His gaze wanders from one to the other of us, resting on Seydou the longest. Finally, he leans forward.

"I'm going to ask you a few questions," he says quietly, "and I want you to tell me the truth. I don't need to know your names, but I do need to know this."

We don't say anything. The big man goes on.

"Were you working on the farm I collected *cacao* from today?" He pauses, looking at us. When none of us answer, he adds, "The one that had a fire?"

I'm pretty sure there's only one farm that caught on fire today. Out of the corner of my eye I see Seydou nod, yes. I scowl. It can't possibly help us to have this giant know that we were on that farm. But two years of answering automatically when a big man asks you something or suffering the consequences have sunk in.

"Are you family members of one of the men there?" the *pisteur* asks.

Seydou shakes his head, no.

"Did you get paid while you worked there?"

I can't help it; an unpleasant laugh sneaks out of me. Khadija and Seydou both shake their heads. The *pisteur*'s eyes drift to Seydou's missing arm.

"Last question," he says. "Would you like to go back to the farm and continue working there?"

"*Ayi!*" The word bursts out of my mouth.

"No," agree Khadija and Seydou, right after me.

The man purses his lips and looks at his big hands, spreading them on the table between us.

"I am going to say this only once," he says carefully, after a pause, "and I don't want you to tell me any more about yourselves than you already have because I need to keep a good relationship with the farmers I work with." His eyes flick to our faces. "But I don't agree with children being made to work without pay for people who aren't family."

I feel an odd squishiness in my chest and realize that it might be hope, bubbling back.

"I am driving east with my wares, to Daloa, where I will sell the *cacao* seeds." The man looks me straight in the eye. "I am not offering you a ride," he says. "But I am telling you that I will not be checking my truck when I leave in the morning, and I will probably stop somewhere quiet to look at the scenery. Do you understand?"

Numbly, I nod.

Khadija still looks stunned but, taking her cue from me, nods too. Seydou looks confused.

The big man smiles. He winks at Seydou and pushes away from the table. "I'll have my niece bring you some dinner. You can sleep in this room for the night, but I suggest you wake up early. I leave just after dawn." His smile widens to a grin. "Me and my empty truck."

With that, he walks out of the room. Seydou twists around to face me.

"He's going to help us?" Hope and fear struggle to claim his features.

"I don't believe it," I say honestly. I sink onto the stool next to Khadija and Seydou, not sure whether my knees are still capable of holding me up.

A woman comes out from a side room and puts some food in front of us. Hard-boiled eggs and fruit, bowls of spicy *kedjenou* and fluffy white *attiéké* to go with it. It's the best meal I've seen in years. My stomach rumbles loudly and, despite my uncertainty about Oumar, I thank her sincerely, along with Khadija and Seydou.

Khadija sets the hard-boiled eggs and the fruit aside for to-morrow, tying them into a strip of burlap she must have ripped from a sack in the truck. By the time she's finished, the panic in her eyes has pulled back like the tide. I put a bowl in front of Seydou, hand another to Khadija, and eat the portion that's left. Seydou picks at the food with his right hand, not really eating it.

I reach past Khadija and rattle the little box.

"Should we give more medicine to Seydou?"

She considers. "*Awó,*" she says finally. "It's probably been four to six hours. I suppose we could."

She opens the box and squints at the faded labels again.

"You gave him that one first last time," I say, pointing to one of them.

She takes the one I'm pointing to and looks at it carefully. Then she looks at me in surprise. "You're right! How did you read it from there?"

"Read it?" I ask, staring at her. "It's the bottle with the chip off the bottom, and its plastic is slightly darker than the other one." I laugh. "I can't *read.*" What on earth is that crazy girl thinking? Farm kids don't have the time or the money to go to school. Even in the days before Seydou and I were forced to work for Moussa, we couldn't afford that. We worked all day in the fields then too, but we were with family and growing things for us to eat, not stupid *cacao.* We barely made enough to feed our family, certainly not enough to pay for school uniforms and supplies. I shake my head.

Khadija looks away and shakes a pill out of each of the two vials. She doesn't say anything, but it's pretty clear *she* had been reading them. I wonder again at how much better off Khadija was than we were . . . How much money must her family have had to be able to spend it on all the supplies it would take to send her to school for enough years that she can read so easily? I have trouble even imagining. I'm surprised to realize that, even though I've started to think of her as a little sister, I don't really know much about Khadija at all.

Seydou swallows the medicine and leans against her, and Khadija looks over his head at me.

"Here, let me take him," I whisper, because even though he's only picked at his meal, Seydou's eyelids are drooping. I haul my drowsy brother to the edge of the room and lay him under a window so he'll have the best odds of getting away if he needs to escape in a hurry.

I'm exhausted and the sound of Seydou's even breathing filling the space makes me want nothing more than to drift off to sleep beside him, but there's something we have to decide before we allow ourselves the luxury of sleep.

"It's great that the *pisteur* isn't turning us in," I say softly to Khadija. "But I still don't think we should go with him."

"Why not?" she asks.

"Two reasons," I say, walking back over to the table. "First, yes, he's being nice to us now, but we don't have any guarantee that he won't change his mind. He could get to Daloa and decide that he'd rather turn us in after all, or sell us to someone else. You heard what he said about wanting to keep a good relationship with the farmers."

"I don't know," murmurs Khadija. "If he'd wanted to turn us in, he could have easily done that here. We have no reason not to trust him after he's taken this chance to help us. He doesn't like seeing children made to work." But it sounds like she's trying to convince herself.

I raise my eyebrows. Of course it's possible that he's telling the truth. It's also possible that he's not. We've both been lied to enough to know that either outcome is just as likely. After a moment she looks down at the table again.

"What's your other reason?"

"The other reason is even simpler," I say tiredly. "It's nice that he's offering to take us with him, but he's going the wrong direction. We don't want to go southeast, we need to go north.

"So," I continue, "I think we should all get a couple of hours of sleep and then, when it's close to dawn, we can sneak out into the forest. We know the road we came in on, and we can follow that a lot of the way. Maybe we wait in the bush for a few days, make sure the bosses have given up looking for us, then make our way around the farms to the border. Once we get past the farm we were on, it might be harder, but we can keep pretty good track of our direction from the sun. My trip to the farm from Sikasso was less than a day using motorbikes and cars, so on foot we should be there in less than a week, even going through *la brosse*."

"About that . . ." Khadija says, her fingernail tracing and retracing the grain of the wood in front of her. "There's something I've been meaning to talk to you about."

I look at her.

"Yes?"

"I'm not from Mali, like you," she starts unsteadily. "I'm actually Ivorian. I live with my mama in Abidjan."

Her dark eyes, wide in her oval face, dart to mine to see how I take this.

I can't help but stare. I had figured out she was fancy, but I had always assumed she, like pretty much every kid on the farm, came from Mali. Her name is Muslim, like ours. She speaks Bambara, like us. I had never imagined she was *Ivorian*, like the bosses. I feel betrayed. I lean away from her.

Ivorian.

Rich, city-living Ivorian.

My feelings must show on my face because when she goes on, she won't meet my eyes.

"So you see, Daloa *is* actually going in the right direction, for me. And, if it's a town big enough for Oumar to sell his seeds, then that probably means it's on a main road, which might make it easier for me to find my way home. And I . . . I was hoping you'd come with me . . . ?"

It takes me a minute to remember that Oumar is the *pisteur*'s name. I blink dumbly, not quite believing we're having this conversation.

"Amadou . . ." she says, finally looking at me. There are tears piling on her lower eyelashes, but I don't want to see them.

"*Ayi,*" I say. "No. You can't ask me to go farther into this country full of bosses and *cacao*. You can't make me stay here longer. I need to get home; I need to get Seydou home!" I wrench the med kit off the table and grip it hard. "*You* can get up tomorrow morning and sneak into Oumar's truck and ride all the way south to the ocean if you want to, but Seydou and I are taking the medicine and we're going home. Just because you're rich and . . . and *Ivorian*, I don't have to do what you tell me to do. I'm done taking orders from you people."

"Wait! Amadou, it's not like that!" she says, getting up and walking over to me, but I shake off her outstretched hands. In my head I can hear Moke's voice grumbling about what a rude person his grandson has turned into, but I push that thought away. Why should I care what the wildcat does? Just because we've been looking out for each other for a while doesn't mean that we owe each other anything. It's not like she's really my sister.

"But what about Seydou?" she asks in a whisper.

I whirl on her.

"What about him?" I shout. My chest is heaving as I talk, and I feel like I can't get enough air. "I can take care of Seydou. I did it for years before you showed up, so don't pretend that you're the one who knows what's best for him! I'll take the medicine with me and he'll be fine! We don't need you and your fancy city reading for me to give him the right pills. I don't need you to make him better."

I stop talking and fist my hands against my face because my voice is breaking and I'm never going to win an argument if I'm weak. I have to be strong. I pull shuddering breaths in and out, trying to count them and failing, trying to loosen the metal bands that have been wrapped around my rib cage and are tightening, tightening as I consider leaving Khadija to fend for herself, and taking Seydou safely through the bush to Mali alone. Seydou, who can barely walk; Seydou, who is still spending way too much time sleeping; Seydou, who, in spite of the pills from the dark bottle with the chip at the bottom, is still too warm to the touch and has a swollen stump where an arm should be.

I feel Khadija's hand.

"Don't touch me!" I shout.

But Khadija doesn't listen. Instead, she wraps her arms around me.

The medicine box is a hard lump between us, but she leans her head against my shoulder and says, "It's okay, Amadou. Seydou's going to be all right."

And I stand there stiffly, not reaching around her but not stepping away, and I let the tears fall from my chin onto the top of her head where they collect in the ridges of her frayed braids and sparkle up at me in the low light.

A few minutes later, I step away, still clutching the medicine box in a death grip, and wipe my face with my wrists. Khadija sinks onto her stool.

I fall into a chair and put the medicine box on the table again. For a few moments, neither of us says anything. Then, in spite of how tired and drained I feel, my curiosity gets the better of me.

"So," I say. "You're a city girl who ended up on a farm in the middle of nowhere working *cacao* with a bunch of boys from Mali. You're an Ivorian . . . but your name isn't Christian and you don't speak French. You make no sense at all."

"Actually, I do speak French," Khadija whispers unsteadily. "I just happen to speak Bambara too. My last name is Kablan, because my father is Ivorian and Christian, but my mother grew up in Bamako. I'm named after my Malian grandmother, which is why I have a Muslim first name. Growing up, my mama always spoke Bambara to me at home. It was our secret language.

"And yes, I'm a city girl," she goes on, looking at her small hands with their soft fingers that told me that anyway. "Mama is a journalist in Abidjan. I grew up in the city and I go to the international school there."

I bet it's expensive, I think acidly, but I'm too tired to take another jab at her.

"I'm not exactly sure what Mama was working on," Khadija says, "but she was putting together information for a big report. I'd catch her having whispered conversations on the phone, and she'd leave late at night and wouldn't tell me where she was going."

"What did your father say?" I ask, trying to imagine a world where a woman could sneak out at night and that wouldn't be a problem. Khadija splays her soft fingers on the table, examining them.

"My father doesn't live with us. He lives in France."

I stare, sure now that we don't live in anything near the same world. France? She may as well have said her father was living on the southern tip of the moon.

"Anyway," Khadija continues, "it's Mama and me now, and I wanted to know what was going on. I would ask her again and again, but she wouldn't tell me. She still treats me like I'm Seydou's age. She would only say that it was important, and that important people were involved, and that I was safer if I didn't know anything more. That was a lie."

I'm surprised by her sudden bitterness. Her hands are buried in the material of her skirt and her voice shakes when she goes on.

"Then the phone calls started."

I know what phone calls are. The bosses had a mobile phone that they used every once in a while to talk to people who weren't there, and I've seen some of the *pisteurs* talking on two-way radios. But there must have been something different about these calls because Khadija's voice doesn't sound angry anymore, it sounds scared, and she's stopped twisting her hands in her skirt and is instead holding on to her arms, as if she's cold.

"Who were they from?" I ask.

She looks at me and her eyes are glassy.

"I don't know," she says. "Mama started getting phone calls on her mobile that frightened her. Her phone would ring and she would hang up as soon as she heard what the person on the other end of the line was saying. She never said a word, just hung up. And in the mornings, when she would listen to the messages she got overnight, she would hold the phone so tightly I thought the plastic would break, and her lips would disappear, she was pressing them together so hard.

"I tried to listen to find out what they said, but she would always push me away, and then she would delete the messages right after. I thought that was the worst."

"But it wasn't?"

"No. Then we started getting calls at the house."

I'm pulled out of her story for a moment while I try to understand why one person would need two phones. To call themselves when there's no one else to talk to? Ridiculous.

"Once, I heard a man on the other end of the line," Khadija continues. "When I said *hello*, he asked me what my name was."

I can see that her hands are trembling. "I wouldn't tell him. He laughed and told me to tell my mother that she should be more careful. *You know what happens to people who ask questions,* he said. *And you know what happens to people who answer them.*"

I frown, concerned.

"Did you tell anyone?" I ask.

"*Awó.* But even so, Mama wouldn't tell me what she was doing. I said I was old enough to know, but she said, *Age has nothing to do with it,* and kept working in secret.

"But I was really scared by then," Khadija goes on. "We were getting phone calls every day, sometimes a couple times a day, or in the middle of the night. And when we'd answer there was just silence on the other end. I said *hello, hello* into the phone over and over again, and nobody said anything back. But I could hear them breathing, so I knew someone was there. Somehow, that was even more terrifying than when they were threatening us."

I know what she means. I was quiet at the farm a lot because quiet can be very scary, and being scary got people to do things if I needed them to. The comparison makes me pause and, with a shudder, I wonder whether my quiet menace ever made the other boys feel as frightened as Khadija felt with the man on the phone. I hope not. I don't really want to have anything in common with the men she's describing.

"Mama decided it was too dangerous to stay in the capital. We packed some bags and rented a little house in San Pédro, a port town. She promised we would only stay there a little while.

She said there were only a few more things she needed to find out and then we could be done with the whole project. Maybe we'd go to France, she said, and visit my father. That's when I knew she was really scared. Mama doesn't like to run away and she always said we'd never go to France because it's too cold."

"France," I mumble to myself, trying to picture it. I imagine a village like Daloa, but with everyone shivering.

"I don't think I would like to go to France," Khadija says, picking at the rip in her dress. "I don't have very many friends in Abidjan, but it's the only place I've ever lived.

"Mama worked like crazy those last few days in San Pédro. She would be typing late into the night, and was awake before dawn making whispered phone calls. She told me I'd be safe in the house with Stéphane and Sandrine, but I was never to go out alone. I sat there, day after day, with my schoolbooks, staring through my window at the garden wall. I didn't see very much of her."

I wonder who Stéphane and Sandrine are. Cousins? Uncles and aunts? But I'm more worried by what she just said.

"Those last few days before what?" I ask, hardly daring to breathe. I know what it's like to lose a parent. My mother died birthing Seydou and I remember what it felt like to suddenly have the space she filled in the world be empty.

"Before I was kidnapped," says Khadija. And then everything finally makes sense. The ways she never fit in, her fiery determination to escape. She never looked for work here, never agreed to work for pay that wouldn't come, was never fooled into going willingly. She had been taken by force. That's why she was fighting so hard to get out.

"It all happened very quickly. One night, a little after Mama left for one of her secret meetings, a group of men broke into our house. They had disconnected the phone line, and the electricity . . . but the power goes out all the time and I didn't really think anything of it . . . they knocked out our guard. I tried to fight, and run, I really did . . ." Khadija trails off, and I'm horrified to see that she's crying.

"Don't cry," I say. I hate seeing people cry. "I'm sure you did. You're a fighter." I snort a bit of a laugh. "And a runner. I'm sure you did all you could."

Khadija gives me a weary smile.

"It wasn't enough. There were a bunch of them, and they were bigger and stronger than me, and they were able to tie me up, and gag me, and put a bag over my head." She shudders. "It was so dark with the cloth bag on my head. It used to be a grain sack or a rice sack or something and it was full of little bits of grit that kept falling into my eyes and grinding against my face. But the worst part of it was that I had a gag in my mouth and so I had to breathe through my nose. And I could see the bits of rice or whatever it was clogging the holes and filling my nose with dust and it was so hard to breathe." She pauses. "So hard to breathe," she whispers again. Then she shakes the memory off and continues. "They threw me in a truck, and though I tried to scream and kick, it didn't do any good. Nobody could hear me

190

through the gag and kicking them just made them kick me. I finally lay quietly on the floor because I was scared I was going to suffocate."

I can barely imagine what that would feel like. I shudder.

"We drove forever and the roads got worse and worse," she goes on. "I was tossed around on the floor, and I kept hitting my head because my hands were tied and I couldn't brace myself. A while later we stopped and I was dragged out and handed off to new men. They tied me, sitting up this time, in a van, and took the bag off my head. They left the gag in, though, so I still couldn't scream for help, but I was so grateful to them for taking off the bag so I could breathe again that I didn't even struggle." She pauses and looks at me.

"I hated myself for feeling grateful to them," she says.

I think over all the times I was grateful for the small mercies of life on the farm. How, deep inside, I knew that food or basic medical care or not getting beaten shouldn't be a cause for celebration but I felt that way anyway. How I tried not to think about it, because, if I did, I would have hated myself too.

"I understand," I say.

"I thought you would." Khadija pushes her hands over her face and smooths her braids. She sits up a little straighter. "Anyway, they handed me off once more, this time to a man in a truck, and that last time, they took off the gag. I screamed until I was hoarse, but I was tied up in the backseat and the driver was sitting in front and couldn't care less. He turned the radio up loud and kept driving. We went deeper and deeper into the bush, away from everything I knew, and I kept wondering where he was taking me, whether he would kill me, and then, all of a sudden, we stop and he comes around and pulls me out of the truck, onto the ground, and I'm standing in a clearing in the middle of nowhere, surrounded by boys and this tall man, Moussa. And the man who had brought me is telling him that I have to be kept here because I'm a guarantee that someone will keep their mouth shut back in the city and he hands Moussa money and then he turns the truck around and leaves."

I remember that day. I remember her bruised face and her ferocious eyes. I remember looking away. I do so again.

"And you know the rest, I guess," she says softly. "I realized that I had been taken so they could frighten my mama into being quiet, into not publishing whatever it was that she was working on. And I decided that I wouldn't let them use me that way, that I would escape and get home."

She looks at me again, and her eyes are bleak.

"I thought I was valuable enough that they wouldn't hurt me. I was wrong about that too."

"I'm sorry," I say. My big hands are fists in my lap; the muscles of my forearms are standing out in ridges. But all my strength hasn't been enough to help anyone when they really needed me. When I apologize to her, my voice is a broken thing. "I'm so sorry."

"For what?" she asks.

I don't meet her eyes.

"I didn't stop them. I was right there and I didn't do any-thing." I remember my hope, right as the men came back, that they might be too busy punishing her to come find me, and I feel so sickened with myself that I wish I could die.

I feel a city-soft hand on my arm.

"There was nothing you could have done, Amadou." Tears hit my hands and I glance up at her. Her eyes are dry.

"I could have tried," I whisper.

"You were there afterward," she says finally. "You've been there for me ever since."

I shake my head, not quite able to let the guilt go. But still, it feels good to be forgiven. I loosen my fists and put one of my hands over hers and squeeze it.

"You've helped me too," I say, remembering her pulling Moussa off me so that Seydou and I could get away. "And you did escape," I remind her. "After, what, only a week?" I do the math in my head. "Six days. They were only able to keep you there for six days. They kept me for two years. You're pretty amazing for a soft little city girl."

This gets a small smile out of her. Then her smile fades.

"My mama must be so worried, Amadou. I have to get home and let her know that I'm all right. I want you to come with me."

I feel ripped in half.

"But Seydou and I need to go to Mali," I whisper. "The closer we go to the coast with you, the more likely it is that we won't get home. I have to get Seydou home." I let out a breath. "You should definitely hitch a ride in Oumar's truck. Have him take you to Daloa and then go south and be with your mother. But Seydou and I need to go north."

She looks small and lost.

"But what do I do if those other men find me? What if I can't make it home? What if Mama never knows what happened to me? I'm scared, Amadou."

I'm surprised by how closely her fears mirror my own. I too am worried about the bosses catching us. I too am worried about never making it home. I too don't want to die invisible.

I look over to where Seydou's breath is coming rapid and shallow, then down at where our hands are overlapping. My gut twists.

"I don't know what to do," I whisper without meaning to.

Khadija puts her other hand on top of mine.

"Come with me," she says. "In the city we have access to a good doctor and good medicines. These moldy pills are so old that I don't even know if they're really helping Seydou at all. But my mother can call a real doctor and he can see that Seydou is all right. And then I'll make sure that we find a way to get you home to Mali safely. Mother has connections with reporters, and organizations, and all kinds of people. Let's stay together, please, Amadou. We'll find a way to get you home once we've made Seydou better. I promise."

I promise.

It echoes in my head and, without even wanting to do so, I find myself nodding.

"Okay," I whisper, and it's done.

We're going south.

17

It's not yet dawn when we wake up to the sound of Oumar singing loudly to himself in the next room. We take the hint.

Khadija gathers our belongings and I lift the still-sleeping Seydou against my chest and haul him out to the truck, careful to hold him so that the hilt of my machete doesn't dig into his side. This time we don't have to rush, since we're not afraid of getting caught, and I decide, what the heck, and flip open the tailgate to make it easier. I slide Seydou across. He mutters sleepily about being moved, but he's not shrieking in pain like yesterday, so I pop a few more pills in his mouth and ignore his complaining.

Khadija boosts herself into the truck and pulls Seydou into her lap. I jump in last and pull the tailgate shut behind me. A few minutes later, Oumar walks straight past us, whistling. True to his word, he drives to a petrol station, fills the tank and his spare container with diesel fuel, and gets on the road again, all without looking at us.

Khadija grins, and I can't help it, I grin back. It's hard to believe that this time yesterday I was dragging Seydou around the bush trying to rescue her. Hard to believe it hasn't even been a full day since I set the farm on fire and we got out. I decide that, for now, I will allow myself to be happy with how far we've come and I won't let myself fear what will happen next. I settle beside the other two to watch *la brosse* blur past us as we speed our way southeast.

It's not a comfortable ride. With every rut in the washed-out road we lurch from side to side. I can see why Moussa always told us to lash the sacks really tightly onto the *pisteur*'s truck and I silently send my thanks to the boys who did just that. If they hadn't, we'd be crushed. As it is, I still feel like all my teeth are slowly being shaken loose. Yet somehow, when I stretch out on the dirty truck bed, I fall into a deep, exhausted sleep.

I jolt awake to the feeling of not being able to breathe and open my eyes to see that Seydou is sitting on my chest. I laugh huskily with whatever air my lungs have left.

"Get off!" I roll sideways, gently, so that he falls away but doesn't get hurt. It's only been two days since he lost his arm, after all. "Crazy boy. Why were you sitting on me?"

"To wake you up." Seydou smiles like it's the most natural thing in the world to sit on someone to wake them up.

"And why," I ask, rolling out from under him, "did you want to do that?"

"To show you something." Seydou points to Khadija. It looks like they've been talking together for a while and I'm glad that Seydou's getting over his hard feelings for her. We need to not be fighting if we're going to get anywhere.

Seydou picks up the medical kit with his right hand. My

197

stomach clenches to see him struggle with something so simple, but he fumbles the box into his lap. "Watch," he commands. Wedging the box between his knees, he uses his only hand to open the lid. Reaching inside, he lifts out the bottle with the chipped bottom and rattles it.

"Hmm," I say.

"I'm learning," he says, but I can see the deep hollows under his eyes showing that his illness and the stress of the last few days have worn him out. He leans against a sack, cradling his arm against his chest, staring off into space as he murmurs, "Khadija and I worked on it together. I can do this by myself now. So that if you guys aren't around I'll still be able to take my medicine and keep getting better, right, Khadija?" He looks at her.

"That's right, Seydou," she says encouragingly.

I give Seydou a tight smile.

"Good work, cricket," I say, but inside I don't feel good at all. The image of us not being there to help Seydou with his medicine is a horrible one. I squint at the bottle he's holding and try to count how many pills are left in it.

As Seydou continues to stare vacantly out of the truck, I scoot to sit by Khadija.

"Why on earth would you tell him that?" I ask her in a low voice.

"Because anything could happen," she says. "Anyway, he's really upset about losing his arm. I figured learning how to do something for himself would make him feel better." She points her chin at him. "He's not crying anymore. It worked."

I frown. Maybe Khadija is right and it's good for him to be able to do things by himself if he needs to. But when I look carefully at Seydou, I can see that the hollowness goes deep. The bouncing cricket that was my brother is gone. Now when I look into his eyes, an old man stares back at me.

I shake my head. Khadija is wrong. He may not be crying anymore, but Seydou doesn't feel better.

The day passes in flashes of dense green, cleared fields, and small villages. Khadija and Seydou seem to have become friends while I was sleeping. Khadija tucks one of her arms behind her and she tries to make a game of figuring out all the things she can do one-handed. Seydou plays along with her, soaking up the motherly attention, but when she's not looking he sinks into himself, and now and then, I catch him fingering the air where his arm should be. Every few hours we give him more pills from the two bottles and, for all Khadija complains about them, they seem to be helping. He's no longer hot to the touch and overall he doesn't look any worse than he did yesterday.

Darkness is beginning to bruise the sky when Oumar pulls into the dusty outskirts of a town. Seydou, Khadija, and I look out the tailgate, taking it all in. There are broad streets and many cars and trucks. People are everywhere. So many people that, unlike in a village, no one looks too long at us for being strangers. Concrete buildings stretch higher than one level off the ground and wires running between poles reach even higher than that. Khadija tells us Daloa is small compared to Abidjan, but it's so much bigger than anywhere I've ever been that Seydou and I stare and stare.

A few dozen meters off the main road, down a dusty side street, Oumar stops in front of a walled compound. We hear the sound of the driver's-side door opening, but he doesn't turn the truck off. Over the purr of the idling engine we hear a disembodied voice.

"Well, here we are in Daloa, and this is where I'm going to spend the night. Before I go in, though, I think I'll just take a moment to appreciate this view of the street while I face away from my truck." His voice is loud and clear. I can't help but smile as Khadija and I collect our bundle of food, our refilled water bottle, and the med kit. "Yup," Oumar goes on, "here I am looking off in the distance. Of course there's nothing in my truck but dried *cacao* seeds, but if there were anyone in there, this sure would be a perfect time for them to hop out. Yes, indeedy."

For a moment I feel like I'm living in a universe where all the rules I've learned so far in my life don't really apply. Oumar, a *pisteur* working with the bosses, has let us go. We trusted him and it didn't blow up in our faces. I shake my head in wonder, then drop the tailgate and help Seydou and Khadija to the ground. Khadija lands lightly, but Seydou swings down clumsily, waving his elbow stump, shirtsleeve flapping. He lands off balance, still expecting help from an arm that's no longer there.

Once they're out, I jump after them and shut the tailgate

again. It makes a clanging noise and, as the three of us turn and jog up the street, we hear Oumar stop talking to himself and break into a low laugh. A moment later we hear the sound of the door being opened and closed and the engine revving into gear. As he pulls forward, Oumar blasts the horn a few times.

"That's so they'll open the gate for him," says Khadija as she settles our small burlap bundle on her head and takes Seydou's right hand. I shrug, since she's the one who knows everything about cities and is probably right.

But I think it was Oumar saying goodbye.

"We need to find a place to sleep," says Khadija. "It's not safe to be walking around at night, and I have no idea where the good and bad sections are in Daloa."

I don't know what she's talking about, but I don't argue. It's dangerous to walk around in *la brosse* at night, so it may well be dangerous to walk around here too. After a brief search I find some scraggly bushes in a dip off the side of the road. We crawl under them and try to ignore the rocks and the thorns and the bugs.

"We never had to sleep outside at home," Seydou whines.

"What?" I ask, not really paying attention.

"We had a nice hut to sleep in . . . and there was hay and stuff and no ants . . ." He stops because both Khadija and I are staring at him.

Without thinking I reach out and shake him, hard.

"I don't ever want to hear you call that place home again, are we clear?" I shout.

He stares at me with frightened eyes and then sniffs, *yes, we're clear,* and I leave it at that. But later that night as he and Khadija sleep, I sit there stroking his head and feel my heart breaking. Had we really left when he was so young? Have we really been gone so long? Could Seydou possibly see the farm as home? Would he even recognize his real home when I finally got him there? The questions hurt more than a beating, and even though I know he needs his sleep, I shake his shoulder softly to wake him.

"Seydou."

"Hmm?"

"I'm sorry I yelled and shook you."

"Mmm," he mumbles, and rolls away from me.

I stare at his back in the moonlight, curled around the empty space of his missing arm. I wait a long time, to make sure he's asleep again, and then I go on.

"And I'm sorry about your arm," I whisper. "I'm sorry I got mad that day and left you alone. If I hadn't done that, Khadija wouldn't have been able to run away, and I wouldn't have gotten beaten for it." Tears are tracing their way down my face, and my chest is getting tight. "Then I would have been strong enough to work with you that day. I'm sorry I wasn't there to keep you safe. I'm so . . ." The words come out in soft gasps. "So sorry."

I cover my face with my hands to muffle my ragged-edged

breathing and wipe at the tracks of my tears so that there won't be any way for anyone to know, come morning, that I wasn't able to stay strong.

When I look up from my hands, Seydou is facing me.

The shock of seeing his open eyes makes me stop crying. My chest is still lurching in and out without my permission, but I don't make any noise. I open my mouth to say something to cover my embarrassment but Seydou pulls himself up so that he's sitting facing me.

"This isn't your fault, Amadou," he whispers.

I shake my head, hard, not trusting my voice yet. Seydou reaches out.

"Don't cry," he says.

Which just makes it worse.

I shake his hand off and glower.

"It is . . . my fault," I growl out. My voice is low and harsh, but that's better than being a sobbing wreck. "You can't say it's not."

Now it's Seydou's turn to shake his head. But I'm not finished. Now that I've started, I've got to say it all. "Even if— Even if it's not my fault for that one day, every other day still is my fault. If I hadn't talked Moke into letting you look for work with me, you'd never have been there at all. None of the past two years would have happened to you. You would still be safe, and at home and . . . whole."

And there, it's said. The crushing weight that I've been living under all these years is out in the shadowy, moonlit space between us. I look away. He may have been too small and stupid to have blamed me for this before, but I can't stand to watch his face as he learns to hate me.

For a brief moment, there's silence. Then he shakes me roughly, and I'm startled into looking at him.

"A lot of bad things happened to us," Seydou says, his eyebrows so low and angry they're hooding his eyes. "The drought at home. The fact that none of us could eat. The bosses beating us when we didn't work hard enough."

I blink, not quite understanding the anger in his voice.

"Just because you were there when they happened doesn't mean they're your fault." Seydou sits on his heels and looks at me earnestly. His haunted face wears a serious expression and he suddenly looks much older than eight. "I wanted to leave with you," he reminds me. "I chose to come. If you hadn't convinced Moke, I would have snuck out after you.

"Anyway, I was hungry." He shrugs. "We thought there would be more food in the Ivory Coast. Remember?" he asks, and the ghost of a smile touches his features. "And remember Hawa telling us that in Ivory Coast you could just reach up and pick gold off the trees?"

I remember our cousin's old story as he says it. We used to lie awake at night when we were little, Seydou and I, staring at the breaks in the thatch above us and whispering about how, when we were big enough, we'd go and pick gold off the Ivory Coast trees ourselves. Seydou smiles grimly.

"I believed it," he says. "And there was no way anyone was

going to keep me away from that." He glares again. "It is not your fault I came to the farm, Amadou. Don't you ever say that."

I shake my head, but without conviction. The tears are threatening again and I blink hard to stop them. This time, when Seydou touches me, it's gentle.

"And once we were there, Amadou, you took care of me." His voice is a soft pressure and I feel something hard inside me breaking under it. "You were always watching me to make sure I didn't get hurt. You came between me and the boys who were rough. Between me and the bosses. You took my beatings for me again and again." His voice trembles a little bit. "And *I'm* sorry for that. I'm sorry I was so useless and couldn't keep up better."

"You're not useless," I croak, finally finding my voice. "You're the only reason I didn't give up."

"Me too," he says.

I can't help it anymore, I pull my knees to my chest and sob. Seydou scoots beside me and wraps me in a one-armed hug.

I don't know how long we sit there, but I cry until I feel empty inside and Seydou has fallen asleep leaning against me. Finally, I raise my wet face to the clear night sky and let the breeze dry my cheeks.

And though we still have no plan and no guarantee of safety, I feel just a little bit better.

18

Next day, each of us is exhausted.

It takes all our energy to drag ourselves to our feet and move around Daloa. For a while we wander aimlessly along the main road Oumar was taking yesterday. When Seydou declares he's hungry, I can't think of anything else we should be doing, so I lead them to a spot out of the way of traffic and sit down. Khadija takes the hard-boiled eggs and fruit we saved from dinner and splits them between us.

"We need to get some more food." She sighs around a mouthful of egg.

I agree, but I'm not sure how we're going to get it. I still have the handful of money we stole from the bosses' house in my pocket, but it's not much and I'm no good at haggling. At home, it was always the girls who went to market to haggle, but I'm not sure Khadija knows how to do that.

"Have you ever been to a market?" I ask.

"Of course I've been to a market," she answers huffily.

"No, no, I mean, did you do the shopping at home?" I correct myself.

Khadija looks away.

"Well, no, not really," she admits. "I usually only went to the market if I needed school supplies or clothes or shoes or gifts or something."

"Wait, you went to school?" Seydou asks.

There's an awkward pause. I remember that Seydou was asleep last night when Khadija told me her story.

"Khadija isn't Malian," I tell him. "She's Ivorian and grew up in the city. We're helping her get home so her mama can get a good doctor for you and help us get home to Mali."

"You're like the bosses?" he gasps. That had been my first thought too.

"*Ayi*, Seydou," she says earnestly. "I just grew up in the same country as them, but that doesn't make me like them."

Seydou's eyes are stormy as he processes all this.

"And you went to school," he says flatly.

"*Awó*," she says. "Don't be mad, Seydou, school's not that bad. I think you'd like it, actually. You're a smart little boy."

Seydou gets distracted considering his possible smartness, but I haven't forgotten our real problem.

"Did your mother do the shopping then?" I ask, trying to picture what Khadija's mother looks like.

"No," she says, and from the way she's not meeting my eyes I can tell she's embarrassed by something.

"Well, then, who?" I'm baffled. She said she didn't live with her father. Does she have sisters she never mentioned? An aunt?

"The maid." Khadija's answer is so quiet I can barely hear her. I stare at her blankly, not having any image to go with the world she lived in.

"You had a maid?" Seydou bursts out. "How rich are you?"

Khadija looks down at her hands and the silence stretches. Finally, she whispers, "Please don't hate me."

And I just shake my head because I don't know how I feel about her life and her world and her school and her reading and her *maid*, for crying out loud. But still, I don't hate her.

"Anything else?" asks Seydou dryly.

She looks up at him, a question on her face.

"Is there anything else you want to tell us? Can you fly? Are you a princess?"

Khadija bursts out laughing.

"No, Seydou. That's it. My mama's a journalist and I grew up in Abidjan. That's all of my secrets."

"Well, okay then," he says.

"So." I sigh, looking at Khadija. "You're not really going to be much help in a market, are you?"

"I can do it!" says Seydou, surprising us.

We both turn to look at him.

"What?"

"I can go to the market and get us some food. I used to tag along with Auntie when she would go shopping for us at *home*."

I don't miss the emphasis, but I also think it's a terrible idea. My blank stare must have been answer enough.

"I can help! You never let me help!"

"What?" Some women walking on the other side of the street with plastic jugs on their heads turn and stare at us, eyes lingering on Seydou's missing arm and the machete at my waist. I lower my voice a bit. "There's no way I'm letting you wander off without us. You're still sick."

"You always think I shouldn't help," he argues. "But I can! When you were chained, I kept up with the other boys and brought you food. I can help, you just never let me!"

"Yeah, and look what happened to you when I wasn't there!"

The words are out of my mouth before I can stop them. I never meant to throw his injury in his face like that, but at the same time, it's the truth.

"I can do this, Amadou," Seydou whispers miserably. "Let me help."

I stare at him. His ribs stand out like fingers against the thin fabric of the bosses' shirt when he breathes. His right hand trembles slightly by his side and his face is covered with a fine sweat, showing how much energy this fight is costing him. His other arm ends in a dirty bandage that I know we need to change soon. He is small and breakable. I want to hug him and make everything go away.

And yet his eyes are fierce, and I can't deny that what he says has some truth in it. I take a very slow, very deep breath and reconsider all the things I was about to say. I remember Khadija insisting in the truck that Seydou needs to be able to do some things for himself. I know his arm's not coming back,

209

but maybe if I let him do more, we can get him to be whole again on the inside.

"Okay," I mumble, pulling him against me and resting my face on his head. "Okay."

Seydou's body goes slack in surprise. Then I'm getting the breath squeezed out of me.

"*I ni cé*, Amadou," he mumbles into my shirt.

I glance at Khadija. Her eyebrows are high in her oval face and her mouth hangs open a little. She looks like she's about to say something that might make me feel uncomfortable, so I push Seydou away and rub my hand over his hair.

"Don't thank me," I say. "I'm just too lazy to do it myself. What's the point of having a younger brother around if you don't make him do the boring stuff for you?" And though Khadija looks about ready to kill me, I see a small spark flash in Seydou's haggard eyes and he snorts a laugh.

Forcing a smile while trying to ignore the gnawing fear in the pit of my stomach, I reach into my pocket and hand Seydou our precious money.

"He'll be fine," Khadija whispers, but the muscles in my neck are tense and my hands are in fists by my sides as I pretend not to follow Seydou as he walks into the Daloa central market.

I can see the looks he's getting from the men and women there—wary, pitying—and I try to forget that he's my brother and see him as a stranger would. Young, skinny, maimed, wrapped in torn, oversized clothes and filthy bandages, he looks like a beggar. I swallow my feelings like gravel and continue to follow him.

Seydou doesn't look back. For a moment he puts his hand on his hip, a pose that makes me even more aware of his missing left arm, and then he heads toward a tall square woman who is slouching against a cart, talking to a skinny man. She is not the vendor I would have chosen. She looks hard and is very loud. I regret giving in to this idea.

Seydou lists a little to the side as he walks up to the woman. I wonder when he'll find his new balance.

"*Aw ni sógóma,*" Seydou says politely. "What are you selling?"

The woman and the man stop their conversation and look at him.

"Eggs," she says in a monotone, clearly not impressed, "and corn. Go away, beggar boy, I only sell to customers, I don't give charity."

On the farm I would never have let any of the boys speak to Seydou that way. It's only Khadija's hand on my arm that keeps me from running over there.

"I'm a customer!" says Seydou brightly. I don't know how he's not bothered by what she's saying, but his shiny smile is still in place. He pulls all of our money out of his pocket and holds it up. "My auntie sent me to buy some things, but she said I could get myself lunch too. How much for three eggs?"

"Three eggs just for you?" She bellows a laugh. "How are you so skinny when you eat like that?"

"Maybe after I've eaten them, I won't be so skinny," Seydou jokes easily.

For a split second the woman and her friend stare at him. Seydou's smiling, open expression never wavers. Then, almost grudgingly, the woman tells him the price. Seydou haggles a little, but not so much that it seems rude, and they agree on a price that makes me cringe. It's not too far off the price for three eggs, but at almost a third of what we had, it's certainly more than I wanted to pay. Seydou asks her for help counting out the bills while he puts the eggs carefully in his pocket with his one hand. Another thing I would not have done. I would never have trusted a stranger to hold all of our money.

A one-handed boy trying to put hard-boiled eggs in a shallow pocket is a fine show and many people have stopped what they were doing and are now watching him. I feel twitchy with so many eyes on my brother. Once the eggs are safely tucked away, Seydou takes his change and thanks the woman politely. Then he turns, with a big smile for the whole market, and walks to a kindly-looking fat woman sitting beside a blanket covered in dried peanuts. He kneels in front of her in order to be at her eye level and starts chatting. A voice at my elbow distracts me.

"Your brother is so clever," Khadija says in an awed whisper. I tear my eyes from Seydou for a brief second to give her a look of disbelief.

"You've got to be kidding. He just paid more than full price for three eggs to that witch over there." Now it's her turn to stare at me.

"Don't you see what he did?" When my silence answers for me, she goes on, waving her hands around as she makes her point. "He picked someone who was loud and stingy so that everyone would hear that he had money and wasn't a beggar. Then he paid a good price and was all open and trusting and sweet, smiling so much, being polite, handing her the money. Didn't you notice how everyone's expression softened when he was struggling to put those eggs in his pocket and she had to hold his money for him? He may have paid full price for those eggs but I bet he doesn't pay full price for anything else. He melted every heart in this market."

I turn in time to see a woman from two stalls away walk to where Seydou is still chatting with the fat peanut lady and pinch his cheeks. Within half an hour Seydou is trotting out of the market with a bag of roasted peanuts, three hot ears of cooked corn, a small papaya, and a length of sugarcane balanced in the crook of his only arm. A small handful of leftover coins jingles in his other pocket.

Khadija shoots me an *I told you so* look.

I shrug, and shuffle out of the market after him.

One full meal of roasted corn and peanuts later, we all sit in the shade sucking on the ends of the sugarcane I sliced open for us with my machete. We leave the three eggs in Seydou's pocket for later and I have plans for the papaya. As the sweetness of the sugarcane floods my mouth, I finally feel the knot of uneasiness in my gut over sending Seydou into the market alone unclench. I squeeze his shoulder.

"I'm proud of you," I tell him.

Slouched against the alley wall, exhausted and shaky with fatigue, Seydou beams. He knows he did well. I stare into his eyes and see a little of my brother come back. Maybe Khadija had a point after all.

Finally, I force myself to my feet and reach out to help the others stand.

"Let's go," I say. I want everyone to get walking while they still have sugarcane to chew on and are happy, and not after all the food is gone and they only want to sleep.

"First let's clean this up," Khadija says, pointing to Seydou's stump. I use my machete to cut the little papaya into thin slices and we rebandage Seydou's arm, using the last of the gauze. I try not to think about what that means.

Once we're moving, the realization that I don't know where we're going or how to get us there pounces on me and won't let go. I walk confidently ahead, and the other two follow me. Maybe they haven't realized yet that I don't have a plan.

We're pretty much out of Daloa now, passing big industrial compounds, and soon I'm going to have to stop and talk to the others. Then, out of the corner of my eye, I spot a familiar truck.

"Isn't that Oumar's truck?" I ask, without thinking.

"What?" asks Khadija.

I take the sugarcane stump out of my mouth and repeat myself. Khadija and Seydou squint in the direction I pointed. A few blocks farther down, a battered truck is pulling through an open double gate.

"I think it is," Seydou says, letting go of his arm in order to shade his eyes to see.

Maybe it's the lack of sleep or maybe it's the sugar, but I wonder what's inside that gate. I check my curiosity against my usual caution. But the farm is far away and Oumar showed that he was someone we could trust. Curiosity wins. I lean down to Seydou's level and smile.

"Want to go find out what happens to all those seeds we collected?" I ask.

Seydou considers for a moment, holding on to his left elbow. "*Awó,*" he says.

The three of us walk across the street to the compound where Oumar's truck disappeared just moments ago. When we get to the gate in the high wall we peek through.

The cinder-block edge is warm in the morning sun, and rough under my fingers. I stand there, struggling to take in the scale of what I'm seeing. A series of long, low pavilions, covered with tin sheeting mounted on poles, are stacked to the roof with bulging sacks. Oumar has parked next to it, and men and boys are hefting the sacks off his truck and onto a flat metal square.

"It's a scale," whispers Khadija beside me. "They're weighing the seeds."

The combination of the familiar earth-and-paper smell of dried seeds and the sight of boys working is making me reconsider the wisdom of this. I watch our farm's sacks pile onto the giant scale.

Seeing those sacks gives me a strange feeling. Once the seeds left the farm, I forgot about them. I had always been too focused on Seydou and on getting through the day. Now, seeing hundreds upon hundreds of sacks crammed into the long pavilions, I wonder who wants them all.

Whistling, Oumar gets into his cab and drives his now-empty truck out through the gate. He doesn't see us hiding off to the side, but Seydou gives a small wave anyway.

"Let's go," I say, to get everyone's attention again. I hustle us across the street.

"What do they want so many of them for?" murmurs Seydou.

"I have no idea," I say, "but we shouldn't stick around here any longer. I don't want to get caught."

Seydou nods solemnly, but Khadija seems distracted, staring at the bustling compound.

"Khadija," I say, "let's go."

"Huh?" She half turns to look at me, clearly not having heard a single word I just said.

"Let's go," I say again. I'd really like to get out of sight of that gate. All these men work with the bosses from our farm, one way or another. I'm getting a crawling feeling all over my skin. I can't get away fast enough.

"No, wait," she says, "I think I might have figured out—wait here!" And with that, before I can stop her, she's off, running into the compound. For a moment I'm so stunned I don't do anything. By the time the shock has worn off, she's already across the street and through the gates.

"*Khadija!*" Seydou whispers after her, as loudly as he dares.

"Stupid, crazy girl," I mutter under my breath. Then, to Seydou, I say, "Come on!" There's nothing I can do for her now that she's in. I take Seydou's hand in mine and run into a narrow alley between the walls of two compounds across the way.

"Wait," he says, pulling against me, "we're not leaving her behind, are we?"

I don't know what we'll do if she gets caught, I think grimly. *You wouldn't survive being returned.* But aloud, I say, "No, we're hiding so that we don't all get into trouble and we can help her later if we need to."

This seems to be good enough for Seydou because he follows me without another word. We crouch between the crumbling walls, quiet as two geckos on a rock. From where we're hiding I watch Khadija walk to the nearest man stacking sacks. He pauses his work to talk to her. My heart is in my throat as I watch the two of them, waiting for the man to grab her. But after a few minutes, she waves to him and skips out of the compound. For a minute our view is blocked by the arrival of one of the biggest trucks I've ever seen, but then there she is, standing just outside the gate.

Seydou pops his head out from where we've been hiding.

"Khadija!" he calls, and when her eyes find us, the lost look leaves her face. She hurries across the street.

"What are you doing over here?" she asks accusingly.

"We were hiding so that we could help you later if you got into trouble," Seydou says.

She shrugs.

"Well?" she asks. "Aren't you going to ask why I went to all that trouble?"

I glare at her. No information could possibly be worth the danger she put herself into. All her promises are worth nothing to me if she gets caught and strands us in the middle of the Ivory Coast.

"See," she goes on, "I had this feeling, and so I went up to that man and pretended I was a Daloa girl who was sweet on one of the drivers. I thought he might be willing to tell me where the trucks go." She can hardly keep the excitement from making her voice squeak as she goes on. "See, I had this hunch. I thought to myself, *This is just a weigh station. I bet they're taking the seeds from here and shipping them off for further processing,* you know what I mean?"

I don't have any idea what she's talking about. Khadija rushes on.

"So anyway, it turns out I was right. Guess where they're taking them?" She doesn't wait for us to guess, even though I see Seydou open his mouth to do so. "*San Pédro!*" She bounces on her toes, making her tattered blue dress swish around her knobby knees. She grins at the two of us as if this news should make our day.

"So?" I finally ask.

"San Pédro is the last place I saw Mama. Maybe she's still there. And if we can get into one of those big trucks, they'll take us all the way to the coast. Even if Mama's not still in San

Pédro, we'll know for sure and we can go find her in Abidjan. We won't have to walk, which Seydou can't do, and we won't have to take the bus, which we can't afford."

I think over Khadija's idea again. Seydou looks like he's considering it too. I guess, through all our morning wandering, Khadija has been thinking of how to move on from here too. A bus had never even occurred to me, probably because we barely had enough money for one meal, let alone bus fare for three.

"Well?" she prompts.

"I don't see how we're going to get into one of those trucks without being seen."

I mean it as a criticism of the whole idea, but only as it leaves my mouth do I realize that it can also be seen as agreement. The grin that stretches across Khadija's face makes me realize my mistake just a little too late to fix it.

We spend a few hours watching the weigh station without trying to do anything. The trucks are like giant metal boxes with arched bars on the top instead of a lid. They roll into the drying compound empty, hinges rattling and wind whistling through the bars. When they lumber out filled with sacks of dried seeds, a canvas is stretched over the metal ribs to protect the cargo, and the high metal tailgate is locked. The fully loaded trucks drag along the road and the wind sucks the canvas against the metal ribs, making them look like giant starving dogs.

I turn to Khadija.

"There's no way we're going to be able to get into that truck while they're loading it." Many men carried the sacks onto the waiting trucks and there was a man with a clipboard, watching them. Far too many eyes.

"Once it's moving—?"

I shake my head.

"These trucks aren't Oumar's pickup. They're huge. The metal sides are taller than the men loading them, and a man with a clipboard makes sure the sides of the tailgate are latched. No way could we manage to sneak into that once it's moving."

"Another roadblock?" Seydou suggests. "Maybe if it stopped, we could—"

"No." Khadija shakes her head definitively. "That won't work here. We're not on some bush path anymore. There are too many people who could see what we were doing, or try to stop us, or fix what we'd done before the truck got there."

We muse in silence for a minute. I turn and watch the latest truck rumble out of sight, so tall that it rips some leaves off the branches of one of the trees growing by the side of the road. And that gives me an idea. I turn to Khadija, feeling like an idiot even as I say it.

"How do you feel about climbing trees?"

***

I sit in my tree, about two kilometers from the drying station, and chew my lower lip nervously as I see the giant truck lumber into sight in the distance. I am ferociously counting seconds in my head because how long it takes for the truck to get from one spot to another really, really matters.

The idea is simple, but there are so many things that could go wrong, it makes me dizzy to consider them. The plan is to jump onto the top as it passes under us, then scoot to the rear where the canvas is open and drop into the truck bed. Khadija is in the first tree and I climbed the second one with Seydou on my back. If she doesn't make it onto the truck, we won't jump. But if she does make it, then Seydou and I will jump after her.

Seydou is gripping my neck in a near chokehold with his one good arm and his legs are wrapped tightly around my waist. I've taken off my shirt and tied it around my machete, using the sleeves to secure it flat against my thigh so that the blade is less likely to hurt us if we fall wrong. I don't know if it's the heat or the fear or the lack of my shirt, but I'm sweating heavily into the space between us.

It's the only plan you've got, I remind myself. But it already hasn't worked twice. The first time, Khadija was too nervous to jump, so none of us did, and then the second time, she missed and fell from the tree right onto the ground, after the truck. I don't know that I've ever moved so fast in my life, afraid that she had hurt herself horribly.

When I got to her, she was lying in the dust, dazed. I pulled her off to the side of the road and checked her over. She had only twisted her arm slightly, but we were all scared by the close shave. I tried not to imagine how badly Seydou could have gotten hurt if it had been him that fell.

I watch the truck grow larger as it speeds toward us and I swallow against my suddenly dry throat. If only they weren't going so *fast!*

I hold my breath as the truck rumbles up to the first tree. My hands are gripping the branch of my tree so hard that I can feel the bark cut into my skin, but I don't look away. *Please jump at the right time,* I beg Khadija in my mind. *Please don't get hurt.*

I see her fall, gangly and flailing, from the tree. *Too soon!* I think, and my heart nearly stops because I have visions of her falling under the wheels of the truck and dying in front of my eyes. But she lands with a jolt that pulls the canvas between the ribs into a deep hammock of cloth.

My heart lurches in my chest.

I thought she had jumped too early. *That truck is going way faster than I thought it was.* It zooms at me.

Terror overtakes me. What if I miss and land on the ground like Khadija did and I crush Seydou? What if I break my neck and can't help anyone ever again? What if *we* fall under the wheels of the truck?

"Jump, Amadou," Seydou whispers into my ear from where he's clinging to my back.

I struggle to let go of the branch, but my heart is hammering in my chest and I'm afraid. The front of the truck passes underneath us and I know I have to jump *now*, but I still don't do it. It's only as I see Khadija's panicked eyes flash past beneath me that I find the strength to uncurl my hand from the branch and launch myself into the air.

As I fall, I see the canvas roof streak past below me and I realize I've let go too late just as I hit, hard, against the very edge of the truck.

The cloth of the roof scrapes past my face as I struggle to pull breath back into my lungs and scrabble to get a handhold on something, anything. Seydou's arm around my neck is cutting off my air and black dots are starting to swim in front of my eyes as I swing my legs to try to get purchase. I find myself pedaling against nothing but wind.

Seydou screams in my ear and my panic mirrors his. *We're falling off!*

The truck lurches and I grab at the cloth-covered rib, hoping to have the strength to pull my body on top. Knuckles straining, arms burning, I hold myself up as the wind slaps my face, trying to get my feet into the truck. All of a sudden, I feel hands on my ankles. Khadija must have found a way to get under the canvas and inside. Though my arms feel like they're ripping off with the torture of holding my entire weight and my brother's, I relax and let her guide my legs into the truck. I twist so that I'm not blocking Seydou's access and manage to croak, "Go." Once Khadija has Seydou inside, I drop into the bed of truck.

Gasping, I sprawl across the giant nubby sacks of dried seeds while the canvas roof snaps against the metal ribs above me in the wind. I can feel myself trembling but can't stop.

"It's not as easy as it looks, is it?" asks Khadija from beside me, and I have to give a shaky laugh because I can't possibly imagine jumping more than once.

"Not nearly."

"I thought you weren't going to make it and I'd have to jump out again," she says with a sigh of relief. I roll my head to the side. She makes a face. "I was *not* looking forward to having to do that a third time!"

For a moment I just savor the feeling of lying safe and secure inside the truck and moving without effort. Then I pull myself into a sitting position.

"We did it," I manage, untying my machete and slipping my shirt on again.

They smile.

As we sit perched on the nubby burlap, picking the bits of shell out of our smashed hard-boiled eggs and flicking them over the high back of the truck, I take inventory of my various aches and pains and think that, on the whole, whatever hurts now was worth it. *It's been more than two days since anyone forced you to work or beat you,* I remind myself. *That should be worth some discomfort and uncertainty.*

I refuse to think about how all these risks are only taking us farther and farther away from Mali. Staring out the rip Khadija put in the canvas covering to get into the truck, I watch clouds flash by against the flat blue sky. This is a great way to get Khadija home, but I just hope she keeps her promise and helps us do the same.

Lulled by the hot, tentlike feeling under the cloth roof, and surrounded by the spicy, dusty smell of the dried pod seeds, I let the exhaustion of the past few days win and I sleep.

When I wake again, the truck is still moving. But the sky through the rip in the canvas is dark and studded with smudgy stars.

I crawl from my perch on top of the sacks near the cab to get a better look over the tailgate. We're trundling through a large town, choked with dust and cars and taxis that weave around us, horns blaring. The regular flashes of light are streetlamps, and everywhere there are people. They're filling the sidewalks, spilling out of buses, ducking in and out of shops. Music blasts from windows of buildings and cars alike. I don't know how I slept through the noise as long as I did. I look to where Khadija and Seydou are both still asleep, sprawled on top of the sacks like I was. I cross to Khadija.

"I think we're here," I whisper so as not to wake Seydou until we absolutely have to. "Now what?"

Khadija looks around the darkened truck for a moment and then wriggles like a fish to peer out as well. When she turns around, though I can't see her face, I can hear the concern in her voice.

"It's really late, Amadou."

"So?"

"The men who came and kidnapped me came at night. It just makes me nervous, is all."

I nod. The darkness and bigness of San Pédro make me feel lost and small too.

"But we have to get off this truck."

Khadija stretches her neck stiffly and she doesn't have to say anything for me to know what she's thinking. I don't want to do any more jumping either.

"Where is it going to stop?" I ask.

"I don't know," says Khadija.

"What? I thought you talked to the man at the weigh station?"

"Well, yes, I did," says Khadija, sounding slightly put out. "But I didn't talk to him for very long. I only got the basics."

We lapse into silence, each looking out, considering.

"Maybe we should jump after all?" Khadija finally ventures, but just then, the truck pulls to a stop and honks its horn.

"Oh, now!" I say, scrabbling my way to Seydou. "It's stopped now—we should go!"

"Wait," squeaks Khadija. "Where's the med kit?"

"Seydou! Seydou, wake up!" I shake him.

He does wake up, but his movements are sluggish with sleep, and he cries out when I bump into his arm stump by accident. I slow down, worried I'll hurt him.

"Come on," I whisper to him. "Come with me. We're going to jump now."

Seydou lets me help him toward the tailgate.

"Khadija!" I whisper-shout over my shoulder.

"I can't find it!" comes her panicked answer.

"What?!"

"The medicine box! It must have fallen somewhere and I can't find it!"

For a moment I'm torn. We need to get out, but I'm not going anywhere without those two pill bottles. Seydou's fever is finally going away and, except when I do something stupid like bump him in the dark or hurl him onto a moving truck, he seems to be in less pain too. Despite Khadija's repeated assurances that we'll be able to find him better medicine when we find her mother, I don't want to lose the medicine that we do have.

Letting go of Seydou's wrist, I move to help Khadija. The truck lurches forward again and I'm thrown off my feet.

"Too late," whispers Seydou, and I twist around and see that's he's right. The truck has made it through a giant wall and men outlined in pools of yellow light are closing a massive metal gate behind us. Wherever it is that the truck is going, we're locked into going there too.

Behind me I hear Khadija whisper, "I found it." I don't turn around again. Instead, I crawl to where Seydou is keeping watch and try to figure out what we do now.

"Where are we?" Seydou asks, licking his lips. "Why does the air taste funny?"

The wind that's making the slits in the canvas slap against the metal ribs has turned damp and has an unfamiliar tang to it. I shrug.

"That's salt you're tasting," Khadija says, finally joining us. "We must be getting close to the shore."

"The shore?" Seydou echoes.

"Yes, you know," says Khadija, "the ocean?"

Seydou is still confused and Khadija shoots me a look that says, *How can he not know about the ocean?*

"You know the ocean, Seydou," I mutter, bristling at the things she didn't say. "It's like a big lake with salt in it, so there's different fish. Remember, Moke told us about the ocean once."

Khadija looks away.

That's right, I think. *Just because we didn't go to a private school in the city doesn't mean that we don't know anything.*

Khadija peeks outside and I do the same. Huge, shadowy containers, taller than our truck, stretch in rows off to our right. I look out the other side. They stretch off to our left too. It makes me feel trapped and slightly nauseous. I can't see over them and I have the sinking, nightmarish feeling that they go on forever in all directions and we'll never escape. Our truck turns left. I can't see the gate we came through anymore.

"We need to get out," whispers Khadija beside me. "And maybe you should keep the pills."

I push the small box into my pocket and nod in agreement. I don't want to get any farther into this maze and I really don't want to be found when they unload the truck.

"Let's go," I say. I help Khadija to the edge and grip her forearms as she braces herself against the truck. Then, leaning as far as I can without falling out, I lower her to the ground. I let go and she drops lightly to her feet. The truck has slowed enough, navigating its way through the containers, that she can keep up with us as I do the same thing for Seydou. Because I can only hold on to one of his arms, it's hard to lower Seydou without him being banged against the metal. He hisses in pain when this happens but doesn't say anything. As soon as Khadija wraps her arms around his legs, I let go.

Vaulting out after them, I land with a jarring *thump* I feel in my knees and at the base of my skull. Then I jog over to where they're standing in the road. Worried that another truck might come behind us, or that someone might glance into the side mirrors of the truck we just left, I lead us farther into the container maze and we vanish into the shadows.

We head in the direction we came, toward the giant metal gate. All of us are tiptoeing and whispering. Other than a distant shushing sound, which I figure must be the ocean, the night is broken only by the sounds of the fading rumble of our truck, the dripping of water off the containers, and the sound of something creaking in the wind. I'm shivering with cold and fear, three times convinced that we're going in circles and lost forever, when the wall looms in front of us again. Off to our right is the vast metal gate, shut and guarded. Above us, the cinder-block wall looms almost beyond what I can see. The glint of what must be barbed wire at the top makes me reconsider climbing it.

"So now what?"

"I wish you would stop asking that!" moans Khadija.

"Well, we're where *you* wanted to be," I remind her.

She makes a face and says nothing, considering our options.

"We can't climb the wall," she muses. She's right. Even if there weren't any barbed wire at the top, there's no way that Seydou could get over it with only one arm. I look around for Seydou and see that he's slumped, exhausted, against the closest metal container. Reflexively I touch the pocket that holds his pill bottles, but Khadija only lets me give them to him three times a day, so I don't offer him any.

"Why don't we just wait until the truck leaves and then go through the gate?" he mumbles.

I'm about to tell him to not be so silly but then I pause and consider his plan. I look at Khadija.

"I bet they're going to unload the truck soon," I say.

"If not right away, then probably first thing in the morning," she agrees.

"And they'll have to open the gate to let them out."

"And when they do we can run really fast," Seydou chimes in, getting excited that we're considering his idea.

"It's actually not a bad plan," says Khadija, smiling at him. "They might not even chase us that much because we're trying to get out, not in."

"Okay," I say. "We'll wait for them to open the gate and then we run for it."

It's hours later, when Seydou is fast asleep and Khadija and I are both dozing in and out, that the squeal of the giant hinges makes us jump to our feet. I pull Seydou up, not wanting to miss it, and we creep forward as far we can. He slumps into me when we pause, still half-asleep. I decide to forget Khadija's stupid rules, it's been long enough, and pop two more pills into his mouth.

"You good to run?" I ask him.

"*Awó,*" he mumbles, swallowing, but I'm not sure if I believe him. Hoping the pills will kick in soon, I rub his neck and lean forward to see better. When the gate swings open all the way, a truck the same size as ours pulls forward into the compound.

"Now!" I say, and start running. I can hear the slapping of the others' feet behind me as I lead the way.

Once I'm out in the open, I feel terribly exposed. There's a minute, when the truck is blocking the gate, where the man on the far side doesn't see us and we can just run, but too soon that moment is over.

The man on the far side shouts, holding up a hand. The man on our side of the gate spins around to look where his friend is pointing and sees us.

He shouts at us too, and even though I don't understand their language, it's clear they're telling me to stop.

I pick up speed.

When the men see this, each of them does a very different thing. The one on the far side shoves on the heavy metal door with all his might to make it close faster, trying to trap us inside. The one closest to us lets go of his half of the gate and stands to block our path. I realize that, if we don't make it out right now, then not only will we still be trapped inside the compound, but the men will chase us. I wish one of us had been awake enough to realize this back when we were all thinking Seydou's idea was such a great one.

Too late for regrets now. I consider my rapidly shrinking options and decide we have no choice: we need to get out. I'm ready to put on a final burst of speed to dart around the man blocking the gate, when I hear a stumble behind me. Pausing,

I look back and see that Khadija is holding Seydou against her side, helping him run. They're moving, but they're going too slowly and Seydou is clutching the stump of his arm against his chest. I guess running was too much for him.

I whip my head around and see that I'm almost upon the men. My options have narrowed even further.

"Get him to the doctor like you promised," I shout to Khadija, and then I brace myself and run as fast as I can right into the man who is trying to stop us, knocking us both off our feet, allowing Khadija and Seydou the time they need to scurry out the half-open gate into the night-darkened port beyond.

20

I have a moment to celebrate the view of their four ankles disappearing into the dark, knowing I've done the right thing, before I'm hauled up by the second man and held firmly in place. With my arms pinned, I can't reach my machete. The man I knocked over pulls himself heavily off the ground. He's younger than I thought, with a skinny neck poking out of his uniform collar and bulging eyes. He looks like a cross between a chicken and a frog. When he's on his feet he cuffs me in the face.

The one who's holding my arms, older by the sound of his voice, rumbles out a question to the younger one in the language I don't understand. That must be what French sounds like when you're angry. The younger one, Frog Face, cranes his head to see out the gate, then answers with an angry shrug. Clearly, they got away.

Frog Face swings the big metal gate shut and padlocks it from the inside. Something tightens in my chest when I hear the lock *click*. I'm not sure if it's anger or fear. Then he asks me a question, but he's still not speaking a language I understand, so I just shake my head.

"You," the man behind me asks in Bambara, giving me a little shake that pulls uncomfortably on my shoulders. "What were you doing here, huh?"

I'm surprised to hear him speaking my language, but I still don't answer him.

Frog Face cuffs me again and now I can taste blood in my mouth.

"Answer my uncle, you street rat." He also switches to Bambara. "What were you doing here?"

I glare at him. He hits me again.

"Stop hitting him," the uncle says, and I'm grateful. It doesn't take much getting hit in the head to make you dizzy, and I need to not feel that way if I'm going to escape.

"Why? He could be a spy!"

The older man laughs and I feel his grip loosen slightly. I tense, waiting for the opportunity to run like crazy. If I were to slam my head into the uncle's face I could probably outrun Frog Face. I consider reaching for my machete again. But I see the gun at his belt and I reconsider. There's no way to outrun a bullet.

"A spy?" says the uncle, behind me. "You watch too much television, you and those friends of yours. Who would he be spying for? Another company? Another country? Look at him, he's skinny as a dog and his hands and feet are like rocks. He doesn't even speak French. He's just a poor working boy from the north."

The nephew scowls, fingering his gun.

"We still need to know why he's here," he grouses.

The uncle lets go of one of my arms and turns me so that I'm facing him. He is square and solid. There's not much resemblance to his cold-blooded frog of a nephew.

"I'm of a mind to let you go, but you need to tell me what you were doing here," he says, looking into my eyes. His eyes have rings of tiredness under them and his voice is patient. A quick image of Oumar standing off to the side of his idling truck, talking to a wall while we walked away, flashes through my mind. For the first time, I wonder if I can get out of this by using words. It feels really uncomfortable, trusting so much: first Khadija, then Oumar, and now this guard. But I look at him with the most honest expression I can muster and I tell him the truth.

Mostly.

"We were tired of walking, so we hitched a ride on one of the trucks. But then we fell asleep while we were in it. We woke up to the sound of the gate closing. We got out of the truck but didn't know how to get through the gate, so we decided to run out the next time a truck came in."

"And why did you run into me instead of around me?" Frog Face demands.

"We were afraid of getting caught. And you were blocking the gate. I ran into you so my brother and, um, my sister would be able to get out."

For a moment they just stare at me, taking in my story and my rough hands.

"Where were you coming from?" asks the uncle.

"A little farm outside of Man," I lie, giving the name of the district where the cacao farm was located. I hope that these men will accept that my lack of French comes from being a backwater kid instead of from being Malian. No one here loves a foreigner.

"And why did you want to come to San Pédro?"

"To see my . . . aunt?" But my tone goes up at the end, betraying the lie for what it is. I close my mouth. Let the nephew think I'm a spy if he will, but I'm not going to tell them that I'm a runaway from one of the farms that supply them with their job.

"What? Why? What are you not telling us?" The nephew is in my face again, shouting.

My pleasant look melts without my permission and I find myself scowling. The uncle's voice cuts into our fight.

"You have a lot of scars," he says quietly. "Were you a plantation boy?"

My stomach feels like it's dropped out of me.

"*Ayi!*" I say, louder than I mean to. But the uncle is looking at me with old eyes and I know I can't leave it at that. I flick my gaze along my own arms. Yes, you can see the lines left there by the bosses. I just don't think about them very much. On my legs too, I guess, but hopefully it's too dark to see them. "Um . . . my . . . uncle made us work for him on his farm near Man," I say. "He . . . um . . . was not a patient man, so . . . um . . . that's why we're running here to live with our aunt."

For a moment the big man and I look at each other, and I know he knows I'm lying. But then he lets go of my arm. It feels cold where he was gripping it and for a moment we all stand there, frozen by the surprise of what he did.

"I had an 'uncle' like that once," he says softly, and rolls up his shirtsleeve. Old machete cuts trace a light web on his dark arms, and chemical burns dot his hands. Those hands worked *cacao* at some point too. After a moment, he walks to the metal gate, unclips the padlock, and holds it open a shoulder's width. "Be on your way. But I warn you, you and your family better not come back in here. We'll turn you over to the police next time."

I'm out the crack in that gate like a fish through fingers before I pause. A thin slice of light spills from the inside. The nephew looks angry. I can tell he wants to argue with his uncle, and there's a calculating look on his face that makes me feel deeply uncomfortable. I know I should get a move on before they change their minds, but I make myself wrestle the rarely used thanks off my tongue.

"*I ni cé,*" I say to the uncle behind the closing gate.

"Be safe," comes the soft reply a second before the gate clangs shut and the street is plunged into darkness.

I stand there for a second more, wondering at it all, but then I come to my senses and run away as fast as my legs will carry me.

I've only made it a few meters when two forms hurtle out of the shadows to my left and barrel into me.

"Amadou!" Seydou's shouting, grabbing me. Both of Khadija's arms are thrown around my neck.

"*Gak!* Don't choke me!" I manage to get out.

She lets go immediately and steps away, grinning.

"I'm just so glad to see you," she says.

"We thought . . . we thought," Seydou gasps, still attached to my waist like a lichen, "that they were going to kill you, or give you to the police! And then we . . . we were standing here fighting and I said, *We need to get in there and save Amadou,* and she said, *No, we need to go get help.* And then I said, *What if he makes it out and we're gone?* And then she said . . ."

"Seydou! Okay, okay," I say, pushing him off and laughing in spite of myself. "I made it out fine." I look gratefully between my brother and the wildcat. "And I'm glad you waited for me." I hug him against my side and smile at her. It feels good to be back with them. "Now that I'm here, though, we really should get off of these dark streets as quickly as possible before something else happens."

"I agree," Khadija says. "Come on. Let's see if we can find the house where I was staying."

We wander the streets for almost an hour.

Khadija's excitement seems to override her nervousness about nighttime kidnappers and pushes her forward, but once we've put a few blocks between ourselves and the big metal gate, Seydou's terror no longer drives him. He's stumbling along miserably, tripping over his feet and holding his arm. Through it all, he keeps his lips firmly pressed together, not complaining. I've learned over the past few days that Seydou can do more on less strength than I ever thought. Even so, there comes a point where I can't take seeing him struggle.

"Khadija, we need to stop."

"What?" She looks at me, anger creasing her face. "We made it all the way to San Pédro and you want to stop?"

"*Awó.*" Seydou's weight slumps against me. "We need to."

She glances at Seydou and her eyebrows crumple together.

"Okay," she sighs.

I point with my chin to a vacant lot a little ways farther on.

"How about there?" I ask.

"Ugh, no," says Khadija. "There could be snakes, or broken glass, or drug dealers in there."

"Drug dealers? Like the antibiotics?"

Khadija looks at me as if my stupidity were a hideous rash she can't quite bear the sight of.

"No, Amadou. *Drug* dealers. People who are selling illegal drugs and would kill you for interrupting a deal."

I look at the wild grass and scraggly bushes. Snakes only come out in the sunlight, and though Seydou and I have no shoes, our bare feet are so callused we probably wouldn't even notice if there were broken glass. As to drug dealers, well.

"Where would you rather be unsafe?" I ask. "In the street, in this lot, or at the docks? Because unless you have a better idea of where we can go and be perfectly happy and comfortable, then I think we should get some sleep while we can."

Khadija hesitates.

"What's wrong, city girl?" I say in an ugly voice. "Aren't you glad to be home?"

That's all it takes. One unpleasant word and the scared girl is gone. A wildcat glares at me instead.

"Argh! You have no idea what you're getting into. Fine! We'll sleep here for the night. But we're going to take turns keeping watch with your machete, and if anyone comes by, we run."

"Fine," I say, pulling my machete out of my belt and using it to part the long grass. I wave her into the vacant lot. "Your snake-infested, broken-glass-lined, drug-dealer paradise is waiting for you."

Khadija practically snarls as she stomps past me. I wink at Seydou, who's looking at me curiously.

"Well," I whisper, "she went in, didn't she?"

Seydou shakes his head.

"You're bad, Amadou," he says with a laugh. Holding the long grass aside with his one hand, my brother stumbles in after her, not seeming concerned about snakes, broken glass, or drug dealers when it means he can finally get some sleep.

"I guess I am," I say, and follow the two of them into the vacant lot, smoothing the grass behind me.

We don't sleep well that night. Though there are no snakes or drug dealers, there is some broken glass as well as cans, wrappers, and other trash that I have to clear away before any of us can lie down. And there are ants. The biting kind. After a few attempts to brush them off, we give up and walk on, hiding in the shadows of the buildings, staying off the main streets, and collapsing in empty doorways for a few stolen minutes of sleep when we can.

One of us always stands guard with the machete when we stop because, even though I'd made fun of Khadija, I can't shake the feeling that someone might be following us.

It's the tiny hours of the morning and it's my turn to stay awake when I find that I'm right. Khadija and Seydou are slumped against the wall in a small alley and I'm sitting in front of them, machete across my knees, trying to stay awake when I get the feeling again. It's like ants are crawling up my neck, but this time they're inside my skin. I don't know who's watching us, but I can *feel* the eyes on me. I squint up and down the dark street.

Was that a twitch of movement in the doorway there? Did I hear the noise of a footfall? My tired eyes and ears are playing tricks on me. I find myself gripping my machete handle so tightly my knuckles ache.

Then I see him: a young man in a guard's uniform, slinking toward us. It's too dark to be sure, but he looks an awful lot like the nephew from the docks.

Why is he *following us?*

242

I don't know the answer and I don't want to find out. I consider what to do. I don't want to be caught, but I doubt Seydou has the energy left to run again. Even though we're not blocked in, I feel trapped. I do the only thing I can.

I step out into the open, machete held high, and face him. When the nephew sees me, he stops.

There are barely a few meters between us and I can see the bulge at his hip where his gun is. I only have my machete, but I don't back down.

The nephew holds my eyes only for a moment, then glances to where Khadija and Seydou are sleeping behind me. He fumbles in his pocket and takes out a small piece of plastic. He holds it up, and presses a button. A little light flashes and there's a clicking sound. He turns around and jogs away, leaving me standing in the empty moonlit alley, pointing my machete at nothing but shadows.

Of all the things I was expecting, this was not one of them. I wait for him to come back. I wait for the sound of a shot and the feeling of blood pouring out of me. Finally, I can't take the silence anymore. I jostle Khadija and Seydou awake.

"Let's go," I say.

"What? Why?" Khadija mumbles sleepily.

"I think someone's following us."

That wakes her up. She gives me a look of pure terror.

"Who?" she whispers.

I glance at her face and decide this is not an extra fear she needs right now. I change what I was about to say.

"Probably no one." I help Seydou to his feet. "I just have a creepy feeling and I don't want to stay in one place too long in this town at night." I attempt a smile, but I don't think it comes across. "Maybe it's one of your drug dealers."

Khadija swallows hard, then gets to her feet. But all her muscles are tight, so I don't think she buys my explanation. Her eyes cut from side to side, checking every street, window, and doorway for her kidnappers. Stumbling with exhaustion, we carry Seydou through a maze of streets until I'm sure the nephew can't get to us again.

Hours later, dawn finds us huddled together in the shadows underneath a parked truck. We're invisible to anyone passing by, and it has allowed Seydou a few hours of unbroken sleep, but I keep jolting awake to nightmares of getting run over. Once it's light enough to see, the three of us are off again, though this time Khadija is not nearly as excited as she was before. Even though she doesn't know about Frog Face, she hasn't been the same since I said someone might be following us.

Now, with daylight beginning to filter between the buildings, we trace our tired way, looking for landmarks Khadija recognizes. Finally, we find them. Even so, it's nearly noon when we're standing in front of a tall metal door set into a stucco wall, considering it.

I look up and down the street, expecting hordes of men, led by the nephew from the docks, to jump out at us, but it's eerily silent. Khadija turns to me.

"Should I knock?" she asks.

I shrug. "Your house," I say, as lightly as I can.

"You're right," she says. "It's only going to be Stéphane, or Sandrine. Or Mama. There's nothing to be afraid of, right?"

I give her a thin-lipped smile.

She pounds her fist against the door, causing a hollow clanging that makes us all wince. Almost instantly a small section of the door screeches open to reveal a hard, pitted face with a crooked nose. It must be the Stéphane she mentioned.

There is a second of silence. I look at Khadija. Only because I know her so well can I tell that she's terrified.

"Who are you?" she asks.

The man behind the door barks out a question in French. When he speaks, the pockmarks on his cheeks stretch, making him even uglier.

Khadija stares at the man for a moment, then answers him, switching out of Bambara.

He replies in clipped tones, and slides the little metal window shut in our faces.

"*Ayi!*" Khadija pounds on the door. "You have to let us in!"

The guard doesn't answer. I take in her tattered clothes and dirty face, our overall ragged appearance. There is no way he's ever going to let any one of us in, even if she can speak French. Khadija starts to cry.

I bang on the gate, ready to take on the rude guard. The metal square slides open again, but before the ugly man has a chance to say anything, he's distracted by a high, light voice behind him.

"Fabrice?"

Fabrice pulls away from the peephole and I see a tall, slim woman in the yard behind him. Her face is long and thin, with high cheekbones, nothing like Khadija's oval face, but I can see the same determination in her mouth, the same fire in her eyes.

"*Je—je suis désolé, madame,*" Fabrice stammers. "*J'étais juste . . .*"

He doesn't get to finish. As soon as she hears the woman's voice, Khadija leaps to her feet and grabs at the little opening.

"Mama!" she screams.

"*Khadija!*"

Lurching forward, Khadija's mother pushes Fabrice out of the way. She swings the door open with all her body weight and the two of them hurl themselves into each other's arms.

"You're all right!" her mother keeps saying, holding her face, stroking her hair. I'm surprised to hear her speaking Bambara until I remember that Khadija said it was their secret language. "Oh, you're home, thank God, you're home. How did you get here? Thank God you're all right."

I wrap an arm around Seydou. My fear of being seen by the nephew again overrides my manners and I steer Seydou through the open metal door, past the embarrassed guard, and into the garden. Once off the street, I stop.

"Do you think our mama would have done that too?" asks Seydou in a whisper, craning his neck to watch the scene. An ache spreads through my chest as I remember that Seydou never knew our mother. He never knew our father either, since he had left even before that. Moke, Auntie, and I are the only family Seydou's ever known. I think over what I remember of our mother. She was kind and took good care of us. I'd like to think that she would have run out to us like Khadija's mother did.

"*Awó*," I whisper, giving him a squeeze. "She would definitely have come out running for us when we got home."

"I thought so," Seydou mumbles, and he rubs his face into my ribs.

We stand there, waiting to be invited into the house, until Khadija and her mother reach us, tightly wrapped around each other and murmuring softly through tearstained faces.

"Mama, this is Amadou and that's Seydou. They helped me escape and get home." Khadija points to us, but doesn't let go of her mother. Her mother frowns slightly.

"Khadija! *Pourquoi tu ne parles pas français?*"

"Amadou and Seydou only speak Bambara, Mama."

"Oh," she says, and switches over too. To us she says, "Why do you only speak Bambara?"

"We're just poor boys from Mali, *madame*," I say, trying to be as polite as I can. "We never learned French."

"From Mali? Really?" Her eyebrows shoot up. She looks at us all again, this time really seeing us. I remember that she's also from Mali originally. "Goodness gracious, you're all filthy, and I bet you're hungry too."

Seydou tucks his head behind me, suddenly shy. I see her staring at the stump where his arm should be. It reminds me why we came.

"Seydou lost his arm a few days ago," I say. "They cut it off because it was infected. Khadija said you could get a doctor to look at it for us?"

For a moment, she blinks, taken aback. Then she snaps into action.

"Of course, of course! Let's get you some new clothes and a bath and some food and we'll all feel better to talk then. Please, boys, come in. I'm Fatma Kablan, Khadija's mom. You can call me *madame* or Mrs. Kablan. Now, come!" And with that, Mrs. Kablan ushers us into the house.

Once inside, I tense again. Khadija's mother's blouse is a shimmery pink fabric that looks like it would rip if I touched it and the house around us is bigger and better-kept than any I've ever been in. *You don't belong here,* the house whispers.

Seydou is so overwhelmed with the grandness of the house that he walks in a slow circle, eyes wide, taking in the solid concrete walls, the sofa and table, the tiles on the floor, the decorative bars on all the windows to keep robbers out. And, sure enough, glass in the windows. I stay stock-still, afraid to touch anything. Seydou runs his fingers over everything in sight.

"Stop it!" I snap. He startles.

"Oh, he's fine," says Mrs. Kablan absently.

I tell myself to relax. "You're fine," I say. "Sorry I yelled."

But he comes and stands beside me, afraid of making me angry. I sigh. I should be happy. We got off the farm. We crossed the entire country. Khadija is back with her mother. But the luxury of the house makes me feel farther from my own home than I have our whole trip. It, more than the journey, makes me realize just how far I've gone in the wrong direction.

Mrs. Kablan picks up a plastic rectangle like the one Frog Face had last night and pushes some buttons on the front of it. It's only when she starts talking into it in French that I realize that it's a mobile phone. I've never seen a phone so small before.

"She's calling the doctor," Khadija whispers to me, and I feel myself relax.

Mrs. Kablan stops talking and puts the phone in her pocket. "Now," she says, shuttling us through a door on our left, "food."

Seydou and I follow her into the strangest kitchen I've ever seen. There's no fire pit, no hole to let out the smoke, no bucket for water. Instead, there are a table and chairs, some wooden cabinets for storage, and a gas stove. Khadija's mother walks to the cabinets and opens one, her hand still holding Khadija's. It's as if, now that she has her again, she isn't going to let go of her for the rest of her life. My stomach rumbles and I fall into one of the chairs at the little table at the edge of the room. Mrs. Kablan pulls out some vegetables and a loaf of bread. She walks to the stove, puts a pan of water on it, turns the gas on, and lights it with a match.

"Sandrine!" she yells.

A moment later, a young girl not much older than me comes in. She has long-lashed eyes set in a heart-shaped face, her puff of hair held back by a band. She's pretty, and she could have been any of the girls in my village, she looks so much like Seydou and me. As soon as Sandrine sees Khadija, she runs over to her and throws her arms around her, exclaiming in French. Khadija hugs her back. Then Sandrine lets go and, wiping at her eyes, turns to Mrs. Kablan.

When Mrs. Kablan starts ordering her around the kitchen in French, I realize that Sandrine is the maid Khadija had mentioned. She helps Mrs. Kablan cook the food; then Mrs. Kablan sends her out. Khadija tells us it's to buy more food, as well as some new clothes for Seydou and me.

It makes me uncomfortable to sit there and have Mrs. Kablan order her to go out and buy us things. It makes me notice Khadija's and her mother's long, soft fingers. I glance at Sandrine. She may be Ivorian but her hands are thick-knuckled and callused, like mine. As she walks past me on her way out, I whisper, "*I ni cé,* Sandrine." I don't know whether she understands my thanks, but for a split second her eyes latch on to mine, and she gives me a slight smile. Then she's gone.

Mrs. Kablan puts a bowl of a thick stew in front of me. I see chunks of chicken meat and tomato and onion and my mouth starts to water before I even taste it. She hands us each a thick wedge of soft bread and a tall glass of fruit juice and tells us to eat. We haven't eaten since the lunch of smashed hard-boiled eggs on the truck yesterday. I don't need to be told twice.

The stew is hot and filling and the juice is sweet and cool. It's amazing. When we finish, Khadija's mother gives us second helpings.

"Eat until you're full," she says.

When none of us can eat any more, Khadija's mother leans

her elbows against the kitchen table. "Now," she says, "tell me everything."

For a moment, Khadija looks at her mother, her mouth hanging open a little, as if she's trying to talk, but the words just won't come. I think about everything she's gone through. For all the times I wished desperately for someone to know where I was, and what was happening to me, I never thought how hard it would be to actually tell someone.

"Khadija was brought to our farm nine days ago." I surprise all of us by talking. Everyone's eyes swing to me. I take a quick glance at Khadija. She still looks too shaken to take over, so I continue. "Seydou and I have been working on a farm near Man, helping them grow *cacao*."

Mrs. Kablan's eyebrows shoot up in surprise. She studies the three of us, taking in our bruises, Khadija's bedraggled hair and clothes, and Seydou's missing arm.

"Go on," she murmurs, the image of calm. But I'm sitting next to her and I can see her hands in her lap. As soon as I mention the farm, she starts pulling at the edges of her fingernails. I go on.

"Well, it was odd because girls don't work on the farm and kids never arrive alone—it would cost too much for the man driving the truck." Mrs. Kablan's eyes have gone a little vacant and she's pulled so hard on the sides of her fingers that blood is dotting the edge of her delicate blouse. I want to tell her to stop or she'll ruin it, but I don't. "Anyway, she pretty much kept trying to escape every chance she got and then, three days ago, we got away together." I'm leaving out so much. "Seydou had just been hurt and she told us that if we helped her get home you could get a doctor, so we came here with her."

At this point, Khadija breaks in.

"No, Mama, Amadou's not telling it right at all. He's the one who finally helped me escape. He set the farm on fire! He protected me from the other boys too while I was there." She turns and looks at me. "I wouldn't have made it here without him," she says.

At that moment, Fabrice opens the kitchen door and says something to them in French.

"Oh, good," Mrs. Kablan says to us, "the doctor's here." Her tone is even and in control but I take another peek at her hands. Hidden from her daughter's eyes by the table, she has pulled her fingertip to shreds.

I'm amazed by how quickly the doctor has gotten here, but I follow Fabrice into the front room with Seydou, Khadija, and her mother. There, an old man in crisp slacks and a collared shirt smiles warmly at Mrs. Kablan and they begin to talk rapidly in French. I put an arm around Seydou and scoot closer to Khadija.

"What are they saying?" I ask in a whisper.

"Mama's explaining that Seydou had his arm cut off and . . . No, wait," she says, frowning. "That's not right!" She jumps in, speaking to the doctor in rapid French too, leaving Seydou and me standing off to the side self-consciously. Finally the doctor motions for Seydou to come forward.

He won't go by himself, so I walk with him.

The doctor unwinds the gauze and *tsk*s under his breath as dirt crusts off and falls to the floor. We haven't had a chance to change the bandage since before we jumped on the freight truck. We ran out of clean gauze in Daloa.

I hang my head.

He looks carefully at Seydou's stump and pokes at it, this way and that. Seydou hisses between his teeth, but doesn't pull away. The doctor says something to the Kablans, and Khadija says, "Show him the medicine we've been using."

I reach into my pocket and take out the two vials, all that's left of our little kit.

The doctor squints at the labels, then shakes his head and throws the bottles out. Later, when no one's looking, I go through the trash and pull them out, hiding them in my pocket. These rich people might have doctors who'll visit them whenever they want, but Seydou and I need to look out for ourselves. The pills worked well enough once and, if we ever need them again, I want to have them.

The doctor turns to Mrs. Kablan, speaking rapidly in French once more.

Khadija comes over to us and whispers a translation.

"He says that Seydou's got a mild stump infection with some surrounding cellulitis, whatever that means," she says. "He's going to give him a few shots now and a script for penicillin to take tonight. He's supposed to take it four times a day until the pills run out."

"What are shots?" asks Seydou.

"It's medicine they put into your arm through a needle," Khadija says. Then, seeing the look on Seydou's face, she adds, "It only hurts for a second and it keeps you from getting sick." To me she adds, "You'll be getting some too."

"Me? But I'm not sick."

"Like I said"—she sighs—"they keep you from *getting* sick later. Just hold out your arm and get it over with quickly."

Seydou inches closer to me, but Khadija is already talking again. She goes on for a while, trying to keep up as the doctor rambles on about how to tell if infection is setting in, fevers, and something called "phantom limb syndrome." Seydou hasn't really been paying attention ever since the mention of shots, but I listen the best I can. I know whose job it is to take care of him once this old man leaves.

Khadija also says the doctor mentions something called prosthetics—fake arms, and where it might be possible for us to find a hospital that will give one to Seydou. I've never heard of anything like that, so I don't know what to think. How much will this new arm cost? Surely they're not so advanced here in the city that they can simply give Seydou a new arm and everything will be fine? I have a sudden image of Seydou waving around an arm that is large and covered in gray hair like the doctor's and I'm not sure whether to laugh or vomit.

At this point, Sandrine arrives and hands a bundle to Mrs.

Kablan before disappearing again into the kitchen. Soon, Seydou and I are both rubbing the hot, sore spot on our arms where the shots went in.

When the doctor begins packing up, Khadija's mother presses some money into his hand. I can't tell how much it is exactly, but it's probably a lot. My family couldn't afford a doctor even when my mother was dying. I can only imagine what it must cost to have a city doctor come to your house.

I look sharply at Khadija, who is staring vacantly into the far corner of the room.

"*Psst!*"

She turns.

"Don't you think you should get some shots too?" I ask. "Or at least have the doctor look at you?"

She looks away. "I don't want . . ."

Seydou is standing between us, all ears, so I don't want to say too much, but still, maybe there's something the doctor can give her to make her feel better too.

"You need to let them take care of you, Khadija," I say, my voice serious. "They won't know how to if you don't tell them anything."

Khadija swallows. The doctor is almost at the door.

"Please?" I beg. "For me? You made sure the doctor helped us. I need to know you'll get helped too."

Khadija swallows again.

"Mama." Her voice is barely a whisper.

I rub her arm to give her courage. From the door, her mother turns.

"Yes?"

"I'm going to show the boys the bathroom so they can wash up." Her voice trembles, but she doesn't stop. "Could you ask the doctor to wait a moment?"

Then, without waiting for her mother to agree or ask questions, Khadija turns. Three doors lead off the main room, and Khadija brings us through the door on the far right, into a small, tiled room, hands us each a towel, and shows us how to work the shower.

"You can do it, wildcat," I whisper to her as she leaves. I see her clench her fists and press her lips together tightly with determination, just before she closes the door on us. For a moment Seydou and I both stare at the odd tap coming out of the wall. Neither of us have ever used a shower before. "Okay," I finally say, "who's first?"

Seydou's eyes gleam at the challenge, even though he's still cradling his stump against his chest.

"Me," he says.

I brace him by the upper arm so he doesn't slip on the tile. The doctor left his stump unbandaged until after we could get clean, and I'm careful not to jostle it as I help him into the stream of water.

"It's like a hot rainstorm." Seydou laughs, holding his injured arm out to the side to keep it from getting wet. I hand him the soap and let him scrub all the places he can reach by himself and then I scrub his back. My soapy hands bump over the network of old scars there, but for once the echoes of his screams don't haunt me. I realize I finally kept my promise. I got him out. I smile to myself and wash his hair while I'm at it. The side of my head and Mrs. Kablan's floor are getting wet, but I'm not going to let him out until he's clean.

"Okay," I say. "Now your arm."

The puffy stump glistens angrily at us. I take a hard look at it, searching for any of the things Khadija told us the doctor said to look for. But though it looks painful and unnatural, there's no pus coming from it and there are no streaks of infection on his arm. I slather both of my hands with soap and look him in the eyes.

"This will probably hurt," I say. He takes a deep breath. I do the same and then rub my soapy hands over his mangled arm. By the time I've rinsed all the soap off, he's crying freely, but he doesn't pull it away.

I turn off the water and help dry him with one of the towels Khadija left for us. Then, after Seydou pulls on the clean clothes that Mrs. Kablan bought for us, I pick up the Vaseline jar and the new gauze the doctor left. He hadn't thought much of the papaya. I smear some of the clear goop onto Seydou's arm and rewrap it carefully. And, with that, I am left to the shower.

I have never felt anything so good in my entire life. For a while I stand there and let the hot water run over my head and pelt at the knots in my shoulders, then I take the soap and clean myself with a vengeance. The water goes down the drain gray and foamy, but I don't stop washing until it runs clear. I imagine that all the anger and hurt and fear of the past two years are one layer under the dirt from the farm and I scrub until I feel raw.

Finally, I step out of the shower into the bathroom. The curling steam wraps around Seydou and me like smoke from the cook fire. Looking up as I'm drying off, I catch sight of myself in the small mirror above the sink. My eyes look like they belong to a hunted animal. The shower may take care of the old dirt in my hair and on my skin, but there are some things that being in a nice bathroom just won't wash away.

I slip on the new clothes that Khadija's mother bought for me. They are perfectly clean and a pretty good fit. No rips anywhere. I swing my arm around my brother and walk out of the bathroom feeling very, very good.

Mrs. Kablan is waiting for us outside the door.

I look into the front room, but it's empty. The doctor has gone. I look at Mrs. Kablan. She gives us a big smile but I see that more of her fingertips are bleeding and I know Khadija must have told her about what happened in the shed.

"Khadija is taking a rest and I'm sure you both could use one too," says Mrs. Kablan brightly. "We'll all talk more later, but for now, I think you should get some sleep." She hands us each a pile of blankets. "You can sleep here, in the front room. I'll be in the kitchen or my room if you need anything. Otherwise, I'll come wake you in a few hours. Sound good?"

"*Awó*," Seydou mumbles.

"*I ni cé, madame,*" I say, taking the blankets.

"No, Amadou," she says softly, resting her hand on my arm for a moment. "Thank *you*."

Even as she turns away, I can see her smile starting to crumble.

———

The floor of the sitting room is even and clean, and I quickly make two simple pallets with the blankets from Mrs. Kablan. After the bad night, the stress of running, a big lunch, the pain of the shower, and all those shots, Seydou falls asleep almost instantly.

I'm exhausted too, but my eyes keep twitching to the barred windows and the unlocked front door. This is the house that Khadija was taken from. Between that and Mrs. Kablan's fingers, I just don't feel safe enough to sleep. I lie awake, waiting for the bad men from my past to break in and take me where I don't want to go.

For a little while I distract myself by daydreaming of Mali, and going home, and how happy everyone would be to see us and how wonderful that would be. But the dream feels thin now, and like the fabric of Khadija's mother's blouse, I'm worried I'll rip it if I handle it too much. Because underneath the fancy shimmer of the dream I know that the reality of going home would not be perfect. Yes, Moke and Auntie would be glad to see us safe, and yes, it would be good to see their faces and look over the fields of our farm. But there was a reason we left in the first place.

I remember the cracked dirt between the dry, shaky rows of millet and the way the eyes of the little children in the village seemed to get bigger as their arms and legs shrank. It was a hungry time. A thirsty time. Any boy who could left to go make some money in a place that wasn't as drought-stricken. That way he was one less mouth to feed and, in a few months, he would come home with a small roll of money, maybe some seeds. I had watched boys leave for the farms, and girls for the rich houses, every season of my childhood. As soon as I was old enough, Seydou and I went too.

But we never made it somewhere that paid us for our work. And the truth is that neither of us has anything to show for our years away. Less than nothing, because now I'm bringing Seydou back as a cripple.

I splay my fingers on the cool floor and push myself to my feet, then fold my blanket gently over Seydou. My thoughts are driving me crazy. I look out the window. The guard is nowhere to be seen and the yard is empty.

I pad to the door on silent feet, push it open, and let myself into the yard, holding my breath until the familiar feeling of grass and gravel replace tile under my toes. I'll do one lap around the house to double-check that no one's here but us, the maid, and the guard, and then I'll go in and make myself sleep beside Seydou. Even if it still feels like my heart is wrapped in barbed wire, I hope the fresh air will at least clear my head.

But when I turn the corner of the house, I see Khadija's mother through the open kitchen window, chewing on her fingernails, pacing, and talking on her phone in Bambara, no trace of her earlier smile left on her face.

Not wanting to be seen disobeying her command to sleep, I crouch under the window and crab walk my way forward. The cut grass tickles my feet and my calves ache from squatting but I'm almost at the next corner of the house where I can stand again when a snippet of her conversation makes me stop dead in my tracks.

". . . *awó*, tomorrow. If you can't do it tonight, then you need to get us out of here tomorrow." I lower myself to the ground and listen. There's a pause while the person on the other end speaks, then, "*Ayi!*" Mrs. Kablan quickly catches herself and lowers her voice. "No, my article isn't finished yet, Alain. But that's not the point! My daughter was *kidnapped*, do you understand? And it's no coincidence that she was dumped in one of those hellhole farms—they knew what I was doing and did that intentionally. Do you have any idea what she went through there? Looking at her and those poor boys she brought with her . . . the little one is missing an arm! No, Alain, no! I can't finish the article for you. It's more than another assignment for me as well, but my daughter's safety has to come first. I just got her back. There's no way I'm staying here a moment longer than it takes for you to get us visas . . ."

I feel strangely disconnected from my body as I hear her continue to argue with Alain, whoever he is. Mrs. Kablan is leaving the Ivory Coast.

Khadija's going with her.

We're not.

22

I crouch there, listening, until she's done with her call and has slumped at the table. Then I sneak around the house and slip in through the door to the front room, where I'm supposed to be asleep.

For a few minutes I lie there and stare at the ceiling, trying to get my racing heart to slow. Finally, unable to bear it alone anymore, I let myself into Khadija's room without knocking. Khadija leaps up. I was right. She's not asleep either. Instead, she is sitting on her bed, rebraiding her hair into tight, straight lines and staring out her window.

"What are you looking at?"

"Just . . . checking," she says, sinking back onto the mattress and glancing out. I see that, through her window, she has a clear view of the gate. Fabrice, absent a few minutes ago when I did my lap of the house, is now leaning in the open doorjamb, chatting to Sandrine, who seems to be leaving again, and we can see into the street beyond. There are people passing by and others linger in small groups, having conversations. I scan them all automatically, looking for the nephew, but I don't see him anywhere. Then again, since I don't know who else I should be looking for, that one absence is not very comforting.

"Did you see anything?"

"No," she says. Her tone makes me think she doesn't know what she's looking for either. "But I still can't fall asleep."

I remember Mrs. Kablan holding Khadija as soon as she got her back, saying, *You're all right.* Looking at her now, surrounded by her things, wearing a clean yellow shirt and navy skirt, braiding her hair—even with all that, I can see that she's not all right. Her eyes are still a little hollow, her smile still a little slow. She pauses before she leaps now, calculating the possible cost. This is not the same Khadija who left this house. Getting home did not make her all right. I wonder whether she will ever be all the way right again. I sigh and push away thoughts of what it will be like to take Seydou home to Mali. It hurts too much to think that, after all this work, there may be some journeys that you just never come all the way home from.

Khadija rubs her forehead. "I keep feeling like any second someone could come here and take me again."

"Well, you won't need to worry about that for too much longer," I say, scowling. "You're going to France tomorrow."

"What?" Her hands drop from her hair.

"I heard your mama talking on the phone to someone and she's making plans to get out of here." Khadija gapes. "Plans for *two*," I can't help but add, bile churning in my stomach, "not four."

"What?"

"Is that all you're going to say?" I snap.

"I . . . I don't understand why she wouldn't tell me . . ."

"How should I know why she isn't telling you?" I slump on the end of her bed and sink my head into my hands. "I know why she's not telling *us*. She's no kin to us and doesn't care about us, but that doesn't make it any better." I know I should stop talking but the words keep trickling out. "You said, you *promised*, that she would help us get home and now Seydou and I are going to be left behind, to fend for ourselves in an Ivorian town we don't know. I wish I'd never listened to you—I wish we'd never come here with you." *Shut up.* "I wish we'd never met you!"

I finally make myself stop talking.

A silence puddles around us and I wish I could take back what I said. It's just all so hard and I'm so, so tired. I finally look up. Khadija is looking at me but her eyes hide whatever she's feeling.

"Come on," she finally says, and gets to her feet.

"Where are you going?"

"I'm done trying to figure out what's going on by myself." Face set, she pulls open her door and heads toward the kitchen. I scramble after her. "That didn't work before. We're going to go talk to Mama."

"Um . . ." I follow her half-braided head. She's not letting me catch up. "Are you sure that's a good idea?" I spare a moment, since I'm already worrying, to worry about Seydou waking up and finding me gone. Other than the few nights on the farm when we were punished with sleeping separately, we've never been apart. I don't want him to wake alone in this strange house and panic.

"You made sure I got home," Khadija says. "I'm sure as hell going to do the same for you." A step ahead of me, Khadija stomps into the kitchen. Her mother whirls around, clicking her phone shut.

"Khadija," she says, smiling, not sounding pleased at all. "Amadou. You're awake. What are you two doing?"

Khadija's chin goes up.

"Trying to figure out why you're lying to us!"

For a moment there is silence. Then Mrs. Kablan's false happiness peels off her face like bark stripped from a tree. The looks she and Khadija exchange make the room crackle like the air before a lightning storm. Now I know where the wildcat got her temper. Then Khadija's mother looks away. The silent war has ended.

"I'm not lying to you," she says softly. "I have never lied to you. I'm only trying to keep you safe."

"Well, that didn't really work either, did it?" whispers Khadija. I'm horrified at her rudeness but her mother crosses the room in three steps and scoops her into her arms.

"I know, baby, I know. I'm trying to fix it," she whispers, her ruined fingers stroking the sides of her daughter's face.

"By taking me to France and not telling me?" Khadija pulls away. Mrs. Kablan goes still. "By abandoning Amadou and

267

Seydou? By pretending nothing ever happened? It *did* happen, and they matter to me, and you can't just keep hiding everything. I deserve to know. *We* deserve to know what's going on."

I lick my lips, worried that Khadija has pushed too far and gotten us in trouble. It would only take one angry word from Mrs. Kablan, and Seydou and I would be out on the street. Whether Khadija liked it or not, there would be very little she could do about it.

Mrs. Kablan sinks into one of the kitchen chairs and covers her face with her hands. Then she gets control of herself. She looks at us carefully, measuringly.

"Amadou," she finally says with a sigh, "please go to my room. On the table by my bed you'll see a pile of papers, a large brown envelope, and a small notebook. Could you bring them here?"

Happy for the chance to move, I leave the kitchen. There is only one door that I haven't seen open yet: the one in between Khadija's and the bathroom. I decide it must be Mrs. Kablan's room. I glance at Seydou, but he's still fast asleep. Opening the door, I see the things I'm looking for on the table beside the bed, where she said they would be.

As I cross the room to get the papers, I run my blunt fingers over tiny vials of makeup and perfume on the dresser, brush my calluses over the silky touch of the pile of clothes stacked on a chair. I briefly wonder what it would cost me to have given this kind of finery to my mother when she was alive, but I can't imagine the numbers that must be attached, and every one of them would matter. And anyway, thinking about numbers makes me remember other numbers that matter, like how few coins remain from the money we stole from the bosses and how few hours are left before Mrs. Kablan takes Khadija to France. I squeeze my eyes shut to block all the numbers out, then pick up the pile of papers and head to the kitchen.

By the time I get there, Khadija is sitting on a chair next to her mother, and they have their arms around each other. I guess they used the time I was gone to get rid of any hard feelings left between them. I'm glad. I put the pile on the table in front of Mrs. Kablan and take the seat across from them.

She gives her daughter one more quick hug and a kiss on the forehead, and then she lets go of her to reach for the papers. She opens the notebook and I see that it is filled with small, neat handwriting and pencil sketches. I can't read what any of it says, of course, but I recognize some of the things shown in the sketches: pods, seeds, trucks, drying flats, docks. Then she reaches into the large envelope. It's filled with pictures. Mrs. Kablan fans them out in front of us on the table, then sits back to let us have a look. There are clear photos of *cacao* trees, the pods, the seeds, a ground dark-brown powder, and shiny, colorful packages of candy. Then there are blurry pictures, ones that are difficult to make out, of people far away working in fields and at the docks.

Khadija holds up one of the blurry pictures.

"What's this even of?" she asks.

Her mother shrugs ruefully.

"Mobile phone pictures don't make very good evidence."

"Phone pictures?" I ask. Phones are for talking. I don't understand how now all of a sudden they're giving Mrs. Kablan pictures too.

"*Awó*," says Khadija. "Like this." She lifts her mother's phone from the table. She points it at me and presses one of the buttons. Then she turns the phone around so I can see it. There on the screen is a picture of my face. It's grainy and dark and the colors are slightly off, but it's definitely me. It makes a sick feeling churn in my belly, though I can't quite put my finger on why.

Khadija has moved on from taking pictures of me, focusing again on the photos in front of us. "So, what is all this?" she asks.

Her mother turns on the electric light that hangs from the ceiling, banishing the evening shadows that had begun to settle around us.

"This," she says, "is the report I've been working on. This is the reason they want me shut up before I can publish it. This is why you were taken."

Khadija and I stare blankly at the pile of pictures on the table in front of us. For a moment, Khadija flips through the notebook. Then she takes a comb out of her pocket and continues braiding from where she left off, as if she can't stand for her fingers to be idle when her brain is churning.

"I don't understand," I admit.

"Well." Khadija's mother sighs. "I don't really understand it either. But the truth of the matter is that this country's main export is cocoa, and the chocolate lords will do a lot to make sure that the story of how it's grown doesn't get out."

"Wait, chocolate?" Khadija's face is slack with surprise, her fingers frozen mid-movement on top of her head. "This is about *chocolate?*"

I glance over.

"What's chocolate?" I ask. "I thought we were growing *cacao.*"

"You've never even tasted chocolate," Khadija's mother says, shaking her head. "That's just not right. Here." She pushes herself away from the table. "Let me give you something to taste while we talk."

She pours milk into a small pot and starts to heat it. Then she adds sugar and a dark powder. After a few minutes, an amazing smell reaches me.

"What's she making?" I whisper to Khadija.

"It's hot chocolate," she says. "Mama always made it for me as a little girl when I couldn't sleep."

Khadija's mother pulls the saucepan off the flame and pours a steaming liquid into three mugs. "Try it and tell me what you think," she says.

I lift the mug up to my face and breathe in the rich steam. Then I take a long sip.

Khadija's mother gives a soft laugh at the look on my face. The liquid is deep and dark and sweet and bitter. It's hot and rich and tastes like comfort and secrets. I imagine what it would be like to have this waiting for me every time I couldn't sleep.

"It's good, isn't it?" Khadija's mother says with a sad smile, tasting her own mug. For a few minutes we sip in silence, then she says, musingly, "You know, it's not really true that you've never had chocolate before . . . maybe not in its refined form, but I'm sure you must have at least tried the seeds. Didn't you?" she asks, looking at me with interest. "Didn't you ever try the beans in the pods you picked?"

For a moment I'm not sure why she's changed the subject, but then I think through what she's saying and a cold feeling enters me.

"Wait," I say, "you think that the pods we were growing on Moussa's farm make *this*? No, you're wrong. That was *cacao*."

"*Awó*," Mrs. Kablan says. "You were growing *cacao*. But that's what they make cocoa and chocolate from. Once the beans are fermented and dried, they get shipped out to other countries, where they're roasted and ground into a paste that they turn into cocoa solids and cocoa butter. Then big companies take the solids and the butter and make it into every kind of chocolate—chocolate bars for snacking on, chocolate for baking, chocolate fillings, frostings, hot chocolate. They even use it sometimes in hand creams and such."

I'm staring at her, trying to process what she's saying.

"You mean . . . you mean that for the last two years we were kept on that farm to grow something that's a treat for city kids who can't sleep?"

Mrs. Kablan nods, staring into the creamy swirls of her hot chocolate. I look into mine too, but the taste has changed in my mouth. Now I know the secrets of the dark, sweet liquid in my cup. The smell washes over me again, and this time I gag on it. It's no longer the smell of a loving bedtime routine, but the smell of pain, and working for no pay, and not being able to go home. It's the taste of Seydou with only one arm and I can't get it out of my mouth.

I push the mostly full mug across the table, away from me.

"I think I'm done," I say.

"I don't want mine either," Khadija says beside me.

"I can understand that," says Mrs. Kablan. "These beans were grown on a farm that I know not far from here where no children worked without pay to grow it, but I can still see why you wouldn't want it."

We stare at her blankly.

"Chocolate," says Khadija's mother, rubbing her temples as if she's getting a headache just talking about all this, "doesn't have to be grown the way you were growing it. On small farms, yes, that's the only way *cacao* will grow. But sometimes farmers make enough to pay their workers a fair wage for their labor. It's just not the way that a lot of the chocolate in the world is grown. Usually, the big companies make huge profits, the middlemen in Abidjan get fat off the taxes, and the farmers make next to nothing." Her tired eyes meet mine. "And so the farmers find workers they don't have to pay. Usually, those workers are children."

I remember how Khadija thought the bosses' house was

so small and run-down. It's true that, compared to the houses I've seen since, the bosses' house was more of a shack. They didn't eat all that much better than us boys, and they worked alongside us too. I try to imagine what it would have been like to work on a different kind of farm, but can't. Then another thought hits me.

"Do you mean to say that kids are being forced to work on *cacao* farms everywhere, not only where we were?" I ask.

"Thousands," she says, gripping her mug with her abused fingertips. "But I'm having a lot of trouble finding all the information I need for my article. Some of the children working are family members of the farmers, or say they are, and others work but can still go to school. It's hard to get a good count of how many children are being kidnapped and forced to work against their will.

"And once the cocoa cartel bosses got an idea that I was working on a chocolate piece, they began to threaten me, and the people who were willing to talk to me before suddenly stopped talking, or disappeared. I was in the process of getting us out of the country because it was becoming too dangerous, but then they took you." Her voice breaks and she reaches across the table and strokes Khadija's cheek. "I couldn't leave then, even to go home to Abidjan, because I had to hope that you were alive and, that if I was quiet and stopped working like they told me to, I'd get you back. I've been offering money to everyone I can think of for information on where you'd gone, and I wouldn't leave San Pédro because it was the place you would know where to find me . . ." She stares into Khadija's eyes. When her hand drops to the table it curls into a fist. "I care a great deal about the injustices of chocolate. But not at the expense of your safety. Now that you're back, I'm going to get you out of here before they can find you again. From the beginning, I've tried everything I could think of to keep you safe. You don't know how sorry I am that it didn't work."

Khadija is staring at her mother, but I'm stuck on something Mrs. Kablan just said.

"Wait a minute," I break in. "If the cocoa people have so much power, why do you think we're safe here? This is where they kidnapped Khadija from before!"

"Well," says her mother, spreading her hands, "they don't know she's here and they've left me alone while she's been gone. The only people who have seen you are Fabrice, Sandrine, and the doctor, all of whom I trust, so there's no reason to think that they'll come here again."

A horrible, prickling feeling creeps up my spine and digs its claws into the back of my neck. I suddenly realize why I'm upset that phones can take pictures. I reach out and grab Khadija's hand.

"But Khadija," I say, squeezing her arm, "I think they *do* know that you're here."

Mrs. Kablan's head whips around to me.

"What?" she asks.

"We caught a ride on a truck," I explain, "and it dropped us here." I shuffle through the pictures until I find a shadowy one of the dock. "When we got out, one of the guards followed us, but when he found us, I think he took a picture of us with his phone." Khadija is looking at me like I just announced that I wanted to be a *cacao* boss when I grow up. My stomach churns. "I didn't want to make you more scared last night, so I didn't tell you then, but don't you see?" I shake her arm again. "The man who followed us last night works at the docks that are run by the chocolate people! Once he had your picture, he went away again. The only way that makes sense is if he knew where to find you later."

For a moment Khadija and her mother both stare in silence. Then Mrs. Kablan bolts out of her chair, pulling Khadija with her.

"We have to get out of here!" she says, dragging her to the bedrooms. "Now! Go, get your shoes on. I'll get the passports and some money. Meet me at the front door!"

"No!" Khadija and I both say at the same time.

"This is not a joke!" her mother snaps at us. "Move! Now!"

"What about Amadou and Seydou?" Khadija asks.

Her mother's eyes are glazed with fear, but she focuses on me again for a moment.

"Go get your brother," she says, "and hurry! You'll have to come with us. We'll figure out where we're all going once we're out of this house."

I pound into the front room, not waiting for her to change her mind and leave us here in San Pédro. I run to where Seydou is still asleep on the floor and grab him into my arms, blankets and all. He thrashes awake.

"Let go of me!" he screeches.

"Shh! Seydou, it's me!" I shove the blankets away and grab his right hand. "Come on, we need to run. Be quiet!"

Instantly awake, Seydou follows me without another sound. When I get to Khadija's mother's bedroom, I see her shoving papers from a desk drawer into a satchel.

"Where's the medicine Sandrine bought for Seydou?" I ask.

"On the table by the front door," she says over her shoulder. Her movements are jerky, panicked. I run.

Sure enough, on the little table by the front door I see a small brown paper bag. When I pick it up, it rattles. I take a moment to look inside and check: it's medicine. I shove the bag in my pocket. I can still hear Khadija and her mother shouting at each other about what to take or not take and I'm considering what food I should grab from the kitchen when the lights go off.

Though Seydou is next to me and I know that Khadija and her mother are only steps away, the sudden darkness makes me feel like I'm completely alone. Fear does that. I grab Seydou tight against me. I can hear Mrs. Kablan whispering Khadija's name and the shuffling footsteps of the two of them in the dark.

"There's nothing to worry about," I whisper to Seydou, trying to make myself believe it. Just as the words leave my mouth, I hear a *click* from behind me, and the front door swings open.

23

Whirling from the opening door, I push Seydou ahead of me into the kitchen and shove us both under the table. I tuck my head so that my eyes won't shine in the darkness and give us away. *So much for having a guard,* I think. I listen with every fiber in my body, my mind racing for what I can do to help, my heart leaping around in my chest like maize thrown into a pan of frying oil.

I have to get out of here.

I hear men's footsteps start across the front room, heading for the bedrooms.

I can't leave without Khadija.

They're not trying to be quiet about it.

I won't let Seydou be hurt again.

I bite my lower lip so hard the rusty taste of blood floods my mouth. I force myself to stand and peek around the kitchen door frame, Seydou pressed to my back. I see the shadowy forms of three men, but I can't do anything about that.

I'll get Seydou to safety, then I'll come see what I can do here. With that thought, I turn and slink to the kitchen door,

Seydou's hand gripped in mine. I don't really have a choice: I have to get out of the house. I crack the door and peer out into the dark yard. When I see shadowy figures hurrying through it, I nearly bolt back into the kitchen. But something stops me. I look at them again and realize I know those shapes. I have no idea how Khadija and her mother got out, but taking one more quick look around, I dash to join them.

They freeze when they see us running at them, but then I catch up to them and grab Khadija's hand. Mrs. Kablan takes her other one. Behind us, I hear the men shouting ugly things and a steady smashing sound. They're trying to break down the bedroom doors. They don't yet know that we're out here, but we don't have much longer. A tug on my hand tells me that Khadija's mother has realized this too and is pulling us to the big gate. I see Fabrice's slumped form in the shadows off to the side. I hope he's all right.

Mrs. Kablan goes over to him and feels at his neck, then rejoins us. Khadija dashes ahead and pulls the bolt open slowly so it doesn't squeak. She pokes her head into the street, then turns to her mother.

"What if they're out there too?" she whispers.

"Doesn't matter," Mrs. Kablan murmurs. "We have to get away from here. Run to the right, as fast as you can, and if we get split up, meet me at the newspaper headquarters. We'll borrow one of their cars."

I have no idea where her newspaper headquarters is, so I clench my teeth and decide not to be left behind.

"Ready to run?" I whisper to Seydou as Khadija's mother slips out the gate.

He nods, a well-controlled fear hiding behind the courage in his eyes. I give his hand a quick squeeze.

And then we run.

We dash from their house into the street and around the corner. I'm sure we've been seen, but right now no one is chasing us. As I dodge behind Khadija I wonder whether this will be my life—always needing to run, never feeling safe.

Up ahead Khadija's mother slows to a walk and takes her daughter's hand. I copy her casual pose as we turn another corner and now we're on a street lined with shops. Music pours out into the dark spaces between the lights, and people linger together. I try not to look too suspicious as I follow along, but I know that my breath is still fast from running and I can't help my eyes darting from face to face, looking for danger. I feel wound tight inside with uncertainty as we walk, block after block, past people and cars. Some stare at us, some ignore us. All of them make the prickling fear climbing my neck stronger.

Finally, just when I think I can't take it anymore, we get to a high wall. Khadija's mother knocks on the gate and the night guard lets us in. But even when the gate closes behind us and the guard hands her a set of keys, Khadija's mother keeps walking quickly. We're not safe yet.

She takes us around to a low car shelter.

"Get in," she says, stopping by a white Jeep, and we all do. The cold plastic of the backseat crinkles under me as I slide in after Seydou. Khadija sits on his other side. As soon as we're in, her mother drives the Jeep to the front gate. The night guard comes to her window. Mrs. Kablan speaks quickly and urgently. I hear Fabrice's name and see the guard nod. After their quick conversation, he opens the gate.

Khadija's mother cranks the window closed again and says over her shoulder to us, "Stay down and don't let anyone see you."

The three of us scoot onto the floor. It's uncomfortable, but we stay still and silent as Khadija's mother drives out of the newspaper compound and navigates through the traffic. I watch her neck as she drives. I can see the taut muscles pulling against the skin there. I tell myself that when I see her relax, I will too. Until then I stay on high alert.

It feels like hours, though I'm sure it's not nearly that long, when Khadija's mother finally says, "Okay, you can get up now."

I hoist myself off the floor and feel the other two settle onto the seat beside me. Looking out, I see the taller buildings and brighter lights shrinking in the background. Ahead, I see darkness. We're driving into the countryside. I feel darkness inside too.

"Where are we going?" asks Khadija.

"Right now, we're just putting some distance between ourselves and San Pédro," her mother replies, drumming her fingers on the steering wheel. "That was too close. Far, far too close." Her voice is shaky but I can see that the tension has gone out of her neck.

I collapse against the seat.

"Try to sleep," Khadija's mother says. "Once we've gotten away a bit, we'll stop and have a think about what we're going to do next."

Khadija makes a small sound, which I take to be agreement. Or maybe it came from me, I don't know anymore. It's been too long since I've slept, too long since I've felt safe. Seydou tucks his feet up beside me and leans into Khadija. I rest my head against the window and close my eyes. With every slow jostle of the Jeep, my head smacks against the glass. I was hoping that it would be enough to keep me awake since I know that I need to be paying attention but, against my will, I find myself falling asleep.

When I wake up later, there is no vibration of a motor and moonlit leaves are plastered against the glass beside my face. I glance around, disoriented. Out the window over Khadija's head, I see a brighter patch that is the road. I realize Mrs. Kablan must have pulled off into the bush. Seydou and Khadija breathe evenly beside me, but I hear a soft muttering from the front of the Jeep that tells me Khadija's mother isn't sleeping.

"*Madame?*" I whisper.

The noises stop abruptly.

"I'm sorry, Amadou. Did I wake you?"

"No, I just woke up. I think because we stopped. Why have we stopped?"

I see her wave a shadowy hand in the near darkness.

"I was getting too tired to drive safely. I figured it would be better to pull over and get some sleep before going much farther."

I take a chance and state the obvious.

"You're not sleeping, *madame*."

Khadija's mother gives a tight laugh.

"You're right. I was only able to turn the car off, not my brain."

I sink my head against the cold plastic and let my eyelids drift closed. I know exactly what she means. The exhaustion of the last few days washes over me. The worry about what's going to happen next follows close on its heels. Though it feels like heavy weights are pushing on them, I force my eyelids open. There are things that need to be decided.

"*Madame*, when we go again, where are we going?"

I see her rub tiredly at her forehead. I wonder if she has a headache.

"I've been trying to decide. What we really need to do is get as far from here as we possibly can. I won't let Khadija get taken again. And San Pédro is no place for two Malian boys who don't speak any French."

"So . . . ?"

"So," she says, rubbing away, "I think maybe the best thing to do would be to find some rural border crossing into Liberia. Somewhere out of the way, somewhere so small we can hope they don't have a functioning radio . . . From there, the paper should be able to get us out to France, and no one in the Liberian government is likely to detain us on our way out."

Liberia. I've never heard of it.

"Is Liberia near Mali?" I ask.

There is a brief silence. Then, in a soft voice, "No, my dear. And that's a problem I haven't figured out yet. Liberia is on the coast. Mali is to the north. All of Guinea is in between. We're nowhere near Mali. I'm so sorry. I know that Khadija promised you that I'd get you home, but she didn't understand the situation." Her voice breaks slightly as she crushes my hopes. "I'm going to have to leave you somewhere as safe as I can manage here, or in Liberia. I can't take you to Mali."

It feels like my heart is a handful of packed mud thrown into water, dissolving away until there's nothing left. To get Seydou home I now have to cross an entire country. I look over at his small form curled against Khadija and force myself to breathe again. I don't know how, but I'm going to take care of him.

Really, when I think about it, my main problem was assuming that she would be able to help me. I remind myself that I've learned no one really helps you.

Not true, whispers a little voice, and I want to brush it off, want to stay angry. But the fact is, I can't. Though she got us into a heap of trouble, Seydou and I would never have made it off the farm without Khadija. And, though her mother won't help us get home, she did feed us, and give us new clothes, and get a doctor for Seydou, and take us with her when she was escaping the chocolate men. Unbidden, other images flash through my mind: Seydou, putting mangoes in the sack of pods, and the other boys, especially Yussuf, being kind when they could and when I would let them.

Thinking of Yussuf makes my heart clench unexpectedly. I wonder where he is right now, what he's doing. I realize that I will probably never see him again. I'll probably never know whether he escaped or is back in the padlocked hut with a new crop of boys. I've spent more than two years telling myself I didn't care about anyone but Seydou. I'm surprised to find that, all that time, I was lying.

"*Hakéto.*"

"Yes, Amadou?" Her voice is so tired, I almost regret speaking again, but I need to know.

"And your article? What's going to happen with the article you were writing about the boys who work in the chocolate fields?"

There is a small pause, and when she speaks her voice is heavy with regret.

"Nothing."

"Nothing?" That's not what I was expecting. Not from a woman who was so dedicated to the story that she kept working even in the face of threats and silent phone calls. Khadija's mother sighs.

"There's nothing to be done. I won't stay in this country one minute longer than I have to, not with what happened to Khadija, but there is still so much that's missing from what I was going to write. The newspapers and magazines will never publish a half-researched article."

"No!" I say, gripping the side of her seat. The strength of

my feeling has pulled me forward. It's lucky that Seydou wasn't leaning against me, or he would have fallen. "Your story must go out there, *madame*! If you don't write it, then we won't have anyone to speak for us."

Her exhausted silence is its own answer. After what seems like a long time, she whispers, "I'm afraid I have no good answers for you tonight, Amadou. I'm sorry."

I uncurl my fingers from the upholstery and push my shoulders into the seat, but I can't relax. After a few minutes, I hear her breathing even out, and I know that exhaustion has finally overtaken her and she's fallen asleep. But I feel like someone has kicked a hive of wasps inside me. Feelings swarm around my belly and chest with no way out, stinging my heart and filling my thoughts with venom.

Khadija is being taken away from her home. Seydou and I are being dumped in a country where we don't know the language, with no one to help us. Mrs. Kablan's article isn't going to get published, and no one will ever know the fate of all the chocolate boys.

Thousands, Mrs. Kablan had said when she was first telling us of her article. There are thousands of kids like us, working across the country to make a sweet for rich kids in other places. Thousands. It's a number that matters so much I can't wrap my mind around it. Yussuf's face stares at me, the boys huddled behind him the way they looked when I knocked the lock off the sleeping hut. I decide, in that moment, that Seydou was right all along.

If we're going to escape, we need to take everyone with us.

I reach over and shake Khadija and Seydou. They startle awake silently, tensed to run.

"We need to talk," I say, pitching my voice low and soft so as not to wake Mrs. Kablan.

"What is it?" asks Khadija.

I take a deep breath.

"I was talking to your mama before she fell asleep," I say, "and she says that she's not going to finish her article."

"So?" yawns Seydou.

"I think," Khadija says slowly, "that we have bigger problems to think about right now, don't you?"

I grind my teeth in frustration.

"*Of course* we have bigger problems right now," I say. "But don't you see? If we only ever deal with our problems right now, then everything else never gets talked about. Your mama has to write her article so that people find out about this."

"What difference is that going to make?" Khadija asks.

"I don't know," I admit. "Maybe none. But I still feel we owe it to the kids who are stuck out there . . ." I struggle to find the words for what I mean. "Think of Yussuf," I say to Seydou, "and all the others on the farm. And it's not just them. Mrs. Kablan said there are thousands of kids on farms like ours all across Ivory Coast. And you"—I turn to Khadija—"you've only been gone for nine days, but even so, weren't there times when you wished you could tell someone where you were? When you needed so badly for someone to know what was happening to you that it felt like trying to breathe with rocks on your chest every second of every day?"

Seydou nods.

"*Awó*," Khadija whispers, so softly I can barely hear it.

It's quiet, but it's enough.

"We can't do much for those kids," I say, "but they may never get away and have a chance to tell their story. We do."

"You're right," says Khadija finally.

I feel like the sky has opened again and my feelings pour out of me into it.

"So what do we need to do?" asks Seydou. He sounds so grown-up. I look at him for a moment in the moonlit darkness and realize that he is no longer my clueless baby brother. My heart twists a little, wondering whether my cricket might be gone for good.

"When Mrs. Kablan wakes up, we get her to finish writing her article," I say. "We make her listen to our story, and write it down. That's what we have to do."

"Why should we wait?" asks Khadija. "Let's do it now."

"I don't think—" I say, remembering how tired she was just moments ago, but Khadija is already leaning forward and shaking Mrs. Kablan's shoulder.

"*Mama!*"

Mrs. Kablan lurches awake, grabbing the wheel.

"What? What is it?" she gasps.

"We need to talk," says Khadija.

24

"*Mun kéra?*" she asks, looking from one of us to another, concerned.

"We need you to write your article," Seydou says, leaning forward.

"What?" Mrs. Kablan is still half-asleep.

"I know you want to get to Liberia right away," I say, "but before you go, could we take a little time to help you with your article? It's really important that people know about this."

"I—" she starts. Khadija doesn't let her finish.

"You can change your article if you have to, Mama! You can make it an interview of three kids who lived through the farms and add in the stuff you already have."

The sudden gleam of interest in her mother's eyes makes me feel like maybe this is going to work after all.

"Please," I say. "Think of all the other mothers in Mali. They may never have their children come back to them. We want to tell our story, *madame*. We owe it to all the kids who didn't get away. Please help us."

Mrs. Kablan's lips purse tightly. She reaches into her bag and pulls out a notepad and a pencil.

"Very well," she says, knuckling the sleep out of her eyes and sitting up straighter. "Let's begin."

We take turns, each of us telling the specific story of how we ended up on the farm, with Mrs. Kablan asking questions to fill in the holes in her research as we go: How many boys worked with us? What were their names and ages? Where was everybody from? How long did we work in a day? Did we ever get days off? What happened when we got sick? How did we get out? The questions go on and on.

We answer each one as thoroughly as we can and Ms. Kablan scribbles furiously, jotting down everything. By the time dawn's orange fingers stroke the hood of the Jeep, we're almost done.

"You see," I say, finishing my story, "in Mali, it's traditional for young people to leave home and go work somewhere else for a season while the old people and the women and little kids stay home and tend the crops as they grow. It didn't feel odd to trust the bus drivers in Sikasso. They were offering jobs, and it seemed like a good place to start.

"Even when we got to the farm and I saw them arguing with Moussa, I still didn't understand—why was this farmer giving out money before we had worked for the season? And why was he giving it to the man with the truck and not to us? I decided he must be giving a portion of what we would earn to the man to cover the trouble he took getting us there. Then the man with the truck drove away and Moussa handed us some tools and put us on a work crew with the other new boys."

"It was only that night," Seydou cuts in, "when they first locked us in the sleeping hut, that we heard the truth. The boys who had been there for a while started to whisper and we found out that we weren't going to be able to leave at the end of the growing season."

"The bosses said we could leave when we'd earned out our purchase price," I add. "But they wouldn't tell me how much we owed, and in all the time we worked there, I only saw boys arrive or die, never leave when they wanted to. And we never once got paid."

Mrs. Kablan drops her pen and massages her hand for a moment.

"I am so sorry, boys," she says. "So sorry that you were caught up in all of this. It's a vicious, vicious cycle." She splays her fingers across the notes she's been taking like she can soothe the truth out of them and, for a moment, there is silence in the Jeep. Then Mrs. Kablan motions briskly for me to go on with my story. But as my mouth parrots out the facts of our imprisonment, my mind wanders. Because, though I'm glad to my bones to know that our story will get out into the world, Khadija was right: we have bigger problems right now. As I come to the end of my story, I'm faced with the more pressing problem of what Seydou and I are going to do once this interview is finished.

Forced to be honest with myself, I can finally admit that going home is not a good option. If the drought hasn't broken, I'll have to leave again to make money, maybe get trapped on another farm. And what life will Seydou have with only one arm? There's no way he'll manage well enough as a farmer to stay alive. I'll have to take care of him too.

Then an idea occurs to me.

A perfect idea.

A terrible idea.

It makes my stomach churn sour to consider it, but by the time we've wrapped up the interview and Khadija's mama is putting away her notes, I know there is only one answer.

"*Madame?*" I ask.

Her eyes jump to meet mine in the rearview mirror, though her hands continue to pack her things.

"Yes, Amadou?"

"I have a favor to ask."

That stops her hands. Slumping, she says, "I'm sorry, Amadou. But I don't have any legal papers for you. I can't bring you to France with us."

I'm surprised. France still seems like the tip of the moon to me. Even though I was upset at her for leaving us, I've known all along her taking us there wasn't possible. But deep inside it makes me feel warm and wanted that she's been trying to figure out what to do with us too.

"That wasn't what I was going to ask," I say.

"Oh?"

"I was wondering if you would be willing to make one more stop before you go to Liberia, and take us to that other *cacao* farm you mentioned. The one where they pay the people who work there?"

She looks at me in the mirror, her face blank. Khadija and Seydou are staring at me. I gulp and finish what I need to say.

"I was wondering if you could ask them to give me a job."

Though it's far, far out of their way, she does it.

Khadija, Seydou, and I sit in the backseat of the Jeep and watch the landscape move past us. Now that it's light out I sit in the middle so that Seydou can have the window.

A long time later, we pull out of a tunnel of bush and roll past cultivated groves of *cacao* trees. I feel myself tense up just looking at them, but then a warm hand slips into mine and gives a little squeeze. I look down, expecting to see Seydou's small fingers laced through mine, but instead I see that they're Khadija's.

I look into her face and see that her eyes are shiny.

"It's going to be okay," she whispers to me. The rattling of the Jeep over the ruts in the road keeps the sound from the others. "Mother said it'd be different here. You'll be safe. You'll get paid."

But her voice shakes as she says it and inside me a little worm of fear whispers, *Maybe*. Both of us want to believe it, but neither of us is sure we can.

It occurs to me that, one way or another, Khadija's about to leave our lives, probably forever. I squeeze her fingers and try to memorize the details of her face. Almond eyes, like her mother's, oval face, fuzzy braids finally finished and tied in a fresh knot at the base of her neck. Like it or not, over the course of everything that's happened, I've learned to care for the wild-cat, and the thought of losing her grinds inside me like broken bones.

It's hard to believe that only yesterday we were still in Khad-ija's house in San Pédro. Hard to believe that it was only last night that we were drinking cocoa in the dark. Impossible to believe that ten days ago I didn't even know she existed. Now we're driving through villages and fields that look achingly fa-miliar. Finally, we pull into a little village.

"You stay in the car until I've had a word with Abdoulaye," Mrs. Kablan says, and gets out of the Jeep and heads inside a low, mud-walled building.

"Are you sure about this?" Seydou's fear is a whisper at my elbow.

I consider the building and the groves stretching behind it.

"*Ayi,*" I answer honestly, "but I think we need to trust Mrs. Kablan. If this place is all she said it is, it will be a good thing for us. And if not"—I shrug and turn to look him in the eye—"then we'll get away and make our way home. We did it before. I won't stop until you're safe."

His old-man eyes stare into mine as he weighs my words.

"Okay," he says. He straightens. "I can do this."

"I know you can," I agree.

Khadija leans forward and rubs Seydou's back while she gives the clearing a critical look. "It's cleaner than Moussa's farm. And, as a journalist, Mama knows a lot of things and even more people. She's probably right about this place."

I look out the side window in time to see Khadija's mother come out again with a tall, wiry man. In the doorway, I see her rummage in her purse and hand him some money. The little voice of fear inside me gets louder. I have to swallow hard so that it doesn't choke me. *No,* I tell it. *You've spent enough time not trusting anyone. It's time to let go of that.*

Mrs. Kablan walks to the Jeep and opens our door. "This is Abdoulaye," she says, waving her hand at the big man behind her. "Abdoulaye, this is Amadou and Seydou, the boys I told you about."

"*Aw ni sógóma,* boys," Abdoulaye says.

"*Nbah i ni sógóma,*" I mumble.

She turns to us.

"I've given Abdoulaye some money to get you started, and he's agreed to let you work when you're not in school. If you ever want to go home to Mali, you tell him. He's agreed to arrange the transportation and send the bill to me in France."

I look at Abdoulaye.

"I've worked *cacao* before. I can pay our way."

"So Mrs. Kablan says. How old are you?" Abdoulaye asks me, looking me over.

"How old do you have to be to work here?"

At that, he throws back his head and laughs, the bump in his stringy throat bobbing up and down.

"Well, we try to only have adults work the farm, but since you're the head of your little household, we can probably let you work half days when you're not in school, as long as you're at least seventeen."

"How fortunate," I say, with a completely straight face. "Yesterday was my birthday. I just turned seventeen."

Abdoulaye laughs again. It's a kind laugh and I begin to hope that perhaps this will all work out. Beside me I see Khadija's mother hide a smile with her hand.

"Happy birthday," Abdoulaye says, holding out a hand to me, "and welcome."

Khadija's mother turns to us then. "Goodbye, boys. Thank you for everything you did for Khadija. I'll make sure that your story gets told. I'll even send a copy of the article here so you can see I've kept my word."

I hold out my hand to her.

"Thank you, *madame*, for all you've done for us."

She takes my hand. Then, with a weak smile, she gets in the car.

Khadija scoops Seydou into a big hug.

"Don't go!" he sobs, clinging to her with his one good hand.

"I don't have a choice," she says softly. "But I'll come back to visit if I ever can and I'll write you letters. Will you write me too?" Seydou nods, the illiterate fool, and the two of them are hugging and crying. Losing Khadija is like a knife in my side: painful, tearing. Finally I can't take it anymore and I pull Seydou away.

"All right, enough," I say gently, looping my arm around him. He sniffles for a bit, then wipes his face. Khadija straightens, and the two of us take a long look at each other. There's a small silence.

"Safe travels to France," I say finally.

"Good luck here."

Another silence stretches while we look at each other with nothing else to say. Then Khadija steps forward and wraps her arms around me. To my surprise, I do the same. For a moment we just stand there. Then we pull away.

"I won't forget you, wildcat," I say.

"Of course you won't," she says. "We're family."

With that, she pulls us both into one big hug, and then turns and gets into the car. As the white Jeep disappears into the bush, Khadija twists in her seat and waves to us out the rear window. I hold Seydou tight against me and we both wave back until she vanishes from sight.

EPILOGUE

I still count the things that matter.

We were at the camp seventeen weeks before Abdoulaye was able to take Seydou to a hospital to be fitted for his new arm. It showed up two weeks later. In another four and a half, he was using it easily. It was twenty-nine days after getting it that Seydou stopped complaining of pain in the arm that's not there. Since then he has gotten more and more comfortable. There is still a hint of the old man in his eyes but a bit of my cricket is there too. Now a missing arm no longer stops him from hopping around.

It was also over three months before we got our first letter from Khadija in France, saying she and her mother were safe and well, and a clipping of her mother's article, but it was eight months before Seydou learned enough to be able to read them to me. It was another three months after that before he knew enough to be able to write back. My writing still looks like I dipped two chickens' feet in ink and then made them fight while standing on my paper. My teacher says it's good for a first effort from a boy who has never moved anything smaller than a machete, but it's nothing compared to Seydou. Even with only one arm, Seydou has taken to school like a caged animal finally released.

It was seven months before we stopped hiding food to make sure we would have enough. Two more months after that, I realized that nobody had hit me since I arrived, but it was a whole year before I stopped flinching when the men got too close. It was only last week that I overheard our teacher saying that he thinks Seydou might grow up to be a teacher too. *You don't need two arms to be a teacher,* he said. *You only need a quick mind.* Seydou has walked on air for the past seven days.

We've been paid every Friday for fifty-four straight Fridays. We are going home for the first time twenty Fridays from now. That's when I'll have enough money to pay my own way to Mali, give some to Moke and Auntie, and still have enough to come back. I will miss only three paydays. Seydou will miss only three weeks of school.

There are also some things that I don't count.

Every day when I come home from working in the fields, I have no idea how many pods are in my sack.

I refuse to count the things that don't matter.

AUTHOR'S NOTE

Cacao, "the food of the gods," was once so valued that, in ancient times, its beans were used as money. Today, we have turned it into a cheap sweet we consume thoughtlessly, but *cacao* still comes at a terrible cost. Amadou, Seydou, and Khadija are fictional characters, but their story is one that many children share. Though it's hard to believe, thousands of children today continue to work in slavery to produce a treat for other children half a world away.

Today, almost three-quarters of the world's cocoa is grown in Africa, with 40 percent coming from the Ivory Coast alone. However, multiple factors, such as the low international price of cocoa, civil unrest, and high taxation, mean that small-scale growers (the way the vast majority of the world's *cacao* is grown) earn almost nothing from the production of their crop. They still have to tend their groves, and carry the risk of a bad growing season, or blight. They still often have to pay for what they eat, since they are growing a cash crop instead of food. With so little made on each harvest, many growers don't have enough left over to cover their costs, let alone to fairly pay their workers. Thus, many turn to free labor: modern-day slavery.

Too often, that labor comes from children.

By and large, in the United States, children do not work. We have labor laws, minimum age requirements, and mandatory public schooling. This is not true in much of the rest of the world. In fact, UNICEF estimates that worldwide 15 percent of children, approximately 150 million of them, work in conditions that are potentially harmful to their health.

Repeated attempts have been made to get the world's chocolate companies to be aware of the conditions under which their main ingredient is grown. Again and again, they have refused to take action. An agreement, the Harkin-Engel Protocol, does exist, which lays out steps to eliminate the worst forms of child labor in cocoa production. However, as of today, there is little evidence that any real change is happening as a result of this protocol. The chocolate companies value a low international price for cocoa and maintain that they have nothing to do with bands of criminals selling children into slavery on a distant continent. The organized crime rings on the Ivorian border continue to traffic boys and girls without interference and children continue to be forced to work.

The good news about chocolate is that chocolate companies cannot exist without consumer demand. If you're bothered by the state of the chocolate industry, you, as a consumer, can have an impact. Consider writing, e-mailing, or using social media to contact your favorite chocolate company and ask them to make a commitment to decreasing the poverty of the producers in their supply chain. Or, do some actual (or virtual) reverse trick-or-treating where you tell people about this issue instead of taking mainstream chocolate from them on Halloween. One way or another, decide to be deeply informed about your favorite treat before you enjoy it.

Though security concerns made it impossible for me to visit the Ivory Coast when I was writing *The Bitter Side of Sweet*, in the summer of 2013 I was able to visit RAFAVAL, a fair trade cocoa plantation in Haiti, where the women of the small town of Limonade were using the profits from the sale of chocolate to help themselves, their community, and their families.

Fair trade chocolate, produced by companies that guarantee a minimum price to growers even when international prices dip, is by no means the only answer. Nor is it an answer free of its own complications, as any long-term solution must address empowerment and education as well as economics. However, it is one way of tackling the root problem: the grinding poverty of the small growers who produce *cacao*.

To find out more about the issues raised in *The Bitter Side of Sweet*, including more ideas on things you can do to help end child slavery in chocolate production (or to share ideas of your own!), please visit my website, www.TaraSullivanBooks.com.

Tara Sullivan
June 1, 2015

DISCUSSION QUESTIONS

1   Throughout the story, Amadou "counts the things that matter." What matters to Amadou at the start of the book? How does this behavior help Amadou feel in control of the situation he and Seydou are in?

2   Amadou and Seydou end up doing forced labor at the cacao farm under completely different circumstances than Khadija. In what ways does this inform how each of them behaves at the farm? How do their lives before play into this?

3   Moussa and the bosses use punishment to motivate work and keep the children at the farm in line. Why do you think they vary their tactics depending on who they're dealing with? How do the punishments create isolation among the children? Why is that beneficial to the bosses?

4   "I was quiet at the farm a lot because quiet can be very scary, and being scary got people to do things if I needed them to," says Amadou on page 188. Keeping silent and being quiet are recurring themes in this story. How are quiet and silence used by different characters? Do you think it helps or hinders them?

5   For good reason, Amadou believes he can't trust anyone to help him and Seydou. Yet it's when he starts trusting people that he's able to escape the farm with his brother and Khadija. Who else helps our main characters and in what ways? Consider how trusting each other allows them to begin trusting other people.

6 All three of the main characters endure horrific brutalities while at the farm. What are the lasting effects of these experiences? How do the characters help each other heal and come to terms with those experiences?

7 Amadou feels responsible and guilty for the traumatic things that happen to Khadija and Seydou on the farm. Why would he think these things are his fault? How do Khadija and Seydou respond to his apologies?

8 On page 209 Seydou says, "I can help, you just never let me!" It's true that Amadou has trouble recognizing how intelligent and helpful Seydou can be until Khadija points it out. Cite examples from the text showing Seydou's smarts and resourcefulness. Why might Amadou have had difficulty seeing this?

9 After what happens to Khadija, Mrs. Kablan wants to leave the country, but doing that won't allow her to finish researching her story. How do Amadou, Khadija, and Seydou help her complete her story? Why is it so important to them that she publishes her story?

10 At the end of the novel, Amadou and Seydou choose to go to the fair trade cacao farm Mrs. Kablan told them about. What impact does working there have on each of them? What does this say about fair trade on a larger scale?

11 Over the course of the book, we see a change in Amadou's definition of what matters. What inspires this change?

SOURCES

The Dark Side of Chocolate. Documentary film. Directed by Miki Mistrati and U. Roberto Romano. 2010. www.thedarksideofchocolate.org

International Cocoa Organization. www.icco.org

Off, Carol. *Bitter Chocolate: Investigating the Dark Side of the World's Most Seductive Sweet.* Toronto: Vintage Canada, 2006.

UNICEF. www.unicef.org

World Cocoa Foundation. www.worldcocoafoundation.org

GLOSSARY

Attiéké • (Bambara) Cassava ground into couscous-like grains

Aw ni sógóma • (Bambara) Good morning. Used when speaking to a group.

Awó • (Bambara) Yes

Ayi • (Bambara) No

Hakéto • (Bambara) Excuse me

I ka da tugu • (Bambara) Shut up

I ni cé • (Bambara) Thank you / Welcome

Je suis désolé. J'étais juste . . . • (French) I'm sorry. I was just . . .

Kedjenou • (Bambara) Chicken with braised vegetables

La brosse • (French) The bush. Refers to wild, rural areas.

Les pistes • (French) The tracks / trails.

Mun kéra? • (Bambara) What's wrong? / What's going on?

Nbah i ni sógóma • (Bambara) Good morning. (Response if the speaker is male.)

Pisteur • (French) A man who drives the back trails of the Ivory Coast to the farms to collect the dried cacao beans and bring them to central weigh stations.

Pourquoi tu ne parles pas français? • (French) Why are you not speaking French?

ACKNOWLEDGMENTS

Launching a book is a huge project that takes a great deal of time and many helping hands. My thanks are due to many people for this one:

To Nick, my amazing husband. Thank you for all your love, support, and logistical wrangling. I could never have done this without you.

To the small army of friends who came and played with my children in four-hour weekend shifts so that I could get edits done. Daniela DeSousa, Vanessa Martinez, Alexis Kruza, Trish and Steve Ryan, and everyone else who stopped by or helped out . . . without you, this book could not have been finished on time.

To my children, for continuing to be excited that "Mom writes books," even when that means that she went and hid from you for hours at a time.

To my mom and dad: thank you for your unending enthusiasm, and your constant willingness to talk about your grand-books.

To my writers' group: Katie Slivensky, Lisa Palin, Lauren

Barrett, Julia Maranan, Annie Cardi, and A. C. Gaughen. Also to my amazing agent, Caryn Wiseman. As always, you rock!

To Josie Doak, insightful beta reader and wonderful friend.

To Jerry Fatal, who kindly fact-checked my story based on his experiences growing up in Man, Ivory Coast. And to Lydia Kang, medical doctor and fellow 2k13 debut author of *Control*, who figured out a way for Seydou to get better.

To the women of the RAFAVAL community collaborative in Limonade, Haiti, for showing me with boundless enthusiasm how to make chocolate.

To Alexis Kruza (again!), for coming to Haiti with me. Thank you for accompanying me to interpret, for staying in spite of fallen mosquito nets and cockroaches the size of mice, and for carrying my sickly self home through a variety of international airports. Let us never again mention the moths.

To those whose research went before me and helped me begin to understand the complex story behind chocolate when I wasn't able to travel to the Ivory Coast myself. I learned a great deal from the journalism of both Órla Ryan (*Chocolate Nations: Living and Dying for Cocoa in West Africa*) and Carol Off (*Bitter Chocolate: Investigating the Dark Side of the World's Most Seductive Sweet*). In fact, the chilling lines, "*You know what happens to people who ask questions. And you know what happens to people who answer them,*" are a paraphrase of a line from Ms. Off's book, when one of her sources in the Ivory Coast stopped talking to her for fear of his life. I salute these women for their bravery and their dedication to illuminating the truth.

To everyone at G. P. Putnam's Sons: thank you for loving my stories like they were your children and for taking such good care of them. Special thanks to Cindy Howle, Chandra Wohleber, Kate Meltzer, Cecilia Yung, and Annie Ericsson for all your excellent work on this book.

Lastly, to Stacey Barney. Having you as my editor makes the world sparkle. Thank you.

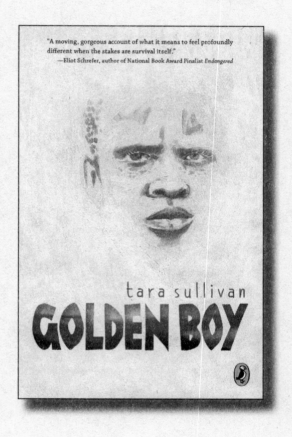

1.

I AM SITTING under the acacia tree on the ridge when I first see them: three men, in nice clothes, coming toward our house. Their shoulders are straight and their fat bellies strain against their belts when they walk. They are the image of power.

I wish I could see their faces, but my eyes aren't good enough for that this far away. I peel off my long-sleeved shirt and my floppy hat with the cloth sewn onto the back and crawl to the edge of the ridge in nothing but my long pants. My skin burns so easily that I could never do this in the middle of the day, no matter how hot it was, but now that the sun is setting I can enjoy the feeling of the wind whispering over me. Our goats mill around me, eating their dinner; the breeze carries the smells of the evening meal my mother and sister are preparing up the slope. The three men walk to our door.

"*Hodi hodi!*" the first man bellows.

Mother appears in the doorway. After a moment, Asu joins

her. Beside the big men, my mother and sister look weak and small. Mother bows her head respectfully and invites them into the house. The men walk in, and now I can't see them anymore, can't hear what's going on. Curiosity crawls over me like army ants.

I toss my long clothes over my shoulder and grab the horns of the lead goat, pulling her down the hill toward the three-sided pen set into the wall of our house. She digs in her hooves and bleats angrily at me, but I push her in anyway.

"I'll make it up to you later," I promise, and shove the other goats in behind her. Pulling the gate shut, I sneak around the wall toward our front door. I rest my hand against the mud wall; heat from the day warms my fingers. For a moment I feel happy about my cleverness. But as I hunch there, listening, that feeling bleeds out of me, until soon it's as if it had never been.

I'm not sure how long I crouch there, but it's long enough. Long enough to hear that the men are the tax collector, the seed provider, and the landlord. Long enough to hear my mother and sister beg. Long enough to hear what the men say in return: No.

No, you cannot have three more months to pay your taxes.

No, you cannot have more seed if you cannot pay.

No, you cannot stay here anymore.

The men leave, closing the door behind them—*thump*. My mother and sister don't come out with them. There are no more sounds of dinner-making. Instead the hollow sound of sadness fills the house.

When I stand up, my knees creak like an old man's. I don't go in. Instead I go to the goat pen because I can't think of anything better to do. And that's why I'm the first to see the hole in the side of the enclosure where the goats have kicked and butted and chewed their way to freedom and the dinner I didn't let them finish. They're nowhere to be seen.

I need to get the goats!

I toss my crumpled clothes toward the house and scramble up the side of the hill separating our farm from the rest of the village. No goats. I race off into the brush under the trees. No goats. I call and shout, hoping against hope they'll return to the pen at the sound of my voice. I run home: still no goats. But my brothers, Enzi and Chui, have arrived from working in the coffee fields, and they're standing by the hole in the goat pen with Mother and Asu, waiting for me. The instant I see the four of them there, I know I'm in trouble.

"Habo!" my eldest brother, Enzi, calls out to me, his voice low and angry. "Where are the goats?"

I stop where I am and look down at my feet.

"Well?" Enzi stomps across the space between us until the shadows from his broad shoulders completely cover me.

"Gone," I mumble.

"What?" Enzi is shouting now, which really isn't necessary. My ears are one of the few parts of my strange body that work just fine.

"They got out," I say.

Enzi looms over me. His hands fist at his sides, making his upper arms strain against the thin material of his shirt.

"And just where were you when they got out, hmm?" he asks.

I don't want to admit what I heard. I dart a glance toward Mother, but she is staring off in the direction of Arusha and doesn't see me look at her. In the pause I hear Chui grumble to Enzi, "He looks like a ghost and he does as little work as a ghost. I bet he was sleeping."

I hate Chui for saying it, but it gives me the lie I was looking for.

"I guess I dozed off."

I don't see Enzi raise his hand, but the force of his slap sends me staggering into the wall of our house. Small clumps of mud break off and fall to the ground from the impact of my shoulders. When my head snaps back, I bite my lip and my mouth fills with the taste of my own blood. Mother's head whips toward me at the sound, but she doesn't say anything. Enzi is twenty, and man-grown, and has been in charge since my father left. She rarely questions what he does.

Asu is a different story.

"Enzi!" Asu says with a gasp. "What did you do that for?" She runs over to me and dabs at my bleeding lip with the edge of her khanga, her pretty face all crunched up in concern. Mother looks away over the hills again, her dark eyes strangely empty, her face as smooth as the sky.

"That stupid ghost boy lost our goats!" Enzi points at me when he says this, the muscles of his arms standing out, tense.

"And how is hitting him going to bring them back?" Asu snaps. She stands facing Enzi, her frown pulling her head scarf low over her eyes, hands on hips. She has dropped her hem again and I can see my bloodstain peek in and out of the folds at her ankles.

Enzi throws up his hands and stalks into the house, head low between his shoulders.

"You always defend him," mutters Chui to Asu. His round face twists deeper into a scowl. He kicks a rock by his feet and it goes skittering off into the bush.

Asu turns away from Chui. She pushes the heels of her hands into her eyes, seeming suddenly tired. "Well, none of you ever do," she answers. But she says it so quietly that I don't think anyone else hears her.

As if released from a spell, Mother starts moving again. She wipes her dry face, as though to remind herself that she exists. Her fingers trace the wrinkles around her eyes and mouth. Then she straightens her hair scarf and turns to Chui. "Pack," she says to him. Over her shoulder, to me, she adds, "Go find the goats."

"Why do I need to pack?" asks Chui as the three of them head into the house.

Face still stinging from Enzi's slap, I leave to look for the goats, grateful that I have a reason not to be there when Mother tells Enzi and Chui we have to leave.

I hunt for the goats for hours: until my face is red and sweaty, until my feet are sore and my lungs burn. The darkness soothes my skin, but my bad eyes are worse than useless. It's luck more than skill that sends me tripping into a gully where I land right on top of the goats, who have huddled together for warmth. Not sure whether I want to kick them for running off and scaring me or hug them for still being alive, I tie them together with the length of sisal twine I brought with me and lead them home.

When I get to the front door, I'm not sure what to do since I can't put them into their broken pen. I decide to bring them inside with me. They're still hobbled to one another and they start to walk around the small interior of our house, bleating and getting tangled in people's legs. Mother *tsks* in annoyance and strides out the door with a big burlap sack over her shoulder, pushing the goats to one side with her hips when they get in her way.

"I found the goats," I say unnecessarily. Chui shoves his hands into his shorts pockets and glares at me. When he scowls his eyes become angry little slits in his face. Enzi glares at me, too, from where he's folding his clothes. Asu looks up from sorting the kitchen goods and laughs softly.

"I can see that, Golden Boy. But did you have to bring them into the house?"

"Well, their pen is kind of broken."

"Hobble them outside by the door, then," she says, "and pack up your things. We have to leave tonight."

I pull the goats outside and hobble them with the twine. I tie the horns of the lead goat to the side of the pen, too, for good measure. Then I head back inside.

Even though I know the answer, I ask the question so Asu won't know I heard what happened. "Why do we have to leave?"

Chui's head snaps up. "Because of you!" he snarls.

"Chui," Asu warns softly.

"It's true!" he shouts at her, waving his raggedy-finger-nailed hands around to make his point. "We used to be fine here, fine! Enzi says that Father was able to keep the farm running through worse droughts than this. If he hadn't left because of that stupid ghost, none of this would be happening!"

"*Chui!*" Asu's voice is no longer soft. Chui stops talking and continues shoving things into his pack, his neck stiff and his movements choppy. His face is tight and hard.

There's an awkward silence. I move over to the corner I sleep in and start piling my clothes into the middle of my blanket with my white hands. Not black and strong like En-zi's. Not black and slender like Asu's. Not black and stumpy like Chui's. Not black and calloused like Mother's. Milk white. Bone white. Ghost white.

Mother comes back in and her sack is bulging at irregular angles. I see the outlines of tools. She unpacks them and sets them against the wall, for whoever will have our house next, I suppose.

"Aren't we bringing those with us?" asks Chui.

"No, my dear," says Mother absently as she joins Asu near the food stores.

"Where are we going?" I ask. If we're not bringing the tools with us, that means Mother doesn't think we'll be farming anymore.

"To Mwanza," she says, tying an aggressive knot in a large bundle of cornmeal and dried pigeon peas. "My sister lives there. We'll have to stay with her until I figure out what to do next."

"Where is Mwanza?" I ask.

"Far away." Her voice is a tired sigh. "We'll have to catch a bus from Arusha. Even so, it will be many, many hours before we get there."

"What's it like to take a bus for the whole day?" asks Chui.

"Oh, ask Enzi and Asu," says Mother distractedly. "We used to go up every year to visit when they were small. Before . . ."

She trails off, never saying before what. But Chui shoots me a poisoned look anyway. We all know what "before" means. Before I was born. Before Father left.

Enzi looks up from where he's putting his machete and the last of his clothes into a plastic bucket.

"Ask Asu about the bus," he says to Chui. "I'm not going with you."

We all stare at him.

"What did you say?" Mother asks, suddenly very alert. Her hands clench and unclench by her sides. I don't think she knows she's doing it.

"We need the money," says Enzi, not looking at her. The light from the kerosene lamp throws shadows across his face, highlighting the jut of his cheekbones, hiding his eyes. "I can make ten thousand shillings a day picking coffee. It just doesn't make sense for me to leave until after the harvest is finished."

"No," says Mother. "No, I won't split the family. We're all we have now."

Enzi moves to put an arm around her shoulders. She's swallowed by his shadow, and now I can see his face. His eyes are sad, but his jaw is rigid. He's not going to change his mind.

"You can't leave us now!" exclaims Asu, slapping her hand down on her bundle. "How will we be safe on the road without a man?"

"You'll be fine. Chui will be with you."

Asu narrows her eyes. "Mother and I are supposed to make it all the way across the country with a fifteen-year-old for protection?" Asu may be nineteen and old enough to be married, but she and Enzi fight like two children about how to run the family.

"Hey!" says Chui. "I help Enzi in the fields and get almost a man's wages. Why do you still think I'm just a little boy? Enzi thinks I can do it."

Asu doesn't respond and instead returns to packing. I can tell she's frustrated, though, because instead of folding things neatly, she's shoving them into the bags.

I'm only two years younger than Chui, but no one has mentioned that I might help on the road, too. Chui may not be a man, but I'm hardly a person. I finish tying off my bedroll and help Asu with the kitchen supplies, handing her things to pack. It slows her down enough that she isn't crushing them anymore. I know if I let her keep doing that she'd be angry at herself later. Chui has stopped packing entirely, staring at Enzi as if he could make him stay with us using just the power of his thoughts.

"You're going to abandon us, then?" Mother has started to cry onto Enzi's shoulder. Her hands make fists in the material of his shirt.

"Just because I'm staying here doesn't mean I'm abandoning you or breaking up the family," Enzi says softly, patting her on the back like you would a baby. "The money here is good. How am I going to make this much money on the road? In Mwanza? It's a fishing city. I don't know how to fish. We need the money I can make here." His hands are huge and calloused from working in the fields, but he holds her softly. He looks deeply into her eyes. "You need the money I can make here more than you need me on the bus with you. I'll come as soon as the harvest is done. I promise."

Mother lets go of Enzi and sinks down beside the packs. She rubs her fingers into her temples as if she's getting a headache. I want to go and put an arm around her like Enzi just did, but I don't think she would want that from me, so I stay where I am.

A vein on Enzi's forehead is throbbing up and down, up and down, drawing a line of shadow across his face, but he doesn't say anything else. Asu wraps a wedge of *ugali*, the thick cornmeal porridge that's the basis of most of our meals, in a banana leaf and hands it to Enzi.

"For your breakfast," she says flatly, and reopens the bundle she just tied shut to leave some other food with him, too.

"Let me stay here with you. I can help!" insists Chui, breathing hard. He has always stuck close to Enzi. Maybe that's why there was never any room left near Enzi for me.

"No," says Enzi, reaching over and squeezing Chui's shoulder. I see Chui's shirt wrinkle under Enzi's fingers. "You need to go with the family. You'll be the oldest son until I join you again."

"But I can help!" Chui says. His eyes are big and shiny even though his hands are clenched by his sides. "We could work together."

"No," says Enzi firmly. "They can't go alone." He looks Chui directly in the eye as he says this, and after a pause, Chui nods at him, like a man. No one looks over at me. Enzi goes on: "I'll put you on the bus in the morning, but I'm going to stay here. I'll sell the goats and, at the end of the coffee season in December, I'll follow you to Mwanza."

Chui nods again, then stalks out into the night. "I'm going to check on the goats," he says over his shoulder.

I say nothing. Enzi is the closest thing to a father I've ever known. Even if he never really liked me, he was all that I had. Now he's staying behind. I want to say something, but I feel like I have no words. Even if I did, they probably wouldn't want to hear them from me, anyway. Other than the occasional bleat of a goat, it is so quiet in the house that I can hear the rustling of the grass outside and the whine of the cicadas and, when the wind changes direction, the muffled sound from over the hill of Chui crying.

It takes us most of the night to organize ourselves: leaving Enzi with the goats and the things he'll need and packing everything else into bundles we'll be able to carry on our heads.

When everything is ready we stand beside our packs for a minute, looking at our house. Mother's hands rattle by her sides like dry palm fronds in a wind. Finally, Enzi says, "Let's go."

With the first step I feel a terrible shift in my chest. This leaving is not like leaving for the river or school. This leaving is the kind of leaving you do at a gravesite. It's a leaving that is also a giving up. Our home is no longer our home. Our farm is no longer our farm. I make the mistake of looking back one more time.

I hope that everyone will think I'm rubbing at my eyes because I can't see well in the dark. But tonight no one teases me, not even Chui.